By Chancey Plagman

1. King of the Capital

The throne was very cold, Aunten had noticed when first he sat on it. Since then, two days had passed, and his totalitarian command of the capital city had thus far been a disappointment. None of the tales he had read growing up ever warned him of the severe dullness and boredom that was granted a conqueror. Every day as mundane as the next. Regardless of who sat on the throne, the sun rose and fell in the same spots.

Still, Aunten had a lot on his mind, but not as much as that of the previous leader, Anek Slank, whom he had slain to achieve this honor. And now, here he sat, bored, but surrounded by thousands who would do his bidding…or perish for disobeying.

When he walked the capital grounds, his feet were bare, his hands covered in black gloves. He sometimes wore a hood, which covered his ghoulish face, but in the presence of his fellow Deadman, who had been raised from the grave with him some weeks ago, that wasn't necessary. Here in the capital, he was not afraid to let the skin tissue that looked barely stitched together reign over the people. He stood about six and a half feet tall, towering over most everyone else in the land.

Aunten spoke in a high, terrifying voice that caught the attention of all around him. His every word annunciated to the perfection of terrifying all who stood beneath him. At this moment, late in the afternoon where the sun began to dip uncontrollably into the northern earth, the only creatures around him were his fellow Deadman, whose appearance was much the same compared to his. Like their leader, all their teeth were filed sharply down, and they had no hair on their bodies save eyebrows.

Sienel, the chief of his twelve Deadman, was the first who Aunten would trust with anything close to the throne, or as much as any king could put into his subjects. True, they possessed some of the powers he did, and were also impervious to every known weapon, but Aunten always seemed to imply his superiority over them, not in word, but in action. Sienel was the only one of the thirteen Deadman whose skin was not white, his being black.

"Jenik, give me the time."

One of the Deadman said, "The time is 4:21, sir."

Aunten sighed. "Then it is late enough for me to hear your reports. Any one of you can go first, I care not who, I will listen nevertheless."

Sienel spoke first. His dispatch to the north of the capital, in the country of Penulton, came south the minute word spread that the capital had been overtaken by Aunten. The mountain men would keep to themselves, but if need-be would be powerful allies to his cause. "The mountain men have reported nothing out of the ordinary, sir."

Aunten replied, "Very well."

Nerenger, another Deadman, said next, "I wish to report, sir, that there is nothing on the horizon of the the Ganglish Sea worth telling." To the west of the capital was Carni, a small town that was the last stop before the sea began. All spots to enter the sea were guarded by the strongest of Carni, and few were able to pass them. They would remain loyal to anyone sitting on the throne in the capital, less they fear their town being sacked or wiped off the map. Like the mountain men, they were early to pay tribute to the new ruler of Winterlon, Nerenger being their spokesman on Aunten's council.

Yenrik, yet another Deadman, spoke next. "Sir, nothing out of the ordinary from Renold." Yenrik had begun a communication with one Jarold Karn, an older resident of the outpost Renold, to the south of the capital. Jarold had been lucky enough to be elected to stay at the outpost while every other soldier of the capital fought and died at the Battle of Arnic Canyon, where Aunten and his army of dark warriors had been victorious two days prior. Always weary of his capital, Jarold was proud to report the few comings and goings of the south.

Aunten sighed again. "So be it."

And finally, Jenik stated, "There is one development out of Carni, sir."

At this, the other Deadman around the table turned, first to him, then almost all of them to Nerenger, who eyed his fellow Deadman suspiciously. The west was his territory, all word was to go through him.

But the development was of little consequence. Jenik continued, "There was a small boat that passed by the town, sir, occupied by two men from Geinashaw, perhaps men sent direct on the order of Prince Hinja."

This caused Aunten to sit up. "Yes? Continue."

Jenik had nothing else to say. "Well, sir, I do not think there is anything else to add. Rumor is the best way to describe it. Neither the prince nor the Weston family has not sworn their allegiance as of yet."

Aunten half-yelled, "Then look into it! I will not sit here day after day waiting to hear only speculations! I want full, detailed reports, and if there is nothing to report, then what these other gentlemen have said suffices. Do you have anything further or not?"

Jenik shook his head.

Aunten turned to Nerenger. "I want you to round up a few capital men. Then you and Jenik go to Carni and try to find out some more details about this boat. If these are the prince's men, see to their intentions. Are they here to try and put a knife to my throat? Are they seeking peace? Perhaps my assistance in ending their conflict."

Aunten spoke of the Geinashaw civil war, which was the longest active feud in Winterlon. For sixteen generations, the Hinja family had battled the Westons, both claiming to have the blood right to be crowned king or queen, depending on who led the family. Lolar Hinja, the current prince, had only lost his father seven years prior, and the supposed word Aunten's predeceasing governor, Anek Slank, heard was that Lolar would lose the war for his family, ending the conflict. His title of prince would be restored to king if he were to wipe out the Weston family tree.

Sienel commented, "Sir, I wouldn't bet it likely they are here to attempt a coup. The last thing he might want to do is attack a man who is beyond death and controls the capital."

Aunten went silent for a minute, then said, "But consider, Sienel. He is a fool. And fools always make rash decisions when situations are dire. There is a reason that people are at their worst when things they love or take for granted are in jeopardy. People are at their worst when times are rank with fear."

Sienel nodded in agreement, turned to Jenik and Nerenger, and motioned for them to go and follow up on Jenik's findings.

The two Deadman rose from their separate spots, Jenik on Aunten's left and three chairs down, and

Nerenger on Aunten's right and two chairs down. Jenik moved quickly, while Nerenger stared after him, fearing there might be conflict between them.

The two invincible men left the hall, a hall which only three days before had been a headquarters for the team that worked on battle plans against Aunten's army. The late Governor Slank had a good idea or two on how to deal with Aunten, but he was not ready to fight against his foe and his followers, and because of his unpreparedness, had suffered the consequence of death.

Aunten rose from the throne and said, "I, king of the capital, wish to go to the map room. Escort me there."

The remaining Deadman surrounded their leader as he went toward a room whose walls were entirely made of maps. The fifth governor prior to Slank had installed the maps and had them stuck to the wall. It proved most useful when the times were right. William Anber, the governor before Slank, had to fight off Kildeno, a devilish man who had nearly taken the capital three years ago. It was Aunten the archer who had taken Kildeno's life from him, though the devil in the man took his revenge swiftly, inhabiting Aunten and leading him down the dark path.

It was only months after that Aunten and twelve of his best lieutenants tried themselves to take the capital, but their efforts ended within an hour, and the thirteen men were executed, overseen by a great capital warrior Halun Leman. Privately Aunten knew it was his next goal to find out what had happened to his executioner, and now that the capital was his to lose, he could track him down.

Aunten and his twelve compatriots were awarded the powers of evil by the devil himself, who could have condemned them to an even worse fate after

Aunten escaped hell, but it was the devil's bidding for Aunten and the others to take over Winterlon. And so the rise of the Deadman had begun, and now they had plateaued no more than two days after achieving the ultimate victory of overtaking the capital of the world.

As Aunten looked about his capital, he saw several citizens walking around aimlessly, in a zombie-like state, never looking up, and when Aunten neared them, they bowed before their king. Aunten did not acknowledge them. Every leader before had.

The city itself appeared as drab as it had under Slank's rule. There were various shops, bars, markets, blacksmiths, but most businesses were closed under Aunten's request. They were to serve him in various other ways, chief among them clearing out all the resources.

A nearby river which encircled all of Winterlon had been fished out, and that fish served as meals for the people, for Deadman feasted on more live prey, like rabbits and walpen (which were kind of like wombats, but with thicker fur that was harder to bite through to get to the meat).

The other jobs of the citizens were more accurately akin to slavery. They were to do whatever Aunten wanted, and immediately, lest they desired a swift and merciless death. Most of the time Aunten himself would kill them, but at odd times another Deadman would be called upon to do the deed.

Part of the fear from the citizens came from knowledge that Aunten had granted them. Along his quest to pillage the capital, he had burned down most of the small villages in the neighboring country to the east, Sadhill. He had also destroyed a good number of villages in the country to the north, Virk. While he had left a few towns untouched in the capital country of Lear, this final notion was left as a warning to those who resisted his rule.

After a five-minute walk, they entered the map room. The center of the far wall was the capital, and nearby it Arnic Canyon, where three days before Aunten and his men had proved themselves against the capital's army. To the west of the city was the small town of Carni, about twelve miles, or a two-hour walk. To the east of the Canyon was the next-door country of Sadhill, and about two-days' journey to the east of that lay the area where Aunten had first appeared after his death and new life, the Endin River. Sure, there were plenty of small towns between the capital and Sadhill, and even more between Sadhill and the river, but most of them had at this point been wiped out by Aunten on his journey toward the capital.

"Sienel," Aunten said, gazing at this map for the first time. "Remove the villages that no longer stand."

Doing his bidding, the Deadman walked over toward the map, and starting in Sadhill, moved around the map for several minutes, taking time to move his palm over each village that was large enough to earn a name on the map and smudging it with heat. The heat emanated from the Deadman, and when he took a few steps back to admire his work, there were more smudges on the map than names.

Aunten now looked toward the south of the capital, where not too far was the country that he had now taken notice of, Geinashaw. It wasn't too large, but at the same time was not too small to not be noticeable. Their debated leader, Prince Hinja, was an ageing man who Aunten knew could be defeated sooner rather than later. The story of the nation at war had many tall tales of how it began, the most famous being that it all started with a decapitation of a rebellious leader by the then king, who in turn was burned head to toe by the rebels. No one in the string of sixteen generations had been able to stop the two factions from fighting, and Aunten could not think of anything to stop them now, not even his insurrection of the capital.

He had ambitions to go after them next in his plans of total control of the world of Winterlon, but he couldn't say for certain if they should be next on the list. Because off to the north, beyond the point his army had traveled, and housing the Wise-Mountains, was Penulton.

Aunten wasn't sure yet, but he knew there likely was trouble in this direction. He had traveled pretty far, and yet a Mainmen army had come to the capital's aid during the battle. Where had they gathered, and who remained, if any?

An old foe of Aunten's from before his Deadman uprising, the Mainmen were a force to be reckoned with, at least when they were at their peak. It was they who defeated the first rule of the Deadman five hundred years ago. For two generations they had ruled all of Winterlon, and the small resistance that had been overlooked grew and grew, and eventually took back the world. That resistance was the Mainmen, who joined forces with multiple armies from around the world.

Penulton was also where the legend of the Wiseman had ended with his creation of the mountains. The world had been created by the Wiseman, or so the stories went, and he ruled as a god over all the world, until his strength gave out and he left it to be controlled by the abomination of mankind. Aunten wasn't aware that this was the country the Mainmen had settled in after their expulsion from the capital, the first action by former Governor Slank.

Further yet to the north lie the nation of Dulon, housing the Benshidi, a people who had known peace amongst each other, and who had closed their borders to outsiders decades ago. Before that, they were even more ruthless and deadly than the Mainmen. Their fighting days were over, but the reptilian brain used in combat must remain, or so Aunten thought. Regardless, he kept several ideas in the back of his brain about what to do if he was attacked by these isolationists.

Fiernan, a brave Deadman and great fighter, asked, "Sir, what is the real reason we have done nothing yet? We have captured the capital, and by extension, the world, yes, but there will be fights to be had, warriors to kill. Correct?"

Aunten smiled, "Yes, Fiernan, and their time will come. For now, my dear follower, we are resting up. Lest you forget, we exhausted our army to that of the capital and the Mainmen, so while I grow another, I only have you twelve.

"We have to look toward the remaining Mainmen. We may have defeated the bulk of their force at Arnic Canyon, but I saw a small band of them before our advance toward the capital. I didn't care where they went, for I first wanted to secure the city, but now it is a decision I have regretted."

Fiernan continued, "When will we make our next move?"

Aunten chuckled, "Be calm, be patient, my dear Fiernan. I am deciding whether to go after our enemies to the north or our enemies to the south. Either way, the news has reached both and each now fear me equally. I am letting it get to them, and soon the fear of their waiting for my attack will get to them even further. Then they will be an afterthought to us. We will wait for the return of Nerenger and Jenik before I display to you my plan."

And with that, he requested the men to be ready at a moment's notice to have the torches lit. It would be important for them to be kept lit all hours of the night, for Aunten was to draw out the possibilities of where the Mainmen had rested while Aunten marched his campaign across Sadhill, Virk, and Lear. He wanted to point out the spots his followers would travel if uprisings began. Aunten wanted to think about where the remaining Mainmen were right now, and where they might be headed.

More importantly, he wanted to form a plan, one that may take years, but would be done nevertheless, to maintain control over all remaining countries of Winterlon, to the north, south, east and west. Billions of people inhabited this world, and it was Aunten they would bow to. He would see to it.

2. The Last of the Mainmen

James Realms and company had been running for a long time. Since their defeat at Arnic Canyon, he, Laura Jacobsen, Amanda Richardson, Ed, Jaenen, and Darven Hotean, Talen Wadenston, Erik Johnson, Ted Browning, Valen McQuint, and Michael Joven had been getting as far away as they possibly could from the capital. It had been four days since then, and the road had been far from a straight one, full of detours and decision making and exhaustion, for they had not stopped besides sleeping and planning on where to go next.

James remembered each one of these moments as he sat by the small fire that Ed and Talen had made. The group had, after their defeat at the Canyon, made one last attempt to save Governor Anek Slank, but he had already given up by that point, and the group had escaped his chambers via trapdoor, then slid loose a few bricks to escape the capital city undetected.

That night they stopped, and Ed and Talen remained on guard as the nine others slept, but none of them slept easily. They were all terrified that the Deadman, or worse Aunten *and* his Deadman, would be there when they would wake up, or kill them in their sleep. There was not one of the eleven who did not have a nightmare that evening. James felt lucky when he awoke the next morning and he and everyone else was alive. They had sat there that whole morning, all dead quiet, except when someone brought up an idea for what to do next.

James Realms was brought to Winterlon moments after learning of its existence. His mother and father, Pam and Roger Realms, had been great warriors in their time, but had retired years before, never telling their son about their true work. That is, until the night of their murders. Ed and his sons had saved him and killed the assassins, and opened a new chapter to his life.

James had light brown hair, light green eyes, and a fair complexion. Since he had arrived in Winterlon, his physical appearance had changed a bit from slightly unhealthy to more muscular and fit. He hadn't been the best student, and ended up working in a department store before his arrival. Since, he had turned everything around and had become a respectable young man.

Laura Jacobsen stood about five feet six inches, was blonde with blue eyes. Like James, her father, Arnold Jacobsen, had been a respected, leading figure of the Mainmen cause in the years before. However, his death triggered a deterioration in her life, leading to her mother, who remained back on Earth, to re-marry and bring her daughter up in a world devoid of the likes of Winterlon.

She had a desire to live up to her father's name, and that had brought her great spirit. She had trained in the Mainmen ways in the last two weeks, and picked everything up the quickest of the three. Her knowledge of Winterlon was also better than James and Amanda's, though only as much as she could recall from her father's stories.

Amanda, on the other hand, was five nine, just an inch shorter than James, and had brown eyes that matched her hair and her skin. Like James and Laura, she had few experiences that would have prepared her for a war in a world she barely knew existed.

Dawn Richardson, Amanda's mother, was another Mainmen warrior of the past who held legends in their ranks, though her death on Earth came from a car accident. Amanda had also lost a brother to suicide, James had learned, and she and her father had moved from the middle of Nebraska to New Mexico.

Amanda picked up the training fairly well, not as quick as Laura, but faster than James, and like Laura was hoping to prove her worth to everyone around her. All three of them shared the age of twenty.

The three youngsters had been trained by Ed Hotean, current leader of the Mainmen, a five-foot eleven inch, graying at the temples, 55-year-old man whose hair was black everywhere else, save a graying middle in a thin mustache. His two sons, Darven and Jaenen, stood taller than their father, Jaenen being the elder of the two aged thirty, had brown hair, brown eyes, and clean shaven. Darven, twenty-seven, had orange hair, blue eyes, and a thick beard. Both had been trained in the Mainmen ways and had remained loyal to the cause all their lives. All three were darker skinned, toned to a Latin equivalent.

They were also trained by Talen Wadenston, one of the tallest men in Winterlon at seven feet two inches, was muscular all over, though both Darven and Jaenen also showed off their strength from time to time. His hair, however, was blonde, except again for some graying, which came with his age, fifty-two, as gracefully as was possible.

Talen had been loyal to the Mainmen cause as well, though he did so at the capital. He had kept Ed and the other Mainmen up to date with Slank's governing, and had rejoined his group after Slank dismissed him from his service.

The other Mainmen who had been with these seven in battle was Johnson, a controversial man whose tendency to drink heavily and bed women consistently was matched only with his zeal for battle, and his skill with it. For a man of forty-eight years, he had short jet-black hair, a goatee, no sign of gray anytime soon, and a small scar on each arm, supposedly from an old flame who cut him when he learned he had been with other women.

The eight were all similarly dressed in their Mainmen wear, minus the armor they had worn into battle, which now was placed in packs they carried on their backs. Their cloaks were all brown and their cloths underneath were white.

Then there was McQuint, who, like Talen, had stuck around the capital after Slank had dismissed the Mainmen from their location. McQuint, however, had decided his loyalty then lied with Slank and the capital, and he turned his back on the Mainmen. Following the Battle of Arnic Canyon, though, he would be happy to join back up, and in these times, Ed and Talen were not afraid to take him.

McQuint had a goatee as well, and dishwater blonde hair that was always flowing with the wind, sometimes unkempt. He was younger than the others who had been with the Mainmen before Aunten's rise, aged forty-five, and was six feet five inches tall.

Browning, a twenty-seven-year-old man who had been a capital loyalist since he was born, was unlike the others in several ways. His five feet six-inch build and leanness made him appear as less of a threat. He also had an attraction to men but had never been public with it. Now was not the time to bring it out, but he couldn't help but look to people like McQuint and Johnson and stare endlessly.

Like McQuint, Browning was quick to join the group, especially after seeing his cousin, Whales, die at the hands of a dark warrior in the Canyon. He took several lives that day, which earned the respect of all who had not already given it to him.

Lastly there was Joven, another man of the capital who had never been a Mainmen. He was the chief guard at an outpost of the capital until Aunten arrived, and was thirty-five, fairly lean, and had light orange hair. His clean-shaven nature helped distinguish him from Darven, though it wasn't uncommon for the two to be mistaken due to their likeness. Sure, Darven had the height advantage on him, but being six feet even, Joven wasn't a slouch.

These three had worn the capital gear, and unfortunately did not have the packs the Mainmen did, so they had shed their armor not too far from the capital. They did not know that the Deadman had found them the day after their escape from the capital, but hadn't really formed any thorough ideas for a search party. What good would it do to have three or four of them stalk the land to find a few guards that, for all they knew, had abandoned their posts?

Underneath the armor all three of them had different cloaks and baggy, old materials on. McQuint's clothes were mostly white, though stained blood from the battle did bathe it. Joven's were mostly yellow and black, and Browning's were red as well, though his had originally been white, but again he could blame the battle for turning them red.

All together, they were an interesting gaggle of men and women from varying backgrounds and walks of life. They would all form a bond as the last of the Mainmen, through thick and thin. This led to an interesting first discussion, and James remembered it as if it were hours ago.

Ed had begun, "Well, we have some decisions to make. We are about all that remains of the Mainmen. The rest are dead. Nothing is left of our force that can possibly go against the capital and take it back, not right now. So, we need to find a force that can."

Talen continued, "We look at four directions to go: north, east, west, and south. Each represents a challenge. To the south is the capital, but beyond it is Geinashaw, a country that is at civil war, and has been for a long time."

McQuint interjected, "And I think it's obvious we can't go east. Aunten came from there and left no survivors, none that could help us at any rate."

Laura said, "But we could. We don't know where he started destroying everything. Maybe it was only a few villages over."

Amanda frowned. "Maybe it was more than a few villages over."

Browning commented, "It's more. I heard some say that he had destroyed the entire country of Sadhill, and we know that he executed Governor Bulde. Sadhill, in ruins, will be of no help to us."

Ed said, "And to the west is the river by Carni, which will certainly be under the control of Schritz after a day or two."

Amanda asked, "Well, couldn't we find some boats or something nearby and get across?"

Talen shook his head, and said, "I don't think so. The river goes all the way up to the Wise-Mountains. It begins there, but all the way down, the town of Carni, and several others like it across the way, defend the river. It is impossible to go down or across it and survive."

James said, "We could go clear around it."

Jaenen replied, "No way. There's a stronghold on the north and south end of the river. No way through, around, nor under it."

Amanda inquired, "Under it?"

Johnson spoke, "Well, we don't have the manpower to dig far enough before we are discovered."

It was James who asked, "We came back from the north, from the Mainmen camp. What is to the north of that?"

Darven answered, "We have our home country, Penulton. And our town, Longell. Should you want to go further north, we have to deal with the Wise-Mountains. There is no path through them. You can only go over them, and that is about as dangerous as it gets. There are animals, creatures, deadly rain-storms and things and the height of the individual mountains are enough to make even the strongest man reconsider climbing."

Joven spoke the obvious. "Any choice we make will be a dangerous one."

Talen said, "And the longer we wait, the greater chance Aunten and his Deadman will find us."

Ed piped up, "But if we keep traveling east, there will be the villages on the other side of the Endin River. They may be of help to us."

"Hotean," started McQuint, "you know as well as I that the territory beyond the Endin River is nothing but wastelands. And once we do reach the villages on the other side of them, the people in them are no friend of the Mainmen."

Joven stood up. "No, but that was a long time before this. Surely they have heard of the Deadman and their quest by now."

James chuckled. "Don't call me Shirley."

Everyone looked at him funny.

James stopped chuckling. "Oh, right. You guys wouldn't get that. Sorry."

Talen sighed. "I have heard tales from the west, though, of the Hundrin."

Browning and Darven simultaneously sighed. "Here we go," said Darven.

Laura perked up, asking, "What's the Hundrin?"

Talen smiled. "They are a nomadic people that trek across the land on gigantic creatures. Bulia. They stand almost thirty feet tall and one hundred feet long, some more than that. And they have huge antlers and a trunk that weighs hundreds of pounds. Well, the Hundrin ride them every forty years or so and find a new location to live. Then the next generation picks up and moves, and so on.

"Point being, they are due for another trek in three years' time. It'll take us a while, but we can move north and find a passage across the river. We'll find and rally them to our cause. Aunten would shudder at the idea of an army of Bulia on his doorstep."

"I don't think," started Ed, who got up as well, "that Aunten would have much trouble, even with them. A regular man, yes, would quiver in his boots and piss himself, but not a Deadman, let alone twelve followers behind him."

Ed had heard enough and decided to put it to a vote, and Darven and Amanda and James voted in favor of going north. Jaenen and Ed and Joven wanted to go east. Talen solely wanted to go west, and Johnson, Laura, Browning and McQuint wanted to go south, but then McQuint changed his vote to north as soon as the campfire was out, so the entire group came to utter chaos.

One accused the other of betrayal, and then Ed changed his vote to north, and Johnson changed his to east. James and Darven and Amanda all were persistent in the group's traveling north, but Talen then reconsidered and changed to south. Browning then wanted to go east, but McQuint said that to go east was suicide, which made Browning go back to south.

Finally, Laura changed her mind and decided north was the way to go, making the vote six in favor on north, and the other five split between two other directions. This was enough for Ed and Talen.

For two days they traveled, hardly seeing any sign of life, and for James, Laura, and Amanda, no easy sleep came, no matter what Ed would try to say to convince them that Aunten couldn't find them, even now when they were far north.

On the next day, things changed. A rainy day, one with little sign of hope of ever reaching Longell. It was this day that Amanda, who was at the time in front of the group, spotted something across the flat plains. It appeared to be a horse and rider, and Ed, right behind her, pulled out his sword, one given to him by the former Mainmen leader, Joren, who fell at the Battle of Arnic Canyon.

Ed warned everyone the rider was unfriendly. And so he was, as almost immediately, the rider jumped from his horse, and came charging at the group. Ed met him in battle, and not more than two seconds after a quick sword clash had Ed been cut in the shoulder. He backed up a bit, and Talen, who had his sword drawn now, took an arm off the rider, making him wince and yell, giving McQuint, who had snuck to the right, an opportunity to take his head.

Getting a good look now, everyone else saw that the man was wearing the skin of an animal, which flopped off him as soon as he had slumped from his horse. Even from the decapitation, James could tell his eyes were mad, his teeth broken in places and some just plain rotten. His tongue appeared black, and his skin course.

Amanda was the first to ask, "What the hell was he?"

Ed, who was being treated by Browning and Darven, answered, "A mountain man. Former capital worker, who is trained to kill anyone who approaches the mountains to the east."

Laura asked, "Mountains? We didn't see any mountains when we were off to the east."

Talen answered, "No, this would be to the area we would have gone to had James not turned us when Aunten's army passed."

James recalled this. One night when the group had been seven, before Browning, McQuin, Joven, and Johnson had joined, James had been visited by the Wiseman, creator of Winterlon, and had warned him his group would be dead if they didn't move to the west. They almost were face to face with the enemy, but were spared an easy death.

"Why would he attack us?" asked Amanda.

Johnson, who was the last to unsheathe his sword and had stayed behind to protect the others, answered, "Because they're sore at Mainmen."

Laura shook her head, questioned further, "But why exactly?"

It was McQuint who answered. "Because quite a number of years ago there was this fellow named Golrook who broke off from the Mainmen and decided to go work for the capital. He said that the pay would be better and convinced five hundred Mainmen to follow him. Within a year, Governor Anber decided he had enough guards and sent all the Mainmen who had come to help to these mountains. They have been shut off from all communication with anyone since, if you believe the stories. Only few handfuls of men or women have ever traveled past the mountains, but none have gone over and lived to tell tales of what they saw."

Ed shook his head, still wincing from the pain. "It's likely that they would now be loyal to Aunten."

James asked, "Do we need to pass so close to these mountains?"

Browning, who was finished bandaged up Ed, replied, "Well, the other option is to continue across these plains. Food will be scarce, but there are a few more animals that creep toward the mountain range."

He turned back to Ed. "Seems we have another decision to make."

And so the group decided not to risk it, voting almost unanimously this time. Only Joven and Browning dared to vote in favor of going toward the mountains. Ed asked for forgiveness from the group for their crossing so close to begin with, but the group was easy to let it pass, especially since it was Ed himself who had paid the heaviest price.

From then on, the journey had been a fine one, and while Browning was correct with the scarcity of the food, they managed. The group was further west then they had been originally, so they couldn't rely on villages like Caricut to feed them.

James could still hear the laughter and sense the joy that village had given them when they were close to reaching the Mainmen camp. It had been nearly a week ago, but it remained his happiest moment yet in this world.

Most of the vegetation in the plains was exotic enough for Laura, James, and Amanda, but they were re-assured once the group arrived in Longell, they would be re-equipped with enough proper food to last another journey. They only hoped it would be a better one than their previous.

3. The Wiseman's Return

The day after, five days from the fall of the capital, was like the previous, though the rain tapered off by mid-afternoon and the sun came out for the four hours of daylight that remained. The eleven travelers had neared the border of Penulton, and would soon be leaving the country of Virk. The progress was a welcome one, and all eleven of them, save James, was quick to fall asleep.

James Realms remained by the fire, which was ill-advised provided the winds had risen out of the south after sundown. The two moons of Winterlon were now bright in the sky, bright enough that James could see where most of what remained of the Mainmen were without aid of the fire, which was quickly dying.

Suddenly, the wind died down from heavy, to nearly nothing, to nothing at all, and James was joined by the Wiseman for the fourth time.

The Wiseman, in usual fashion, was beaming at him, dressed in his white cloak. "Young Mr. Realms," he began.

James stood up. "You!" he cried. "How do you have the nerve to let thousands of warriors die and demons from hell take the capital?"

The Wiseman lifted a hand. "Patience, my boy," he said, "for I will explain."

The Wiseman reached forward, as he had done three times before, and hit James in the chest. Soon he saw the portal that would lead him to whatever picture the Wiseman desired him to observe. Both walked through.

They now saw from a different angle, an angle from the top of Arnic Canyon, where capital guards and Mainmen alike fought against Aunten and his army. James sighed in frustration, knowing that just five days before he had lived through this.

James asked, "What's the point?"

The Wiseman, still beaming, answered, "James, the point is Aunten would have won an even greater victory if this had happened."

James then saw that a guardsman, Whales, was in the middle of a swordfight with a dark warrior, but an archer from the side of Aunten was about to shoot Browning, Whales' cousin. James watched in utter horror knowing what was about to happen, for Browning had told them a couple of days prior his experience in the battle.

Whales had heroically sacrificed himself for his cousin, but what James saw now wasn't that. Instead, Whales stood by and let the arrow hit Browning.

Leaping over to his dying cousin, Whales removed the arrow, and kissed him on the forehead for a moment before running off, back into battle.

James then turned toward the Wiseman. "What would have happened to us if Whales had survived?"

The Wiseman's beaming smile faded. "He would have taken Browning's place in your company; however, the results would not have been the same. If he were still alive, tomorrow he would begin to have doubts of your journey, and feel the grief, the full, real grief, of his loss at the same time. He also has a family back in Abentur, just outside the capital. Whales would feel even more guilt over leaving them in the hands of the likes of Aunten. The result: he would leave your party and die at the hands of illness fifteen years later.

"But that is not the way life has willed it. Whales took that arrow, spared his cousin, and now Browning has in him a vengeance. That feeling can only be matched by a loyalty to the cause, which is now instilled in him. He will remain at your side until the end."

James asked, "You know this?"

The Wiseman chuckled. "I am the Wiseman. I know all, young James."

Now James turned back toward the vision, and saw that with Whales surviving, this triggered a series of events that did not unfold: McQuint is killed by an archer, and Ed loses a hand in combat. Laura is equipped with a tremendous scar on her forehead from a close encounter with a dark warrior. Even James is not untouched now by the battle, missing three toes after a dark warrior's sword falls on his foot.

This image made James shiver. He turned back to the Wiseman. "I think I've seen enough."

The Wiseman's smile returned, and with it came a hearty laugh. "James, I hope you've seen the full reasoning for this vision."

James shook his head. "I don't."

"The reason," the Wiseman continued, "is because everything happens for a reason. Any twist or turn in your fate will not just result in a different future for yourself, but also for your fellow warriors. You mustn't lose sight of that. If you are greeted in the coming days and weeks with defeat, humility, and loss, know that it is all headed in the right direction."

Once again, the Wiseman put his hand on James' chest, and the two walked through a new portal, returning to the campsite.

"Now, James, I must warn you: you must use this to keep this group together. Any man or woman you lose will cost you dearly. Don't let it happen."

James asked, "Will someone die?"

The Wiseman shook his head. "I cannot say."

James replied, "So how do I keep them alive?"

The Wiseman answered, with a smile, "Hope. Hope begins in even the weakest of souls and grows through the strongest. And sure enough, one day the weakest soul will have enough hope to see that deep inside, they are the strongest of souls."

And the Wiseman was gone in a blink.

Back at the camp, James gasped loudly. The campfire was out, and James was lying on a cloth, two paces away from Laura, who stirred in her sleep at first, then propped herself up to face James.

"What is it?" she asked.

James replied, "The Wiseman. He visited me again."

Laura's excitement got the better of her, and though the night air was cool, she had no shame in letting her skin be caked in goosebumps as she asked, "What did he say?"

"To keep everyone together and bring hope. That hope is essential to defeating Aunten, I guess."

The group was split on the notion of the Wiseman. Ed and one of his sons were non-believers, but even Ed had to acknowledge that there was a higher power to warn the group before they were captured, or worse, by Aunten's army when they passed by them.

Laura looked slightly disappointed. "He didn't tell you where to go? Or what the future will be like?"

James stared at his feet, realizing what he was about to say would be of no help to his friend. "He knows the future, he knows everything, but he won't tell. Or can't. I don't know, maybe if he does, he dooms us, and we all end up dead."

"Well, we could use some help with that. I'm no expert, but I think Ed and Talen are planning on stopping at that village, Longell, re-stocking supplies, then God knows what. They'll continue the fight, but they don't know how to find a force like The Mainmen to fight him. And that's just for them. What about us?"

"What do you mean?" James asked.

"We don't have a clue what dangers are going to be waiting for us if we end up going to the Wise-Mountains. We're also no closer to figuring out how to kill Aunten. If Ed is right, there's a way to do it, but we can't do it while we're walking around the wilderness, heading for a village hundreds of miles from the capital."

All the noise awakened Jaenen, who rose from his cloth not far away. Jaenen was the only Hotean that believed in the Wiseman's existence and took in every word he could hear from James.

"I'm sorry to eavesdrop, but you said the Wiseman visited you again?"

James nodded.

"Did you see anything important?"

James sighed. "I guess I can say it again. He showed me that we need to stick together and cling onto hope. Without that, the whole future is in the balance. And it's not just one of us that's affected. It's all of us. Like, he said that if Whales had lived instead of Browning, he would have left us, and Jaenen, your dad would have lost his hand, and Laura, you'd have a gigantic freakin' scar on your face."

He looked down at the ground and continued, "McQuint would be dead, and I'd be missing some toes."

Talen, who was casually listening to the conversation, then rose from the ground as well. "James, can you get him back?"

For years, Talen had been with Ed in rejection of the idea of the Wiseman, but with recent events, his mind was being changed, gradually.

James shook his head. "When he visits me, it's only for a short time. Then he's gone, and he never says when he'll be back."

Talen's face was now slowly flushing with frustration. His tone was meaner, his words coming out more slowly. "And how is that supposed to help us?"

Laura said, "Well, maybe he talks to other people. Maybe, oh, what's his name?" She turned toward Talen now, asking, "That prince you were talking about? Prince of Geinshaw?"

Talen corrected her. "Geinashaw. Prince Hinja. Possibly."

Laura's face perked up. "Maybe if he needs to join our cause, the Wiseman will talk to him, kick his ass until he joins us."

James held up his hand, saying, "He can't do that. He told me before the battle that he can't interfere with anything personally."

Jaenen turned his head in question. "But he told us to move when the dark warriors were passing by."

Shaking his head, James replied, "I think he meant that he can't step in front of arrows for us, or make the enemies' weapons disappear. Sure, he can talk to us and suggest we move, or talk to the prince and try and get him to stop fighting."

James sighed and continued. "It also means that there's almost no way the prince, or anyone else, will ride up to us tomorrow with the secrets to beating Aunten because the Wiseman told them to."

"Speaking of which," started Laura, "Talen, do you know anything about that? Ed said that history repeats itself, and there were Deadman in the past and they're gone now. So there must be a way to do it."

Talen sighed. "I agree with him. But this was five hundred years ago. I guess I never looked, but if it's written down in a book or something, it's probably in the capital. And if it is, with Aunten sitting on the throne, he's probably already ordered it destroyed. We'd need another resource."

Jaenen looked to Talen. "I can ask for them, Talen. Do you know what the plan is after we're back home?"

Talen shook his head. "Right now, your father is thinking five steps ahead. We'll probably spend a week in Longell, maybe more, maybe less, then we'll probably continue north. Or maybe we'll turn east. It will all come to him in time."

Jaenen turned to James. "And if the Wiseman does come back, you should ask him, James."

Talen sighed in disgust. Despite everything, he couldn't betray rational thought to the idea of a heroic, older, deity figure swooping in to save the day.

He turned to James and said, "I'm not sure where all this is coming from, James, all the clairvoyance of the future, but do us a favor and listen to Jaenen. Ed and I will be all ears to any suggestions you have." Talen then stretched, yawned, and went back to the ground, and without another word, went back to sleep.

Jaenen wordlessly did the same. So James and Laura turned their attention back to each other. Laura spoke first. "Remember what we came up with? How we're going to keep each other in the loop?"

James nodded.

Laura pointed toward Amanda, on the far side of the group, and both James and Laura could hear a distant snore coming from her cloth.

"Good idea. I'll tell her everything in the morning."

Laura smiled. She yawned as well, and James prepared to go back to sleep, but Laura said, "You know, I'm tired, but after all that I can't go back to sleep. Not yet."

James, who by this point, was lying down on his cloth, looked back up toward her. "You want some company?"

Laura nodded, and held a hand out for James to grab to help him up. The two then walked away from the campsite a few paces before continuing the discussion.

"I have to admit, I'm a little cool, but I'm not freezing my ass off."

James chortled at this. "That's Winterlon for you. Feels like it should be one way, but it's the opposite."

Laura nodded. All three of them had been whisked away to Winterlon from their homes on Earth. Laura from upstate New York, James from the western reach of Ohio, and Amanda from eastern New Mexico. All three of them just had their Earth clothes but were given Mainmen clothes after they reached the camp. The armor sets and cloth underneath were an anomaly. They kept the warriors cool in the heat of battle, but warm in cold environments.

Laura continued, "I guess. You know, it's a hard time for everyone, especially us. We haven't been home in, what's it been, two weeks now?"

James had honestly lost count of the days not long after the first visit from the Wiseman, when his seriousness about Winterlon kicked into high gear. He shrugged at Laura. "I can't say for sure, but that sounds about right to me."

"I've been meaning to ask; do you miss it?"

"Home?"

"Yeah. I guess you told me you and your parents don't get along, and I've told you how that was true for me, too. But I worry about Amanda. She had her dad to take care of back on Earth."

"Take care of? Maybe. She lost her mom and her brother, but she's only a...I never asked, but I'd figure 20-year-old girl. It'd have to be pretty tough for her to be his only support in the world."

"I'm gonna ask her in the morning. But you don't miss it?"

The two had been walking along all this time, but James stopped at this point. "I guess I miss some things. I miss being able to listen to music. My phone died a long time ago, and of course, no service here anyways."

Laura chuckled. "Yeah, I think we sorted out our priorities pretty quick."

James thought about it some more. "I miss my doodle book. I guess I never told you, like, the day we came here, I found an old doodle book from high school. I hadn't looked at it since, probably, my sophomore year in high school. I spent hours going back through it, thinking about how much time I spent wasting away in it while my college hopes and dreams died."

Laura smiled at this, unsure if he was trying to be funny or not. She stopped when James continued.

"But I'll tell you what I don't miss. Being an absolute, bonafide loser. I don't miss not having a car and having to walk around everywhere. I don't miss my bitch of a boss at Graney's. And I don't miss my supposed friends, who I hadn't talked to in months."

Laura nodded at this. "Good, cause I don't miss my shit-eating stepdad, my spineless mother, and my worthless college courses on British mercantile law."

James gave a funny look. "I don't even know what that is."

Laura laughed. "Trust me, traders and merchants coming up with their own rules of engagement in trade is not fun. And I especially don't miss being alone."

James nodded in agreement.

"By the way," continued Laura, "you're not a bonafide loser. You're actually a sweet guy who knows a lot of important values, like trust and honesty, and you don't have a bad sense of humor, either."

Laura then took a step closer to him and looked down at his hands. Hers began to tremble in nervousness, and James took notice of it.

"What?" he asked.

Laura stopped. Her hands calmed down, and she retreated. "I—I don't know what came over me. For a second I thought about..."

James waited for her to finish, but Laura sighed in disgust and blew a raspberry. "Nothing. Just nothing."

"It sounded like it was going to be important."

"If it was that important, I'd tell you."

He wanted to stop her, but Laura started walking back toward the campsite. James stood where he was for another few moments in thought.

He couldn't help but smile as his imagination started to flow a bit. He knew what she was thinking: take his hands in comfort, they'd walk back to the campsite, maybe have a make-out session. He stopped himself there. He knew better than that.

Though the feeling of being liked didn't hurt him, he knew now was neither the time nor place for a romantic rendezvous. That was probably what stopped Laura from taking that extra motion.

Before James returned to the campsite, his mind went back to forming visions of what would have happened next if Laura hadn't stopped. A smile came back to his face, the smile of a young man who knew that a young woman whom he admired, passionately or not, showed him her thoughts, at least for a moment.

4. Longell

And so that next morning, Ed announced after a rushed breakfast of Culder leaves, the only edible vegetation in the land, that by the end of the day they should arrive at Longell. Jaenen and Darven were all smiles at this announcement, for it meant reuniting with their families.

The three from Earth had learned on their journey to the Mainmen camp that Jaenen was married to a woman named Maryann, and Darven married to Veridey, and they had a child together, a son. They hadn't heard his name.

McQuint was also a native of Longell, as he told the group by the fireside. He had left when he was about twenty years old and hadn't been back since. He told them that was twenty-five years ago.

The three were now the last ones by the fireside as the other eight began to pack their things up. James and Laura had been ahead of the game on that front and had their belongings together. Sleep wasn't easy for either of them, but ignorance was bliss for Amanda, who hadn't awakened after the visit from the Wiseman.

"Amanda," said Laura, "James and I were wondering. We, well, we wanted to ask you something."

Amanda shrugged her shoulders. "Fire away."

Laura took a deep breath, but James beat her to the punch. "We were gonna ask if you miss anything back on Earth. Like your dad or your horse or..."

Amanda hadn't really thought back to Earth for a while, being all caught up in their journey over the past six days. But now James and Laura could both see it in her eyes, a sudden, forceful impact on her soul: she hadn't thought about her past life, and that fact haunted her. A terror visage came over her, and a small sweat broke out on her forehead.

"I guess I hadn't...really thought about it...for a while."

Laura and James knew these had to be the most useless words uttered in some time, for they were summed up in Amanda's face.

Laura put her hand on Amanda's shoulder in comfort for a moment, then pulled it away. "Then you don't miss it?"

Amanda gulped, and a tear came to her eye. "My dad."

That was all it took. She covered her face, and all words of comfort and bringing the three of them together were lost. James motioned for Laura and him to get up and leave her for a moment.

Laura did as James asked her to, but she quickly faced him as soon as they had walked a few paces away. "Any reason why we left her there to bawl?"

James nodded. "Yeah. Anything we could have said to her would have gone in one ear and out the other. She's too focused on it to hear what we have to say."

"But the whole point," Laura argued, "of the Wiseman visiting you last night was to tell you that we need to be together on this. And the first thing you do when she needs us is walk away."

James shrugged. "You can talk to her if you want, but I know how she feels. I lost both my parents the night we got here, and I didn't have a damn clue where I was or what I was doing here, or who anyone around me was. I got over it, but it took time."

Laura nodded in agreement. "I guess, yeah."

By this time, Amanda had wiped some snot off the edge of her nose, dried her tears, and gotten up from the fire. She now approached James and Laura slowly.

"I, uh...I apologize for what happened there. I lost my head."

James shook his head and approached her. "Don't apologize. We've all been through a lot in the last two weeks. No wonder you lost control when all that caught up with you."

"It would put a strain on anybody," agreed Laura.

But Amanda now had a fierceness lurking underneath her. "And I guess that means I'm the weak link, right? James, you got over your parents' death while you got used to being here. Laura, you were almost ready from the word go when we got here. I just...went along for the ride, I guess. I put everything I left behind on the backburner, and now it burned me. Right in the butt."

James sniggered at the comment but straightened up. "You're funny, Amanda."

Amanda nodded. "Good to know. Maybe I'll have a career as a jester."

Laura approached her, but Amanda backed away.

"You two keep doing what you're doing. I'll catch up."

James said, a little louder to her, so everyone else around them could hear, "I had another visit from the Wiseman last night."

This stopped Amanda and everyone else dead in their tracks. Talen and Jaenen had heard everything before, so they took a little less notice to this.

"Is it true?" asked Browning, who now approached Laura and James.

James nodded. "Four times he's visited me now, and what he said was that we need to turn every ounce of fear we have, every feeling of sadness that creeps up on us, every natural diversion away from death that guides us, into hope. We need it, no matter how bad things look. No matter how deep we are in shit, we need to turn it around and open our eyes to the hope that will carry us to victory."

Joven and Johnson nodded in approval. "You could make for a hell of a speechwriter," the latter commented.

Amanda had been facing away from James until he started his little encouragement speech, and as soon as Johnson had said his peace, she darted for the area of ground she had called home the night before and had done in thirty seconds what it took the men around them five minutes to do. She was all packed up and ready to travel.

"Okay then, Mr. Smarty-man, lead the way."

James shook his head and pointed toward Ed, who had already begun walking to the north.

"That's his job."

Amanda and Laura both smiled at this and started to follow him. That's when it happened.

Out of nowhere, a woman jumped onto James' back and tried to bite at his throat. Or it felt like a bite. James couldn't piece it together for a few more moments, but it was a small blade.

Talen was the quickest to react, retracting his blade and preparing for battle. But he saw that this woman was not alone. Six others were approaching from the east.

Their appearances were similar to the man that Ed had battled days before. The mountain men had followed them and were seeking revenge for their lost brother.

All the others in the group started taking out their weapon of choice, Amanda reaching into her pack for a dagger, Laura finding her pack a few paces away and wrestling out her bow. Darven also chose the bow and took aim at one of the mountain men.

Everyone else except McQuint also chose swords, McQuint joining Amanda with the choice of dagger, though his might have been due to it being the only weapon he had. Since he, Browning and Joven had fought with the army of the capital, they had only been equipped with swords.

McQuint had lost his on the run to the capital, but had picked up a dagger from a fallen Mainmen. This was usually done in honor, but McQuint had done it out of desperation. The old adage of passing weapons down posthumously was taken seriously by the Mainmen, so he kept this to himself.

The six mountain men were armed with animal claws and other improvised weapons, most of which were jagged, uneven, and nastily sharp. It was luck that none of the eleven found themselves on the wrong side of a point.

James was still wrestling the woman on his back while the other ten went to battle, save Jaenen, who rushed to help James. After a couple of evasions, Jaenen was able to pull the woman off James, and without hesitation, she had a sword through her gut.

Young Realms felt at his throat, expecting to see blood when he pulled his hand in front of his face, but he was also spared. Jaenen gave him a pat on the back and motioned for him to join the others, who were in the midst of fighting.

Talen had taken care of one of the shorter, seemingly younger mountain men, and Amanda had managed to pierce another one along his arm, but the killing stroke came from Johnson, who hacked at the man's back until he fell forward. Then Johnson raised the sword above his head and split the man's skull in one stroke.

Laura had two mountain men, a man and a woman, with an arrow in each of them, but they still fought. Brave Browning finally landed a killing blow on the man, a stroke against his chest, and the attackers were down to three.

The man whom Laura had hit with an arrow also succumbed to a blade from Ed, who decapitated his foe.

McQuint's dagger repeatedly hit another mountain man, and finally he fell forward and never moved again. Two remained.

And these two threw their weapons at the group in a last-ditch effort, then turned and started to run back east, where they came from.

Laura fired an arrow toward one, and with some surprise, managed to hit him in the back of the leg. The man collapsed for a moment, then tried to get on his feet again. It was all in vain, and soon he was on his stomach, groaning, reaching back to try and take the arrow out of his calf.

While everyone else was watching this one, the other mountain man was some sixteen paces ahead of his partner, and out of range of anyone's arrows.

"Great", quipped Talen. "All we need is one."

Amanda looked confused. "One what?"

Talen sighed. "One to get away. Now who knows how many will come after us next time?"

Jaenen shook his head. "Talen, why not complement our newest member for a fine shot? Otherwise, two of them would be gone."

Once again Talen sighed, then threw his sword down. "Let that be a lesson to everyone: never let a wild one go. Their vengeance is thicker than blood. And it is blood they will spill when we see them again."

Darven joined his brother, and without saying a word, gave Talen a face that convinced him to shut his mouth for a while.

Everyone in the group examined each other and themselves for any battle wounds, found none, cleaned their weapons, and began to start their journey. After the fire was fully out, and no evidence was left of a camp being there, Talen and Darven were the last to leave the site.

Nothing was to be done with the bodies of the mountain men. Perhaps their friend would come back for them someday. If not, thought James, let the birds and animals peck at them until their stomachs were satisfied.

After a few minutes, Laura caught up with James, who was just behind Ed, leading the pack.

"You all right?" she asked.

Amanda now started to quicken her pace to hear the conversation.

James sighed. "Yeah. Felt a little close for comfort there for a second, but I made it."

Amanda was now with them and put her arm around James while they walked for a while. "Good thing you didn't get hurt. I wouldn't know what I would do without you."

"Neither would I", quipped Laura. "You're the one who gets the inside scoop from the Wiseman."

James laughed at this, the first time he had really shown any emotion since the attack. "I guess I am, yeah."

The three stayed together the rest of the day, and other than the occasional pit stop, none left another's side.

* * *

The eleven walked almost another two hours before their next interruption in the journey. Amanda, James and Laura had walked close to a hundred miles in the previous two weeks, so the days of walking now were a small obstacle compared to what had come before.

From the start of things to now, James had probably lost something like ten pounds, and had begun growing in some facial hair thicker than he had in years. He usually kept clean-shaven, but there weren't exactly any motorized razors lying around in Winterlon.

Amanda and Laura, on the other hand, were in better shape than James was when they arrived, so any change in weight for them was smaller in nature, but still noticeable to the crew.

In the last stretch, Browning and Joven had both approached different parties with their interest in taking up Mainmen training, especially given how the fight against the mountain men had gone. While both had started out as warriors in the capital's army, it wasn't the same as being a devoted Mainmen.

Their creed, as Ed had explained on arrival, was to be warriors sworn by blood and oath to defend peace and honor among the citizens who show it. They displayed strength and wisdom equally. Laura, James and Amanda had been trained along the way to the Mainmen camp, and then sworn in by the former leader of the Mainmen, Joren.

Browning had reached out to the youngsters while Joven approached Ed. Both answered in the affirmative, though they would have to wait until it was a better time before training could begin.

It wasn't long after Joven had shown his appreciation to Ed that a thundering sound came from behind them. Ed, who was now the last in the company, halted and called for everyone else to do the same.

Immediately, James and the others had ducked down into some taller dead grass in the flatlands they were still trekking through. But Ed had unsheathed his sword and prepared himself to battle whatever enemy was ready to consume them.

It wasn't more than ten seconds after the ten others had ducked down that Ed began laughing, triumphantly, at what he saw. It wasn't, as everyone had feared, a mass of Deadman ready to take their lives. It was a pack of eight horses galloping up to their owners to be reunited.

As Joren had explained to James before riding down to Arnic Canyon, these horses were not just common stock in Winterlon. They were as devoted to the Mainmen as a Mainmen was to his cause. The young foal James had mounted and rode into battle had grown attached to him, as had happened with Amanda and Laura. And now, like all good steeds, they had tracked down and returned to their masters.

Ed embraced the head of his horse, a dark-brown one about sixteen hands high, who snorted his greeting at him. James also was found by his foal, a dark brown male with white socks, looking a lot like its mother, and a similar greeting was exchanged.

"How did they find us?" asked Amanda.

"They never lost us," answered Talen. "They must have caught our scents along the road. You see, when the rider is lost, the horses return to the last campsite, which would have been not too far east of here. Once they knew we were still alive, they abandoned that and came to us."

James reached down and pulled some grass out for the foal to eat. He turned to Ed.

"What's yours named?"

Ed gave him a funny look. "We do not name them. They have no reason to be named."

Laura dropped her jaw at this. "Why not?"

Ed chuckled and replied, "We may not have the cats or dogs that you possess on Earth, but we understand the idea of what you call 'pets'. And why do you name them?"

"Uh, because that's what we do," replied Laura.

Darven stepped in now, riding his black horse, about fifteen hands high. "You name them because it's a way to train them, right?"

James got it. "I see. The horses are already trained to come to you and listen to you. They don't need a name to answer to. They just...know."

Ed nodded. "Yes."

Amanda asked, "How do they know? How can they pick up your scent and know who you are?"

Ed explained, "Well, when you start a bond with these horses, they don't forget it. Riding into a battle is hardly a forgetful experience, even for a horse."

While Ed was explaining this, his horse was going to town on some grass as well.

He continued, "And each horse born with us follows a horse before it. James, your foal was with its mother, Joren's horse?"

James nodded. "Yeah. And he said to stay close to him because the foal would follow its mother."

Ed held his hands out. "And now it follows you. You made a bond."

"And that bond is never broken," added Talen.

"But what happens if the rider dies?" asked Amanda.

Jaenen, atop his horse, replied, "The horse gets a new Mainmen to bond with, unless it loses its life, too."

42

Laura shook her head. "Wait, you said every horse obeys the one before it. So, every Mainmen horse was bred around the cause, right?"

Ed nodded.

Laura continued, "Then everyone else here can't just find a horse and have the connection."

Talen replied, "Right. Not until it sees the other horses. Think of it as a communal display. The outside horse sees the other horses getting along with the rider, and eventually it follows suit."

Amanda asked, "But what about the other Mainmen? There were thousands of us down in the Canyon, and now we're down to ten people. Where are the other horses?"

Darven answered, with sadness, "I saw a lot of them killed when Aunten was in the Canyon, too. He flung them back. As good companions as they are, I don't know many that could survive the force he inflicted on them."

"He couldn't have killed all of them except these eight," Laura said.

Jaenen shrugged his shoulders. "Dad, do you know where they could have gone?"

Ed thought about it a moment. "That hasn't happened in several lifetimes. If they didn't follow these eight, they probably are roaming free. And I say let them; let the rest of their lives be as simple as possible."

James had seen so many things in the last two weeks and had experienced so much that he didn't care if it all made sense. He told Laura as such. "Laura, I don't think we can explain everything that happens here. Sometimes we gotta, you know, go along for the ride."

Laura couldn't help but laugh at his joke, and Amanda did, too.

Johnson, in the meantime, already had Joven on the back of his white horse as well, a magnificent horse standing eighteen hands tall, the tallest of the horses. He cleared his throat and said, "I think this has opened up an opportunity to reach our destination quicker. We might as well take advantage of that."

Everyone agreed and got ready to leave. Browning and McQuint shared a ride with Ed's sons, both of whom protested greatly to this, and started to ride. Amanda, who had a background with horses, including one at home named Fury, was quick to climb onto her tan foal. James and Laura, however, struggled, as they had when they first rode with the army down to the Canyon.

"You have to swing the leg closest to the horse up. Once it's over the back, you're home free."

None of the horses had saddles but were graceful enough when they trotted along not to bother the rider. James had only ridden horses once or twice before, but never bareback. Even through two days ride down to Arnic Canyon, he was still getting used to it.

Laura had a similar problem in her prior experience, but as with the Mainmen trained, she learned quickly and had beat James to mounting her foal, which was also tan like Amanda's, but had a white star dead center on the head. She was quick to join the others up ahead, bouncing along as gracefully as she could, for her foal was still getting used to her.

James was the last to mount his foal, who stood about twelve hands high, showing he still had some growing to do. He did finally manage to mount him, which was greeting by claps from Amanda.

"Yeah, thanks, asshole," he replied.

Amanda only laughed more so. "You'll have to catch up now." She turned her horse with her hands, which began to follow the others.

James, in the meantime, pat his foal on the neck. "I don't care what Ed says, I've got to think of a name for you."

He thought about it for a while, then it came to him.

"Rohan. Like off *Lord of the Rings*. That's a good name for a horse. All right, let's go."

As James was saying 'let's go', the foal had already started following the others, and James re-adjusted to the slight bumps and rises and falls as Rohan showed off what he could do.

* * *

With the horses back with them, it didn't take more than another few hours to reach Longell. Ed and Talen led the pack, Jaenen and Darven and their riders behind them. Then came Amanda and Johnson with Joven. Then Laura and James bringing up the rear.

The three from Earth were not exactly taken away by how the city looked. It was a fairly simple village of about two hundred, with little houses and shacks every few paces. Not too many horses were in town, but there were a few cows and boars. A few winged creatures that had the same shape as a chicken, but which had red eyes and an extra set of wings on their rears, roamed the streets, moving out of the way of anything bigger that came up to it.

James had locked his attention onto one, questioning what it was. Johnson noticed this and called back, "Velas. We call them velas."

Sure enough, James and the girls came across a few pens full of mobwin, three-eyed sheep with much thicker wool. And a few pens where boars would paw at the ground toward anyone who got too close, and whose tusks looked painful to the touch.

"It's no capital," said Darven, "but we call it home."

Ed took the crew all the way down a mud street, down to the second to last house, which looked deserted. The roof, made of tree bark, was beginning to rot away, and some spots showed holes where bark had fallen away.

The eldest Hotean sighed in hopelessness. "I've been away too long."

"What did you expect? You've been helping set up the Mainmen camp for three months," said Jaenen.

Ed's horse, as well as Jaenen's and Darven's, knew where to go, behind the house, and the other five horses followed suit. James and Laura gracelessly fell from their horses as they started around back, but both managed to stay on their feet. Everyone else started to go inside, James and Laura being the last to enter.

The inside of the house was in as poor shape as the roof. Nothing was in order in the one level shack. A fireplace was on the far side wall, nearest the place where the horses went. Sure enough, Ed's horse stopped in front of a glass window to keep an eye on his owner.

Two tables sat about ten feet apart from each other, with four chairs around both. They sat on the opposite corner of the fireplace. Another window sat on the opposite side of the fireplace, but something must have fallen in and broken it, because shards of glass were in front of it. Ed noticed this first and moved toward the hole.

Elsewhere in the house, wooden floors were used, but the spots above in the roof where the bark had rotted away allowed for rain to make spots on the floor, and some of the wood had begun to rot from all the wet exposure. James happened to stand in a spot, only to see the wood from one slab of the floor fall away as soon as he stepped on it.

"Damn," said Ed. "I suspect this was broken by a thief."

Darven and Jaenen began to uproot one slab from the floor after another, disappointed in what they found below.

"No, nothing here, dad," said Jaenen.

"For Wiseman's sake! You'd think a Mainmen's house would be spared this foolishness!" said Talen.

Ed chuckled. "You've been away for too long, Wadenston. Longell has its good people still, yes, but with them come the mistrustful, the parasites. Any one of them who comes along now will see our weapons and think twice, though."

With this, Jaenen and Darven both became a little excitable. Ed could tell why they were doing this and nodded toward the door. They both ran out and headed for another part of the village.

James was confused. "What is it?"

Amanda replied, "They have wives here, remember?"

5. A Fork in the Road

Darven and Jaenen lived down the mud path a ways, six houses down and on the opposite side of what they would call a street. Their houses were right next to each other.

Darven lived in the house closer to Ed's. His wife, Veridey, was a shorter woman with long flowing brown hair. Her face was plain, but beautiful, nonetheless.

He came running up toward the house, and bust through the wooden door, to find the house empty. Everything seemed to be out of place. Their house normally had a wide range of flowers in every nook and cranny they could fit it: windowsills, shelves, the table they ate their meals at.

But the house seemed totally bare and filthy. At first Darven feared the worst. His wife had abandoned him. She had found another man and taken the child with her. Or worse dumped him with another family in the village.

"Veridey!" he yelled. He heard no answer. A thought sprung to his mind, and away he went to the back of the house. He had forgotten that she had wanted to begin working on a garden.

He rounded the corner of the house, and his eyes met a figure that he recognized instantly: his wife, Veridey, dressed in blue, but with a cloth over her head. A few hairs flew with a slight wind out of the west, the rest were covered under the tight cloth.

Darven had been away from her for two months, time spent in preparing the Mainmen camp. He had imagined in his mind over and over the idea of returning home and seeing her again. But it had never played out like this.

Her face was sad, her eyes puffy from tears, but not new tears. A huge grin had come over Darven when he first saw his wife, but now that grin was fading.

Veridey moved forward to pick up a couple of sticks from a nearby tree, the equivalent of a white ash, and there stood a sight that Darven could not have ever imagined.

He took three paces forward and dropped to his knees. In an instant his face had broken, and with it his spirit. A stone lay in front of him, embedded halfway into the ground, and rubbed smooth. On top of the stone were four letters, spelling out the name Kale.

It seemed like an eternity before he finally bent down to ground level and put his arms around the stone, which couldn't have been more than a foot across and ten inches tall. He cried enough tears to make the brown, dying grass renew itself to a fresh shade of green, and he would do so for a long time.

* * *

At the same time, a much happier reunion was taking place next door. Darven had beat Jaenen to their homes, and Jaenen had passed right by Darven's door, oblivious to what was happening inside as he did.

Jaenen stormed open the door, and found his wife, Maryann, near a fireplace on the back wall. Like Ed's house, the setup was a fireplace in the middle, two windows on either side, wooden floors, and a table off to one corner of the house.

Maryann, red-haired and very young, seven years Jaenen's junior, immediately dropped the velas she was cooking into a large, empty black cauldron and gasped at the sight of her husband.

"Yeah, it's me," said Jaenen, and Maryann rushed across the room and jumped into his arms. They kissed passionately for several seconds, then she put a hand to his face.

"It's been so long, Jaenen."

Jaenen smiled. "Yes, those two months felt like purgatory."

The two walked over to the cauldron. Outside, chatter began to pick up as the others in the town knew that the Hotean family had returned. Jaenen had closed the door before walking over to the cauldron, so most of the chatter was out of earshot, as was Darven yelling for his wife.

Jaenen peeked into the pot and saw the velas by itself. "You've forgotten the water."

Maryann chuckled at her action and nodded. "There is a spot down the street where I have been getting it. Bring back two buckets. The second one you can use for a bath."

Jaenen nodded and chuckled. He hugged his wife and kissed her on the top of her head before grabbing two buckets, made from a blacksmith, and leaving the house to fetch the water.

When he was outside, he looked down from the way he came and saw everyone else making their way toward him. James, Amanda and Laura were spending a good deal of time looking at each house they passed along the way.

Jaenen smiled and laughed, saying, "Friends, Maryann is preparing a large velas for supper. We can all eat here."

Browning was all smiles, licking his lips at the idea of a meal that wasn't made from foliage.

Ed, however, noticed that the front door to Darven's house was wide open, and as he entered the doorway, nobody was inside.

"Where's your brother?" he asked.

Jaenen shrugged his shoulders. "I need to fetch some water for her." He then turned and headed toward the south, to where she had pointed when talking about the water.

There were no windows that could show the back of Darven's house, so Ed became nervous at the sight of it being empty. Talen, however, glanced toward the back of the house, and did see Veridey, facing away from Darven, who was on the ground.

"Ed," Talen said softly. Without seeing it himself, he had already formed in his mind the reality that was about to come before his eyes.

The doorway was empty now and Ed started walking as quickly as possible toward Talen's voice. Talen backed away from where he was, let Ed get ahead of him, but put his hand up so nobody else could pass. McQuint and Johnson were the first ones to try and follow Ed, while everyone else followed Jaenen's invitation and entered his house next door.

Ed had seen a great number of sad sights in his life prior to today. His father had been killed by a treacherous pirate; the morning after it had happened, Ed had woken up to see his father pinned against their wall. His mother had died peacefully on her bed, but only after withering away at eighty-three years of age. Even his wife, Bel, had died seven years previous from felfish, and he had held her hand for three days straight while it happened. But he had never had to see his son in anguish.

Ed dropped everything, his pack, the sword given to him by Joren, and he walked slowly up to his son, who lay on the ground crying. All Ed could do was pet at his back in comfort, but it would do no good. He turned away and scrunched his eyes tightly, tears falling down his face.

By this time, Darven had been on the ground next to his son's tombstone for nearly five minutes. He finally gathered enough strength to go back up on his knees. He turned his face up toward the sky, and tried to yell in pain, but no sound would come from him aside from gasps between sobs.

Ed was back on his feet and facing away. Talen, meanwhile, had covered his chest and bent down to one knee, a ceremonious sign of mourning. Johnson and McQuint had done the same when Talen bent down, and they could see what was happening.

The other six travelers would find out in different manners, at different times. All of them would feel the pain and loss. None of them would be spared of shedding tears for their comrade's bereavement. All the hope and goodwill that James had whipped up earlier that day was exhausted, like the last, small light from a candle blown out. At the moment, no one could say or do anything to light the flame anew and carry it onwards.

* * *

Jaenen was left to be with Maryann while supper was being prepared. Everyone else headed off to the far corner of the village, where the pub was located. Named after the village's founders, Moser's, was the spot for every man and woman to find when their spirits were up or needed up.

Ed found it hard to not drink to excess, but knowing that they couldn't stay in Longell more than a few days kept him from going overboard. The sorrowful loss Darven had experienced fueled him as well, enough to drink three more cups than normal.

Talen and the other men, besides Browning, who didn't drink alcohol, also drank a little more than they normally did, save Johnson, whose eight-cup limit was matched, but not exceeded.

Even James and Amanda, who were just shy of legal drinking age back on Earth, shared in the pain and drank a couple of cups of beer. Back on Earth, James had tried beer a couple of times in high school, but it never sat well with him. It had been a year and a half since his last one, so James had a hard time getting his second cup down.

Amanda, who had lost a brother and a mother, knew the pain of losing someone so close, and managed better than James did, though she did not call for a third cup.

Laura, meanwhile, was the sole person in the company to join Browning in sobriety. She had had a few fun nights back at NYU, but still being underage, she had carried over fears of being carded in a public bar. Even though Winterlon didn't have any laws about minors drinking, she was too far out of it to care.

Ed managed his last cup of beer and was about to call for everyone to finish what they had in front of them, then get ready to go. The light outside was beginning to diminish, and Jaenen and Maryann would worry about where they went to. That's when Ed felt a hand on his shoulder.

"Hotean, old friend. You're back."

Ed turned to find Autman Callus, a man who had never fought before, but was strong enough to be a Mainmen, before him. Autman was younger than Ed, about thirty-nine years old, and had a small scar under his right eye from an animal he had killed in the wild a few years ago. He was bald, his head large, and he wore a brown tunic with a lesser shade brown trousers.

Ed had not much to say to him. Most men of Longell either went off to fight for the country's capital, the capital of Winterlon, or to join the Mainmen cause. Autman had done none of the above, instead staying back to provide for his family and to farm, but he kept in physical shape to cause problems for many at Moser's.

"Autman", he finally greeted him. "Not a surprise to see you here. I believe this is where we last met."

His neutral 'friend' chortled at this, and said, "I'm sure it was. You know, a few men here thought you were dead. News traveled quickly about what happened at the Canyon."

Talen, who was seated next to Ed, started to get up from his stool, and showed off his impressive height to Autman, who was six inches shorter than Talen.

"I see your friend here survived as well. Wadenston, if I'm not mistaken."

"You are not," replied Talen, in an unfriendly manner.

Ed put a hand up to stop Talen from saying anything else. He turned back to Autman and said, "If you don't mind arriving at the point, Autman, we're about to leave."

Autman laughed again, and continued, "Of course, Hotean. We were hoping to meet you outside."

Joven, who was on the opposite side of Ed, now was up. He reached for a sword, but Ed, out of the corner of his eye, spotted this and shook his head.

Ed sighed, then said, "I suspected you might have been the one who robbed my house. Just to encourage me."

"No," said Autman. "I was not the one to rob the house of Hotean. I was trying to tell you that in your absence, and with the idea freely floating around that the Mainmen were gone, that the alliance is coming back."

The company, minus Ed and Talen, were puzzled by this saying, which Autman said with pride.

Talen and Ed both laughed heartily at this. "The alliance? Really?"

Autman shook his head a bit in surprise. "I thought you would have taken it as a sign of pride. The alliance is what stopped the Deadman last time."

Laura was the first to ask, "What is the alliance?"

It was not Ed, but Autman who answered first, with a question. "Who is this?"

"Laura Jacobsen. I'm here with Amanda Richardson and James Realms, from Earth. We're Mainmen now."

Autman once again had to laugh. "Ed, I'm very glad I ran into you now. I had no idea the cause was in such disarray."

Joven had heard enough. He unsheathed his sword, and the pub, which was not very loud beforehand, now was dead silent. The bartender reached underneath the bar and grabbed a pair of daggers.

She called out, "Any fighting is to be done outside."

Joven put his sword away, but kept his intensity unsheathed. "Do not insult the leader of the Mainmen," he said seriously, and for the first time in the conversation, Autman did not have a smile on his face or a laugh coming out of his throat.

Instead, he replied, "I mean, to go to Earth and gather outsiders to try and get the Mainmen back to strength, you'll need the alliance."

Amanda said, "Okay, it's been a long time into this conversation, and I still don't know what the hell this alliance is."

Browning, who was seated next to her, replied, "The alliance was a pact made by non-soldiers back in the first days of the Deadman ruling Winterlon. Because they didn't answer to any rules or code, they were able to grow strong enough to help defeat the Deadman and restore Winterlon. That's what one side of history says."

James heard all of this, and soon after the pub went back to its previous decibel of small talk.

Talen, meanwhile, had replied to Autman, "If you think for one moment we're going to abandon everything we have fought for just to be with you, you're mistaken."

Autman was serious still, and said, "Wadenston, you are one to talk. The stories were that you had already abandoned the Mainmen years ago to join up with the knight force." The capital's best guards made up the knight force, but were now extinct after the loss at the Canyon.

Talen slammed his cup down on the bar, which shattered. "I have always been loyal! A word you fail to have in your vocabulary."

Once again, the pub was beginning to grow silent. Autman noticed it again, as did everyone else, and finally he replied, "Very well. But know this, Hotean, the men of Longell and the towns around are all ready to fight. Not for you, or your lost cause, but for the alliance. Should our paths cross again, we might not be allies."

Ed had nothing to say to this, and as the conversations around the rest of the pub picked up again, Autman Callus left, a heavy step resounding everywhere he went.

McQuint, who was on the other side of James, breathed a sigh of relief when the whole ordeal was over.

"You were awful silent during that," said James.

McQuint nodded. "Yes. I was afraid I would speak out of turn, since I had joined up with Slank. Autman would just cry out my hypocrisy."

"Can you tell us more about this alliance?" asked Laura.

After a few sips of beer, McQuint nodded. "I'm no historian, but what Browning said was right. They have no rules, no honors they are bound to. If they come upon a village, the men and women of the alliance can steal what they want if they are hungry," he paused to take another drink. After swallowing it down, he continued, "and want it badly enough. If they are without horses, and come upon a stable, they will leave it bare. If an enemy surrenders, they will show them no mercy."

After another sip of beer, McQuint shuddered a bit. "Perhaps it would have been wise to ask Callus how many he had with him. Then we'd know the state of things."

Browning shook his head. "What worries me is that this is one village. Imagine if every village around us begins to form their own alliances. They'd kill each other before Aunten could."

The group would only have a short time to think on this before they would leave Moser's. It was almost suppertime.

* * *

What would have been a pleasant, heart-warming welcome-back meal was now a somber, joyless gathering. It was hard to share tales of battle and victories and kinship when a homecoming like this had been ruined.

Indeed, the velas was big enough to feed eleven people. It would have been thirteen, but obviously no one had expected Darven or Veridey to join them. And so, the eleven ate in silence, occasionally a belch would come out of one of the men, and one did come out of Maryann, which brought a brief sliver of laughter to the table, but that was the extent of it.

Alongside the velas, bread was served, or blund, as it was called on Winterlon, which had been cooked the previous day on a stone. The crust had hardened perfectly, and the next day Maryann would bake another two loafs for the travelers to take with them.

There was also some wine, bought from a nearby village, Jelia, which held the largest market in the southern portions of Penulton. If you couldn't make it yourself or have it made by a tradesman, you bought it at Jelia. That was the rule of the land.

After fifteen minutes of silence, when everyone had consumed everything they could, though their appetites were respectably smaller due to the day's events, there came a time when Ed cleared his throat and it was back to business.

"I..." he started. Everyone else leaned forward in their chairs and waited in anxiety until he started up again.

"We've come to a fork in the road. We've traveled north, but now we need to decide what to do. Obviously, what's happened with Darven will keep him motionless in this fight. I think it's best for him to stay here, stay with his wife until he is well again."

James really didn't want to say it, but he couldn't help himself. "Ed, I know it's not the time, but I'm remembering what the Wiseman said to me. I—"

Ed leapt up from his chair, screaming, "You really think there is a Wiseman? Huh? After what I've seen today you can never convince me! A Wiseman that sees over everything in the world would never let anything like this happen!"

He tried to carry on, but he became short of breath, and sat down, caught it, and trembled in his spot for several moments. Everyone became deathly quiet again, and Amanda silently began to cry, as did Maryann. Talen silently shed a tear as well. His emotions had mostly been kept in check, but this last outburst caused it to boil over, even if it was just one tear he could shed.

James continued, swallowing the metaphorical bitter pill, "I just mean what he said about all of us being together. It all happens for a reason."

Ed sniffled and continued, "Then perhaps there's a reason Darven will not join us going forward. And I mean it, he has his own family to look over, and I will not put him through a war knowing he has less to go home to when this fight is done. Family is the greatest motivator we can create, especially in a time of war, but only if they are safe and alive. I'm not going to put the responsibility of forgetting what happened on his shoulders."

Talen nodded. "Then I suppose, Ed, now is the time for us to decide what to do next. What road we must travel."

Laura cleared her throat, then said, "And what we can do to defeat Aunten."

Browning stood up from his chair, saying, "I suppose there must be a way to stop him. After all, the

Deadman ruled all of Winterlon for two generations before one sprung up that could kill them."

Talen pointed toward Browning. "I'm afraid I've already brought this up. If there is a public display, or a book that does reveal it, and Aunten knows about it, he will have destroyed it by now. Unless you know something that we don't, having worked with Governor Slank."

Browning shook his head. "I was a humble guard until the last few days before battle. If anybody knew about it, it was Hilka, his trusted servant."

Hilka had been the last person to die before Slank in Aunten's taking of the capital. A trusted, loyal man, he had been looked upon favorably by every worker, guard, and citizen of the capital.

"Then there has to be another way," said Laura. "There must be. Where else can we go that would know about it?"

Johnson shook his head. "I wouldn't know where to begin. Ed?"

Ed had been silent this whole time, and he put a hand up to his forehead, wiping off some sweat that had built up from all the excitement. "Right now, I'm more worried about protecting the people of Winterlon. And the way to do that is to have a force willing to fight for them."

Amanda piped up, "Didn't we try that? I mean, we had an army of thousands, and we couldn't beat them. The capital had an army, and they all died in vain. We're going up against thirteen demons that have escaped hell. Where are we going to find a place where more people are going to willingly lay down their lives, knowing they won't come home?"

McQuint was able to answer this. "The Mainmen cause exists for exactly that reason. To fight for the good people. We'll lay down our lives if need be."

"We aren't enough," Jaenen argued. "I know what you're going to say, dad. We need to figure out where to go next. Knowing you, the Benshidi would be your choice."

Ed nodded in agreement. "Yes, my boy. But I don't want to speak for everyone. Please consider all of this before we put it to a vote.

"There is a complication with each direction. South means trying to end a civil war in Geinashaw. West means traveling across a heavily guarded river that cuts us off from the rest of the inhabited lands of Winterlon. East would mean going up against the rest of the mountain men, and lest we forget, they're all angered at us for taking some of their people. Even if we get past them, we'd be journeying into the unknown. North means traveling across mountains and not knowing who will be friendly or threats on the other side, but…"

James sighed in disbelief, then said "Now we're back to the same argument we had days ago. We're no better off. We're worse off, for many, many reasons."

The table became quiet again and stayed that way for a few seconds. Then Laura asked a question.

"Is there any chance that the people up north can help us with more than physical force? Could they have a library or a records of some sort that tells of the history of Winterlon, and how to kill the Deadman?"

Ed knew where Laura was going with this and said, "It's possible."

Johnson piped up, "Knowledge and the force to back it up is a lethal combination. This war could be over before it begins. Aunten would be easy work then."

McQuint cleared his throat, "I've been thinking, and there's a reasonable conclusion I've drawn about our enemy. Aunten has already shown us that he has no meaningful reason to keep killing innocents. Some of Sadhill's civilians were left untouched. It wasn't a total annihilation."

Joven added, "And the people in the capital are all still alive. Only the military were depleted."

"That we know of," replied Talen.

James asked, "But what about Merryjae? And all those other Virk and Sadhill villages along his route to the capital? So many of them are ashes now."

"But he stopped," replied Joven. "Governor Slank heard updates from many scouts about villages like Merryjae. After a few days, he quit. Many villages in Lear were spared. We can't say for sure, but Carni probably still stands. He didn't venture north enough to destroy this town, or any of the others."

Ed nodded. "And I suspect he's concerning himself more with Geinashaw".

Talen jumped in. "Now there is a force that would help us defend the people of Winterlon. They may even be brave enough to sacrifice some of their men for the safety of the innocent."

Jaenen replied, "Talen, they've been at war for nearly two hundred years. Even something like Aunten won't make them forget all the bad blood."

Talen continued, "I'm not sure. I think Geinashaw is an eventuality we'll have to face. Prince Hinja has the bloodline to become their leader, and he is someone who can be negotiated with. Sooner or later, we'll have to meet him and try and end their conflict."

Johnson chuckled. "They will not be pleasant to outsiders, so good luck."

Before anybody else could say anything, the door to the house opened, and Darven stood in the doorway, his pack on, sword sheathed, and determination on his face. He walked into the house, looking around for a chair, but found none to sit on. Everyone else sat where they were, except for Jaenen and Talen, who were standing from the previous conversation.

Darven cleared his throat and said, "I'm coming with you. Whatever you're doing, whatever you're deciding, my place is with the company."

No one said anything. Ed sighed, got up, and walked over to his son. "Darven, you're putting on a brave face, and I am impressed by that. We all are. But we need not be. Your place right now is with your wife. She needs you."

Darven shook his head and his voice cracked as he talked, "No. There isn't anything for me now."

"Yes, there is," said his father. "I spoke with Veridey. She had nothing to say to me. She was as still and quiet as a ghost. You need to be here with her until—"

"No!" shouted Darven. "I would be ashamed of myself if you went off and I remained."

Ed got right in Darven's face, saying, "I will strip you of your name if you come with us. You would bring shame to the name of Hotean, and I will not have it!"

The son shook his father off and walked away from the table, looking toward a wall. Jaenen walked over toward his sibling.

"Brother, none of us know what you're going through right now. Your wife hasn't been through this. And you definitely have not been through this. So you can't know for sure what you need right now."

The younger of the two sons turned toward his brother quickly and with purpose. "I need something."

"A distraction? No. Distractions are for the weak."

"This wouldn't be a distraction for me. It would be purpose."

"When you and Veridey had that boy, you were given a new purpose. Even though he—he's buried in the ground, you still have that purpose. And you still have the purpose of a husband."

"So do you, but you won't stay."

Maryann got up from her seat, ready to join in, but Ed put his hand up, signaling for the brothers to talk it out.

"My wife will carry on without me. Yours I fear for."

"You're saying my wife will not know what to do with herself?"

"Yes, and you can give her a purpose again."

"Just have another child?"

"Yes, but not to cover up the one you've lost. Not to replace him."

Maryann said from across the room, "Darven, I've been with your wife every day since it happened. It was only seven days ago, and she is filled with more grief than I've ever seen in a person. She needs someone to be with her."

Darven turned toward Maryann. "A perfect job for you."

"She needs a man to be with her. She needs her husband."

Finally, Jaenen had had enough. "What would he think?"

This cooled everyone down. Darven, however, still had a sour look on his face. "He?"

"Your son. What would Kale think if he were old enough to understand this? Would he be proud of you? Abandoning his mother at her darkest hour? Taking only a couple of days to get over his death? No. He would want you to be a father. He'd want you to be responsible."

Darven shook his head again. "You didn't know my boy." There was a long silence after this, and even Jaenen couldn't think of anything to counter it with. Darven continued to shake his head. "None of you knew my boy."

Darven's whole body then tensed up and his eyes went wide. His breath shuddered then, his eyes squinted, and he began to sob. A realization hit him, like a sword through his gut. As if all the lights in the world had suddenly gone out, all of the determination and attitude toward continuing the journey was gone. "I didn't know my boy."

Without another word, Darven, still wearing his pack, slowly wallowed out the door, closing it behind him.

Once again, the whole house was quiet. Most of the people at the table, even some of the men, now had wet cheeks from the emotions of the argument.

Darven's visit had upset the mood. Ed shook his head after a long silence, and said, "We'll pick up on this tomorrow. Everyone can sleep where they please. I'll get some wood and start a fire at my place. It'll be warm enough there."

The group then slowly started to drift apart. Talen agreed to sleep at Ed's house, as did Joven, McQuint and Amanda. Everyone else remained at Jaenen's house, which was considerably warm given the cauldron cooking the velas in the late afternoon and most of the evening. A lot was to be said for what would happen next, but after this troubling day, nobody had enough gumption to start a conversation after the house had been emptied of everyone who wasn't staying.

6. A Stoke in the Fire

In the days following his last meeting with the Deadman, Aunten had entrenched himself into the library of the capital. In it lay books as old as the city itself, and tales from generations before. One story that Aunten desired to find out about was that of the warrior that had killed him three years before.

Being a former man of life, Aunten's memory wasn't all there when he returned from hell. He remembered the capital, he knew his Deadman, but everything else was spotty. In his prior life, he had known Pam and Roger Realms, James' parents, and Ed Hotean and Talen Wadenston, but if he saw them the moment he had returned to the world of the living, it would be doubtful he would recognize them. It wasn't until he saw the reflection of Roger Realms' face in the Endin River that he fully recognized his former ally, and knew he was going to have him killed.

The warrior who had killed Aunten was unknown to him, and his name wasn't written down anywhere. He had in five days' time looked through nearly every page of half the books in the library, but nothing materialized that helped him.

He was partway through a book on William Abner, the governor who held the capital before Slank, when he was interrupted by Sienel.

"Excuse me, sir. I was here to tell you of an update."

Aunten shut the book and got up from a small table he was seated at. "Ah, a good time for distraction. My eyes were loathing what they read about William Abner. Not a greater coward has ever lived."

Sienel smiled in agreement. "Yes, indeed. A scout from the mountain men have informed me that one of their own fell. At the hands of a Mainmen, they believe."

Now Aunten's curiosity was fully engaged. "You figured they would head north and now we can confirm it. The only question that remains is how far north they will venture."

It had truly been a long night of discussion and planning in the map room earlier that week. All of the Deadman agreed that the Mainmen survivors were retreating north, Sienel the first to suggest it with the others agreeing. Where their destination took them was never decided.

Sienel bowed to his master, then stated, "It would be a great pleasure if we were bestowed the task of wiping out the Mainmen. Let them only be read about in books such as the one you hold in your hand."

Aunten replied back, "Sienel, I grant you a great deal compared to the other Deadman. They only hold council with me on my request. You have been my dearest friend, in this life and the other. But I cannot task you with this."

"Sir?" asked Sienel.

"I realize that you and the others have been presented with a quality that millions wish they could possess: immortality. But Sienel, as you well know, nothing can last forever. One day, even I will be called back to hell. You know there is a danger when you present yourself in battle."

Sienel nodded. "Yes, sir, but it is a danger I do not fear."

"Perhaps you should." Aunten now turned away from him before continuing. "You know when you are struck down in this form you cannot return. The devil will keep you in his stock like mobwin. Never again will you be given the opportunity to walk the grounds of Winterlon.

"If the Mainmen are to be wiped out, it will be done with the other Deadman. Intimidation is a wondrous key to success."

Sienel nodded in agreement. He then asked, "So, do you wish us to proceed? Shall we head after them?"

Aunten chuckled, then exploded into laughter at his thoughts. Once he had calmed down, he responded, "Give them a day more's head start. Let them think they are safe. Only then will they realize their true failure."

Sienel bowed to Aunten once more. "Then I shall speak with the scout and ask for more information. The man was lost not too far from the Virk border, so we know they are not to the Wise-Mountains yet. Rest assured, sir, once we learn from the mountain men their location, they will not live long."

Aunten smiled and dismissed his follower. He then went back to searching the library, where he would spend a great deal of his day, the evening, and the following day before finding what he sought.

* * *

Ed and Talen were up early the next morning, and not by choice. Halfway through the night, their sleep had been interrupted by a noise by Ed's broken window. As it turned out, there was indeed a criminal who had been using Ed's house to sleep in. His intrusion was met with Ed's blade, and the criminal was never heard from again.

In many ways, Ed was pleased to know that Autman was telling the truth. Though that reality also kept him awake part of the night; knowing that indeed, for the first time in generations, the alliance was about to begin to form. Possibly many alliances.

They spent most of the morning cleaning up around the house and making it livable. Ed had gone to a store down the road and paid fifteen colliers for more bark for his roof (colliers being the equivalent of dollars). Talen, Amanda and he had spent most of the morning repairing the roof, while Joven and McQuint continued to make the house as spick and span as possible.

The others five that would continue the journey were tasked with preparing for their departure the next morning. Ed had briefly spoken with them, revealing that during supper at his house that night, he would let them know the plan. What they didn't know was that it would take until then for him to come up with that plan.

Browning and James spent most of the morning going around to the blacksmith and armory shop and sharpening blades, buying more arrows, and fixing and replacing the shields. Laura, Maryann, and Jaenen went to the market uptown, next to Moser's, and bought some other foods for them. Johnson, meanwhile, went over to Jelia to exchange rupten to colliers, then colliers for tadhips, and finally tadhips then for billuds, as Winterlon currency went.

With that money, he would buy food for the horses, more exotic foods than could be found in Longell, some beer and wine for himself and anyone else who would partake and ordered some new clothes to be made for them. He had taken down everyone's sizes earlier that day and would come back to pick them up the next morning.

70

It had been Ed's idea to Johnson the night before that they shed their Mainmen gear, so as not to be so easily spotted. They could pass as travelers, refugees, whatever story they could come up with in case they ran into anyone faithful to Aunten.

The trouble was that each Mainmen was equipped with a scar on their dominant hand, three horizontal cuts and one vertical cut. Any time a stranger tried to inspect their hand, it would give away the true identity of the travelers, that is the ones who had the scars. Joven and Browning were the only two who did not have them.

Ed regretted that he did not have the luxury or the money to buy everyone gloves to cover their hands. Especially in smaller markets, gloves sold quickly when the weather was cold, or if agriculture was a strong proponent of the economy. Too many farmers had sores, blisters, or scars of their own from using their hands all through their lives. And if the gloves were all to match in color, that would take extra money and time. For now, they would take the risk, and ask that once the new clothes were presented to the Mainmen, they try their best to keep their hands in their sleeves, at least the one that was scarred.

James and Laura then returned with Maryann in the early afternoon, while Jaenen went to check in on Darven. Maryann began to bake some blund, one made from wheat, the other made from oat.

During the baking portion, James and Laura were joined by Amanda, whose hands were beginning to get rawer than they'd been in years. Her reward for the work on the roof was to have the afternoon off.

All three of the twenty-year-olds got to know Maryann fairly well. She had been born in Jelia and her family had moved to Longell ten years prior. She had met Jaenen during that time, but his Mainmen training took up most of his hours. When he was fully trained, he began to see her more often, and they fancied each other very much.

Three years prior they had married, and the following year Darven and Veridey had wed. Maryann was heartbroken right after the wedding when she learned that, for the second time, she was not able to carry Jaenen's child. While there were few physicians or apothecaries around that knew of childbearing, the only advice she could receive from the ones she did see were not to try again. It could result in the loss of another child and Maryann as well.

So, Maryann, naturally, took a large affinity in Kale when he was born, and was over at Darven and Veridey's house every day, or nearly. She had been there to witness him take his first steps and proclaim Darven as his 'dada'.

Finally, James asked, "So, ahem, when did...?"

Maryann, who had told nearly all of the story in high spirits, was now less so. "It all started two weeks ago. He came down with the felvish. It's common around here. In fact, Jaenen said when he was a little older than Kale, he had nearly died of the felvish. It took their sister, too."

"Wait," interrupted Amanda. "They had a sister?"

Maryann nodded. "But she was not born of Ed and Bel. Bel had been with a man, not of her choosing, prior to Ed, and he had implanted in her the girl. She died when Ed had just met Bel, so he was not so distressed when it happened. At least that's the story around town. No one could say for certain but him.

"Anyway, this felvish, it took Kale and kept him in bed for four days. On the fifth day, he began to improve. The felvish broke, and he could walk around the house, little kid he was. But then the following night, the felvish returned, and then he would sweat and sweat and sweat, then his whole body went red, and we knew that it was too late."

"Too late?" Amanda asked.

"When they get to that stage, they begin to suffer. Horribly. Their breathing gets so hard that it makes everything else shut down. They can't walk. They can't speak. They can cry, but that's all. They can live for another week or so when they're all red, but each day will be more and more painful for them.

"I...I couldn't do it. Not to my own nephew. So, his mother did it."

Amanda gulped, but asked, "Do we even want to know what 'it' is?"

Maryann choked back tears but continued. "She smothered him."

James and Laura's posture dropped as they sat and listened further, and neither could hold back tears as well.

"H—how old was he?" James managed to ask.

"He would have been two in four months. Darven was there for his birth, but then had to go back and finish his training. He was back in Longell when Kale was nine months old. Other than that, he didn't get much of a chance to know him before he and Jaenen left for war. And now poor Veridey hasn't known what's hit her since."

The four sat in silence for some time before Jaenen returned. His news was not too pleasant as he offered an update on Darven and Veridey. Both of them had spent most of the day lying around, with Darven occasionally going out to the yard to make sure Kale's tombstone and his burial spot were well kept. He did so several times already that day and would do it many times over before retiring to bed that night.

There was no doubt about it, Darven would not be able to come with them as their journey continued. This came as no surprise, but still he would be missed in the fights yet to come.

* * *

That evening, the leftover velas served as the meal for the eleven people gathered in Ed's house. Blund was broken, velas devoured, but still the mood was no less sour.

Ed stood up once the meal was over to let everyone know the scoop. "I suppose I can say that it's official. It'll be us ten heading out tomorrow morning."

Maryann, seated next to Jaenen, grabbed his hand beside one of the tables. They had been pushed together so everyone could gather around the same place.

Ed continued, "And I suppose for those of you who don't know, we should fill you in on the details of our new journey."

He turned to Talen, seated three down from him. Jaenen and Maryann were in between the two men. Talen stood up now, but Ed remained standing.

"Our destination is Dulon, the country that houses the Benshidi."

Jaenen closed his eyes in frustration but kept silent. Joven and Browning were silent as well, but their mouths gaped open, jaws dropped.

"Amanda, Laura, James, I know you probably have never heard of them. But they are famous, or should I say infamous, for what they have done."

James and the girls waited for the shoe to drop, but the table was still silent.

"Are we supposed to ask?" asked Amanda.

Talen nodded, and had Ed continue. "The Benshidi are a proud race from an established civilization farthest north on the compass here in Winterlon. They've had a long history as some of the proudest warriors ever, next to the Mainmen, that is."

Ed lifted a glass of wine, courtesy of Johnson, and nodded toward his fellow warriors, who smiled at this.

He continued, "But about thirty years ago, there was an insurrection. And their leader, Queen Quartha, was betrayed by her own company. A few men in their keep were displeased with their leadership and demanded a retirement. They wanted her to step down because of her warmongering mood. She was prepared to scavenge all the lands of Winterlon and root out all darkness."

James remembered something at this moment, and raised his hand, as if he were in school. Ed looked at him, but not knowing what raising a hand meant, only gave him a questioning look. James realized this and put his hand down.

"Sorry, felt like I was in history class. Uh, I remember you said the guy who killed Aunten three years ago, he wanted to do the same thing, right?"

Ed nodded. "True. It's a certain madness that lies within some people here, I cannot explain it. History will show this to be true. For every person like Aunten Schritz who is taken over by evil, someone else is possessed by good and has an unquenched thirst for domination, one way or the other. Queen Quartha had it, and she ended up having a sword thrust through her.

"Anyway, the Benshidi are a pacifistic culture now, under the rule of King Linus, the man who put the sword through Quartha. They shut their gates to their keep, and no one has entered or exited the land since."

Laura interrupted, "And we're going there."

Talen helped out, saying, "I believe Ed and I have agreed on the appropriate course of action. Our ultimate goal will be to reunite the country of Geinishaw, and riding up to them with the Benshidi at our backs may be the proper motivation. If it goes well, it will trigger a movement across all of Winterlon that we must stand together if we're going to have any chance at taking down Aunten."

James smiled. "And I'm sure one of those people will know how to kill him."

Johnson got up from his chair, a few drinks in him, but not drunk, and started laughing. "Hotean," he started, then walked over from the far end of the table, where he was seated, and brought his hand down sharply onto Ed's shoulder, "I knew Joren chose you for a reason. The Mainmen cause lives."

The man still held his drink, lifted it up toward the ceiling and shouted, "Mainmen!"

To which everyone initiated, that is everyone except Browning and Joven, responded, "Strong!"

This had been the cry before the group had left their camp on the ride down to Arnic Canyon. A tradition held back since the beginning of the Mainmen. It was another proud moment for James, one he wouldn't soon forget.

* * *

That night everyone except Jaenen and Maryann stayed at Ed's house, and the fireplace was quieting down when most everyone else had decided to go to sleep. However, this was not true for Amanda, James, and Laura, who were restless.

Joven and Browning were still awake, so the three decided to have a private conference outside. All three of them took to noticing the air wasn't as cool as it had been in the days previous, so they weren't holding themselves for warmth as they spoke.

Laura started. "Guys, did you notice that something was missing from Ed's plan?"

James shook his head. "He didn't go into much detail."

Laura continued, "He didn't say anything about asking those people up north, Benshidi or whatever, if they know how to kill a Deadman."

Amanda replied quickly, "I'm sure he won't overlook it. Ed knows as well as anyone that if we're ever gonna win this thing, we have to figure out how to kill a Deadman."

James nodded. "It's another stoke in the fire. This whole world has been split apart by different factions and wars. You heard what they said in there: Ed and Talen want to use this as an opportunity to unite Winterlon."

Laura checked to see if anyone was watching them. Then she asked, "So what do we do if Ed and them don't get along with the Benshidi? If they kick us out, we'll have no idea if they know."

James suggested, "Even if the Benshidi don't, someone knows. An old sage or soothsayer, magician, I don't know, somebody. It's a big world, as big as Earth."

"Why would a magician know? Do they even have them here?" Amanda said in ridicule.

James sniggered at this. "I don't know. But I say we make another pact between us: we do everything we can to help the Mainmen, but also work to finding out how to get rid of the Deadman."

The two others agreed. Then, one by one, they looked up to the sky. They were not able to see stars very much in their first journey to the Mainmen camp, for most nights had been cloudy. But tonight, the two moons were out bright, and the stars with them. They appeared much the same as they did on Earth, and with that they gave off a perception of a peaceful time and place where nothing could go wrong.

None of them had ever done the clichéd 'watching for falling stars' act as kids, teenagers, or young adults, so they couldn't directly speak to this, but they knew that if they held up to this plan, and Aunten, his disciples, and his dark warriors were killed, they would one day be able to look up at the stars in peace. Maybe their children, at their belly, watching with them.

7. Dress Code

The sun rose on a peaceful morning in Longell, but before it did, Ed and Talen were already on their way back from Jelia with the new sets of clothing. On purpose, they shoved open Ed's door to startle everyone out of sleep.

"Wake," said Talen. "The sooner we get started, the sooner you can eat."

He then dropped half a pound of balen on the table, the Winterlon name for bacon. James remembered his early conversations with Jaenen and Darven about this, and from his spot on the ground, he shook his head, then pulled a warm, thick cloth over his head.

Eventually the nine of them were seated around the table, eating the balen and some eggs that Ed had fried over the fireplace. The door opened again and Jaenen entered, his pack full of the food Maryann had prepared for him and everyone else, and an unsure smile on his face.

"Son," Ed cried before standing up, "you're here a little later than we demanded."

Jaenen chuckled. "Blame Maryann. She didn't want to let me go. It's hard, you know, to see your spouse leave you again so soon after being gone so long."

There was a silence from the two tables, again pushed together for breakfast, as most everyone knew the experience personally. That is, everyone who had a spouse.

Ed then started to speak after Jaenen was seated. "So, our path lies as such: we must cross the Wise-Mountains, travel about another hundred miles, then we shall enter the keep of the Benshidi. It's about forty miles to the base of the mountain, so that should be an accomplishable goal by the morning after next."

He looked around, as if to give a moment for anyone to ask questions. James had one.

"What about the horses? They can't make it over the mountains, can they?"

Ed shook his head. "They cannot. If they wish to join us again, they'll have to do so through the Lanzman forest. They'll join us on the other side."

Amanda was confused. "Hold it. How come we can't go through the forest?"

McQuint answered, "Because it is forbidden. Any living man who enters pays the price of death."

"And Aunten may be a conqueror," Browning added, "but he is not one to skip tradition. It's likely he's guarded the entrances, like Slank before him."

Talen nodded at this. "Any pack of horses would look a little out of the norm to these guards, but they'll let them pass, let nature run where it wants."

Amanda asked, "You guys said to get over the mountains is dangerous. Why not head south to the forest entrance and make sure first before trying the mountains?"

Ed replied, "The reasons are two. First, no one in this room has ever set foot in the forest. We've no way of knowing which way to go once inside. Second, if we do go south and find the entrance is guarded, they'll know our position, and Aunten and the Deadman will come after us."

No one else had any questions about that subject, but Amanda did ask Jaenen a question.

"Why doesn't Maryann come with? If she misses you so much, why doesn't she travel with us?"

Jaenen shook his head. "She has had no training."

Amanda then turned toward Ed, who sat at the end of one table. "That doesn't mean she can't come with, stay back and out of sight if we run into trouble."

Ed opened his mouth to speak, but it was Johnson who answered, sitting across from Amanda. "The Wise-Mountains that stretch into the north also have their own band of mountain men. We might have to kill them to get over it."

"And you saw what they meant to do to us," Browning added.

This was the end of the breakfast conversation. Everyone else ate in silence until most everything was consumed. Extra balen had already been included in the journey, in the packs that kept food cool, but the leftover from breakfast was happily included in the provisions. Everyone that had been on the journey to the Mainmen camp was glad to know there would be more variety this time in their meals.

Talen then propped up the sack he carried from Jelia, carrying the freshly made clothes.

"We will be civil here and allow the women to dress first," demanded Joven.

This was met by a nod from Ed, who said, "Pick whatever color you would like. I believe the tailor had a variety. Johnson told her that we had two females and eight males, so there should be proper things for you in there. The men will have tunics underneath, as is the custom."

Speaking to Amanda and Laura, he added, "You two can wear them as well, if you please."

James then went with everyone else as they exited the house while Laura and Amanda changed. It didn't take more than two minutes before they emerged, Laura now in a emerald dress made of silk, and Amanda in a blue kirtle. She had also changed her hairstyle, allowing her hair to flow naturally down instead of in ponytails. James had to take a moment, as did several of the other men, to examine the good work done by the tailor and how well the two women looked in them.

"You look like you belong in Oz," James joked. "How did you win the battle for the dress?"

"Really, James, to think that all girls fight over clothes. Amanda took one look at it and said she'd rather dress as a pilgrim."

Amanda defended herself, "Well, I get it's not pilgrim dress, but it looks a lot like it. What would you call these things?"

James turned to the guys, most of whom were deep in thought. Jaenen answered, "I haven't ever had to wear one, so I don't know."

Browning, however, did have the answer. "They would call it a kirtle in the capital."

The group turned to him, curious as to how he knew the answer.

Browning just shrugged. "I worked for a year as a tailor's apprentice. I know a few things."

So now it was the men's turn to dress, and James had recalled from a community bath on their journey last time that underneath tunics, men went commando. He wondered if the same was true for women. The men had given him a hard time over it, especially McQuint.

"What matter is this that you wear extras underneath?" he bellowed to him, followed by a laugh. McQuint then turned his back toward James, who wished he could erase permanently from his mind the image of McQuint's backside.

James shot back, "We call it underwear. You ought to give it a try."

Ed and Jaenen were the first to laugh back, and most everyone did. James chose a red tunic to wear underneath his new set of clothes. He saw a pair of black pants that he squeezed into and tucked in a white linen into it.

James saw that of the clothes provided by the tailor, only two sets of jackets that would go over tunics were available. Sizing them up, one looked to be his size, a russet jacket. After slipping it on and buttoning it up, he emerged first from the house, careful to close the door quickly behind him to shield Laura and Amanda's eyes.

While far from fashion critics, Amanda and Laura both gave him a thumbs up from his picking. Next came Browning and Johnson, who both wore a dark shade of blue for pants and had white linens underneath outer tunics. Browning's was umber, Johnson's was beige.

"I see the men's clothes were slim pickin's. You don't get to choose between dresses and smocks. It's all linens and jackets," said Laura.

"And hope to God they're wearing pants," added Amanda, which brought a snort from Laura, who quickly covered her face from embarrassment.

Ed and Joven came next, again with pants of the same color, canary, and white linens. Ed chose not to have his outer tunic on, instead his was packed away. He had picked one of carmine, but it would stand out from a distance. Well, more truthfully, he hadn't picked it out, it was the last one available.

Joven, meanwhile, had been the one to pick out the other jacket, a traditional black as midnight color.

Amanda had asked Ed where his top was, then showed them in his pack the carmine color, which brought a laugh from everyone outside.

"Yes, you laugh now, especially you, Joven. You're going to bake in that when the sun is high."

Everyone else came out at the same time. Jaenen had on some gray pants with white linen and a yale colored tunic. Talen had on the same canary pants, white linen, and a slate outer tunic. McQuint chose black pants, white linen, and a shamrock top. It was the second silliest by most everyone's standards, but all together the group would look a lot less like warriors.

James now realized that there were three people who did not look like servants: Joren, Laura, and himself. Before he could say anything about it, Ed launched into a short explanation of what to do on the road.

"Now, when we do travel, we can keep our weapons on us. But if we are discovered by others who wouldn't do us harm, we'll have to hide most of them in the packs and put them on the horses, while we have them" explained Ed.

Talen added, "What will help this is the illusion that most of us are servants. Amanda, your...what was it called again?"

He turned to Browning, who said simultaneously with Amanda, "Kirtle."

"Right," replied Talen. "Your kirtle will give off that impression. If we spot anyone coming toward us that could find us out, we'll just have everyone jump off their horses and lead them. Servants are expected to do that."

"Not everyone," Ed added. "Since my sword is so different than everyone else, I'll need someone to take it in my present dress."

He turned to James and nodded to him. James was taken aback. There were so many other guys that could have been a fit for this, but not him.

"Why me?" he asked.

Ed smiled. "We could say you are the son of a lord. You're running the show, telling us where to go and how to get there. If we're stopped, you'll have to play the part. And no son of a lord would not hold the best weapon in his hand."

And so, Ed unsheathed the Mainmen sword, the one Joren, in one of his final moments, had given to Ed to carry on the Mainmen cause. The tradition was for the sword to be passed, and the receiver to bow in honor. Talen motioned for James to do so. Even though this would not be a true passing, and Ed would remain leader, it was James, and not Ed, who would have the sword for the time being.

Not more than a minute later, everyone who had a horse was on and ready to start. Browning ended up sharing a ride with Amanda, Joven rode with Talen, and McQuint was with Jaenen. The ten of them would cross nearly thirteen miles by the end of the day and wouldn't see a sole as they crossed several plains.

Most of them were flat, but an occasional rolling hill would come up. The land was beginning to look greener again, and Ed had pointed out in the distance a few Septipod plants that were responsible for it. On their journey last time, the three from Earth had discovered these plants. Septipods were almost in the exact shape as a sunflower, but with lilac blooms, and a dark red stem and head. They had roots that stretched out, sometimes for hundreds of feet that grew crabgrass, giving the land the green look. They were poisonous to humans and horses, but only to eat. To cut one open would release water that held in the stem, and that was safe to drink.

The weather that day had started out so pleasant, but slowly clouds began to roll in, and by the late afternoon, the party had to travel through rain. The fire James and Ed started that night had to be protected by a pair of thick clothes that were hung far enough away from the fire so as not to burn. It was a night of cooked boar's meat, which again tasted great to everyone. The next night, Ed promised, would be cuts from a cow.

Most everyone got to sleep early that night, and the rain wouldn't let up until late the next morning. James' final thoughts before he came to peace were of sadness, for two reasons.

First, he thought back to his parents, and how he missed them. While he wasn't that close with them back on Earth, he knew they would have been proud to watch him take the Mainmen oath, and elated when he was passed the Mainmen sword, which he still had with him for the moment.

Second, he thought of Rohan, and how he would part with him as soon as they reached the Wise-Mountains. Everybody else would part with their horses as well, but as somebody who never really had a pet, James now understood the pain of leaving one behind, and not knowing when, or if, they'd ever see them again. Back on Earth he did have a cat for a short time, but his mother was allergic and they had to sell it.

He didn't know how, but eventually these sad thoughts left him, and he was able to drift off to sleep.

8. The Wise-Mountains

As the rain continued to fall two days later, Ed announced after a rushed breakfast of balen and Maryann's oat blund, "We're nearly to the base of the first mountain. We'll try to climb it today. My guess is we'll arrive there by just after noon. Finally."

The rain had slowed everyone down and having to eat meals that did not require a fire to heat or reheat it was not nearly as filling for the company. The cow meat would have to wait until the rains stopped.

Jaenen asked, "Should we try to climb it in one going or should we rest on the mountain?"

Ed replied, "Son, resting on the mountain is a dangerous idea. We've no idea what creatures will be waiting for fresh meat while we rest during the night."

James' eyes went wide, and he inquired, "So we don't have to worry about just the mountain men? There are other things here?"

A high voice said, from a few feet away, "I'd worry about them, all right."

Everyone turned to see a hooded figure with an armed bow. It wore a light blue cloak and appeared moderately tall, about five feet nine inches.

Ed put his hand to his sword, ready to unsheathe it. "Who are you?"

The figure replied, again in a high voice, "I would have thought you, of all people, Edward Hotean, would recognize my voice."

The figure removed the hood and revealed a lush woman, in her mid-thirties. Her hair was dishwater blonde and her dark blue eye sparkled. Then she said, "Now maybe you recognize Gwendolyn Asfair."

87

Ed's eyes widened. "Gwendolyn!" He rushed to her, and they embraced.

Johnson couldn't get over something. "I'd like to figure out where her last name came from."

Amanda hit him in the shoulder, and he winced a bit.

In the meantime, Ed announced to the group, "This is Gwendolyn Asfair, who formerly trained under me."

Gwendolyn said, "And it was after I realized the mistake of working for the capital that I yearned to see you and Wadenston again. Hello, Talen."

Talen, who had been walking up to her as she spoke, also embraced his old friend.

Gwendolyn said, "A pleasure to see you again."

Talen replied, "The pleasure is all mine."

Gwendolyn also recognized McQuint, and said, "And McQuint. But you've gotten a little fatter since last I saw you."

McQuint replied, "True, but you haven't lost a touch of beauty."

He bent down to one knee and kissed her hand. After he rose back up, he said, "And what brings you here?"

She replied, "Anyone who ventures even one hundred feet from the base of the mountains could see your company coming. So many bright colors."

Jaenen replied, "Well, you stand out as well."

Gwendolyn replied, "Quite. But the mountain men and beasts know me by sight and name, and not to cross me lest they die a quick death. What is your name?"

Ed said, "Oh, excuse me. I didn't introduce. This is my son, Jaenen. We also have with us Michael Joven and Ted Browning, former workers of the capital, and the man there," as he pointed to Johnson, "is Erik Johnson, a present Mainmen."

Gwendolyn took a moment to nod her greeting, but her eyes stopped on Johnson. "I believe the name Erik Johnson is familiar, but not the face."

Talen replied, "Yes, you left us not long before his induction. After review."

"After review?" Gwendolyn asked. "I don't hear that too often. And what, may I ask, would trigger a review before taking the oath?"

Johnson stood at this and replied, "That's for us to know and you to find out. Perhaps the hard way."

His nature was joking, but he put a hand out toward her. Gwendolyn took the arm and bent it to the point of some tendons popping and a sharp look of pain to come over Johnson's face.

She shook her head at him. "I have fought off advances from several creatures more charming and amusing than yourself, some of them had skin slimier than yours. I don't intend to step into something unless I know the outcome."

Still she held her grip, and Johnson continued to wince in pain. He wouldn't give in, but instead started laughing at his predicament. Part of the laugh was his amazement at what was happening, but also a side effect of the pain.

"Don't let go, don't let go, don't let go" whispered Amanda.

Finally, Johnson stepped back and prepared to have control again, but Gwendolyn didn't release.

"If anything is to happen in that nature, it is started by me, understood?"

Johnson nodded. He had stopped laughing now and was trying to hide his audible cries of pain.

"And that doesn't just go for me, it goes for anyone else around you whom you have an eye on."

Johnson nodded more rapidly this time, but still Gwendolyn held on. Ed and Talen started to take a step toward him to help, but Amanda and Laura, both in a state of elation, gave them both a death stare that kept them back.

Gwendolyn concluded, "If you don't, you'll wish that this would have been the most painful thing I had done to you. Do we have an understanding?"

Before Johnson could do anything else, Gwendolyn released her grip and Johnson gasped. He backed away and returned to his spot, embarrassed and ashamed.

"I just found my new personal hero," said Amanda. Laura nodded along.

Gwendolyn walked away from her previous spot and now looked down on James, Amanda, and Laura.

"And who might you be?"

James stood up and offered his hand, shakily. "James Realms, daughter of Pam and Roger."

Gwendolyn took his hand, and at first yanked it forward, as if to repeat her actions with Johnson, but exclaimed in joy at his horror. Laura and Amanda were giggling, not just at this, but at James' description of himself, which he didn't catch.

"And these fine ladies?"

Seated, both Amanda and Laura waved to her and said their names. Gwendolyn bowed to them.

"It's been some time since another woman has been seen in this area. It'll be a pleasure not to be alone for once."

Ed piped in, "Laura is Arnold's daughter, and Amanda is—"

"Dawn's," finished Gwendolyn. "I could surmise that."

Gwendolyn shook hands with the two now, saying, "Nice to meet you. I had the honor of fighting alongside your parents. We miss them dearly."

Ed frowned at this. "You knew Roger and Pam were gone?"

Gwendolyn nodded. "They would have been the first among you I would have recognized."

McQuint asked, "Won't you have some balen and blund?"

Gwendolyn replied, "I would, gladly, but my meals nowadays are the likes of bretnin and nolos."

"Then this would be a welcome change for you," invited Browning, who stood up and offered Gwendolyn his seat.

She nodded toward him and sat down. "Thank you."

Johnson offered her some balen, his hand shaking in pain, but she shook her head at him.

"I suppose," started McQuint, "you could tell us about what you've been doing with yourself all this time."

Gwendlyn shrugged. "It's a long story, and I'm sure you have one to match it. Why else would you be coming this far north?"

Ed bit first. "Because we are on our way to try and summon the Benshidi to fight against Aunten Schritz. Surely you've heard of his return."

Gwendolyn replied, "Yes. The news of his ascension from hell doesn't fail to reach even the ears of Gwendolyn Asfair."

"Then you must know," said Talen, "that we are all that remain of the Mainmen. Perhaps you haven't heard of the great battle at Arnic Canyon."

Gwendolyn replied, "I did not. But it makes sense. Aunten is now a Deadman, giving him abilities far beyond even an army of Mainmen to best.

And your acceptance of me was a sign of desperation, Hotean. I take it you now lead them."

Ed nodded. "In times such as these, strictness with the old ways is to the detriment of the cause."

Amanda was a little confused. "What do you mean?"

McQuint answered, "You took the oath, did you not?"

All three of the youngsters nodded.

McQuint continued, "Remember you swore to uphold truth and wisdom, to fight for the cause of good—"

"Good as it prospers", continued Gwendolyn. "I swear to die only at the enemy's hand, or when the Wiseman calls me home."

Everyone else who was initiated, and had been for a while, finished, "This I swear". They had been mouthing along with the rest of the words once they knew Gwendolyn and McQuint were reciting the oath.

James got it now. "So, since the Wiseman didn't call you home, and the enemy didn't kill you, you didn't uphold your oath."

Gwendolyn nodded.

Ed picked up from there. "In the old days, to come across a fellow Mainmen who has abandoned the cause meant you had to kill them. But the past two leaders, including Joren, were more favorable. Since our numbers and our resolve was not what it once was, we cannot chop off the heads of warriors who would help us."

It made a lot of sense, but Johnson added, "Though it is worth saying, there are those who held the old beliefs, who would have tried to kill Gwendolyn, or McQuint."

"Or even me", added Talen.

Ed shook his head. "If I had the acumen, and everyone else did as well, I'd do away with that rule. Maybe even remove it from the oath."

This was met with some looks of disgust from some of the Mainmen faithful, even McQuint, who approached Ed.

"You remove that, it changes what we stand for. Radically. Men and women join us to be part of something, and they know the price they pay. I did. I'm grateful for you sparing my life, and allowing me to join you, but how many others will join if they know they can get away with their heart's content?"

Everyone was silent for a moment, and Ed, still young in his leadership of the Mainmen cause, knew his suggestion had gone too far for the crew he had with him. There was an uncomfortable silence that followed for a time, before finally Laura broke it and changed the subject.

"Do you know the stories of the Deadman, from the last time they were here?" She aimed her question at Gwendolyn, who shrugged.

"I know of some stories, of them burning whole stockades to the ground, setting animals aflame, and butchering children in their beds."

Amanda said, "I think she meant as far as how they were killed. Because they can be killed..."

"So I've heard" was Gwendolyn's reply. "But I know nothing of that. I'm no sorceress or enchanter spouting incantations."

James snarkily asked, "Do they not have the word 'witch' in their vocabulary?"

"But," continued Gwendolyn, "I do know that to beat the Deadman is a road that cannot be traveled without many, many, many lives lost. It took two generations to do it last time. And that was at a time like today, of utter tribalism."

Talen agreed, "That is why we are approaching the Benshidi. With the evidence of Aunten's return, and their muster, we can add Prince Hinja to our side as well. Then we would have a force large enough to keep the evils of Winterlon at bay."

Gwendolyn nodded. "Clever, Wadenston. Clever. But that will not keep the innocent alive. What Aunten will do with them is inevitable. One day, death, natural or not, will take everyone into the afterlife. It may be by the hands of the Wiseman, or the blade of Aunten. Either way, an army will only be a nuisance to him."

Jaenen replied, "It's the Mainmen's creed to protect the innocent, remember? What better way than having an army fight against him?"

"This fight is not mine. I am no Mainmen, not anymore."

Amanda and Laura both showed their disappointment. It was a near impossible task to tell between the two who was more so.

Ed shook his head. "We don't ask you to join us, Gwendolyn. You are the master of your own fate. The least you could do, then, is guide us through the mountain until we clear the other side."

There was a silence for some time before Gwendolyn stood up. "I will do that. Hotean, have your warriors pack away their tents and lets us go."

The group did as instructed, and Gwendolyn joined James on Rohan as they rode closer to the mountain that was due north of them. Even Gwendolyn's use of 'lets us go', which was commonly uttered from Ed, didn't go unnoticed by the youngsters. Not that they doubted Gwendolyn used to be a Mainmen, but it was further proof that she had not forgotten her old comrades, and their little idiosyncrasies.

* * *

Back at the capital, the conflict between Nerenger and Jenik came to a head. It was Jenik who had called the meeting, in an attempt to establish dominance over his fellow Deadman. Nerenger had been appointed to his duties by Aunten himself, so Jenik going over his head was an act of treason. The two men were aware of how to kill one another, and that if the act was done, there would be no going back. If the devil had allowed you to come back from the dead and your life was once again extinguished, there was nothing but darkness that would lie before you.

The meeting took place in the spot Aunten had agreed the Deadman could rest, the sleeping quarters on the top floor of the governor's mansion. The room had now been equipped with twelve beds, before only accounting for six. The room was spacious, and really could have accounted for as many as thirty beds. A torch was lit in between each bed on either side of the room, the twelve beds spaced out evenly on each side.

In the middle of the room was a great table, made from some of the strongest and oldest oak trees outside the capital three hundred years before. Since the room had been largely forgotten by the last two governors, the table remained in pristine condition.

Jenik arrived first, ten minutes before five o'clock in the evening. Nerenger was not late, either, arriving six minutes before. In the four minutes that Jenik stood alone in the room, he took little time to reflect what was about to be done. When they were men, Nerenger had been a lieutenant under Aunten, once a strong warrior. But his tenacity to bite off more than he could chew gave way for Aunten's defeat, and Jenik blamed his actions for all thirteen of their collective deaths. The campaign to take the capital gave him all the time he needed to consider the action, and what consequences it would bare. To an extent, calling the meeting meant there was no return from this point.

When Nerenger did open the door, the Deadman stood where he was and sensed the awful action that was waiting for him. While he truly feared there was nothing he could do short of physically stopping his friend from accomplishing his task, a few words beforehand might work in his favor.

"Old friend," he started, closing the door behind him, "I know what you intend to do."

"Then perhaps," Jenik replied, quietly, "I should hasten it."

A sigh came from Nerenger then, one of frustration that sent a slight chill down Jenik's spine. He reached down at his side where he revealed a sword that was attached by a belt. Reality was setting in. "Perhaps you would like to settle this another way?"

Jenik stood as still as one of the statues downstairs in the main chamber, the ones that honored the governors of the past, but only for a moment. Words failed him for the moment, so all he could do was reach down to his side as well and unsheathe his own sword, and mentally prepare himself for what was about to transpire.

A sneer came over Jenik now, and he wasn't afraid to show his willingness to go to battle. "Not while I breathe."

Within a moment, the two met in the middle of the room, their swords clashing. Jenik and Nerenger exchanged blows on each other, Jenik hitting Nerenger's shoulder, and the other hitting Jenik's abdomen. Both men still wore their gowns, with only the hood exposing any flesh.

The blows did expose the blood of a Deadman, a green puss that stained their gowns and dripped slowly onto the floor. At one point, Nerenger made a strike for Jenik, but Jenik's blade hit Nerenger's bony fingers instead, causing Neregener to drop his blade. Calling upon the darkness that gave him life, Jenik made Nerenger's blade melt on the floor, until the iron that had once been a lethal weapon now was a hot pool on the floor, steam rising toward the ceiling.

This gave Nerenger the further inspiration to also use the power he had. Jenik's body suddenly became limp and he also dropped his weapon. Nerenger saw the window on the far side of the room, and made Jenik's body fly through it. The shattered glass stuck into Jenik's head and arms and legs, but soon enough he jumped back into the room not long after Nerenger took Jenik's sword.

Knowing their powers were limited, Jenik tried one more trick, to bring his foe's throat to his hand, his body traveling through the air. He was only so successful, in that Nerenger had overturned the great table in the center of the room then returned to his feet.

With Jenik's sword still in hand, Nerenger charged his enemy and stabbed him repeatedly in the chest, the green puss returning. This only brought laughter from the former.

At this, the lights in the room began to go out, one by one. It was not dark enough outside yet for the room to be pitch black, but the ominous feeling remained. Then the door slammed open, and Aunten appeared, marching with purpose.

"You dare?" he screamed in his high pitch at the two Deadman. In a moment he had materialized a new weapon, a bow and arrow.

Jenik stayed where he was, determination on his face. "Master, I was relieving him of his duties. He failed to report all the happenings in Carni. Need I remind you this was not his first failure?"

Aunten's eyes filled with wrath, one that outmatched Jenik's just a moment earlier. "When did I appoint you the task of attacking your fellow Deadman, or of relieving them of their tasks?"

Almost against his will, Jenik started to move closer to the door, his muscles fighting it every inch of the way. The determination began to fade, and now fear and helplessness took control. "I would only do what you would have done."

A shake of the head from Aunten told Jenik all he needed to know. Jenik continued to move toward his master, against his will. There was no stopping it now.

"Please, please, please, sir, let me live and I will show forgiveness. Don't put me in the darkness. Not yet. We have so much more to accomplish, and I wish to see it!"

At this, Jenik now only had two feet between him and Aunten, who placed the arrow and was ready to aim it at his underling.

"I give you this as your only warning, Jenik. Nerenger's report was satisfactory, yours was not. Overstepping your grounds and covering his territory was in the wrong. If I feel he is following his instructions poorly, I will do what is necessary. Until then, your sins remain unwashed."

Aunten removed the arrow and put the bow on the floor. At this point, Jenik went to his knees, then to his stomach, his eyes glued to his leader. "How do I repent, master?"

No response came. Instead, Aunten left the room, Nerenger followed, only giving one look to his would-be executioner. Not one of thanks or warning, but one of pity.

In Nerenger's mind, he was willing to accept that the fault was his that he and the others had been killed by the knight force three years before. Aunten had selected him to spy on the capital, and inform his general when to strike. The timing was off, and the forces overwhelmed them quickly.

At first everyone thought Nerenger a traitor, but Aunten had relieved him of the blame, saying that he had had his own misgivings about the attempt, and should have trusted his own instincts. Since he had not, the invasion was a failure.

Now he knew that Jenik hungered for more power, and to redeem their past attempt. In doing so, he perhaps thought himself above the other Deadman and second-in-command to Aunten. But seeing how much fear could influence him, Nerenger could only pity the poor soul. He did not have the strength to back up his thoughts.

In the bedchamber, Jenik stayed where he was for some time before the fear passed over him. His master could have sent him to death once again, but spared him. Now at least he knew he himself could not do the same to the others. Instead, they would now see how weak he truly was. He would have to show his worth in some other way. What that was, however, never sprang to his mind that evening. The near-death experience kept him from sleeping most of the night.

* * *

Just short of the mountain's base, Ed stopped everyone and had them get into what he called "servant positions". That meant that the three in the group who appeared more higher up, James, Joven, and Laura, would be on horses. Most of the others appeared as servants or regular townsfolk. Gwendolyn knew she could still act as herself while they were in the vicinity of the Wise-Mountains.

James put a hand on Ed's sword, which caught Ed's attention. James gave a look that said, 'I'll guard it with my life.' It was then that James could feel a pair of eyes watching him. Perhaps more than one.

There they were again, mountain men, dressed in furs, mostly, from whatever creatures they had killed. Several of them looked ghastly, and faded blood still existed on some of them, but they were all armed, and looked merciless.

"Just some guests," called Gwendolyn, who was now walking at the front of the group. Her left hand never left her bow, her right hand ready to feed arrows in case things turned nasty.

There was a mystery yet to be solved to the three from Earth: how were they supposed to get over the mountains? Gwendolyn was leading them right for it, but her eyes never left the mountain men who watched over them.

The entire group was silent with tension, and kept their eyes away from those of the mountain men. Like the ones they had killed earlier, all from a distance they could see that their description was a match for the departed: coarse skin, rough teeth, black or reddened tongues, sunspots all over their faces. If they had been able to see their feet, they would have noticed some of them were missing toes.

Indeed, it had just kicked in now, perhaps more from fear than anything else, that James was now feeling more and more frigid. The mountain bases were met with grass still, but up ahead the grass was whiter and whiter, until it was unmistakably snow. However, from what James could see of the top of the mountains, no snow continued.

From inside her cloak, Gwendolyn took out a tight, black rope and swung it up toward the mountain, where it fitted itself around a strong rock perfectly.

"As you can see," she said, as she turned to face the travelers, "I've had a lot of experience."

Johnson laughed. "Then we'll follow your lead."

Gwendolyn's eyes next went back to the mountain men, most of whom began to disburse to whatever activities held their attention beforehand. A few remained, curious as to how the newcomers would take the climb.

The rest of the black rope was let out, and everyone could see it wasn't extremely long. Gwendolyn sighed.

"I apologize. I've never had anyone with me. We'll have to go in at least two groups."

Ed nodded. "James, Laura, Amanda, I want you to be in the first group. Jaenen, with them."

All four of them complied. Two questions now stood before the group.

"Ed," James began, "you're sure the horses will be okay?"

Johnson replied, "They know they cannot make it over the mountain. Fear not, they will find their path."

Amanda looked around to everyone. "Then they'll meet us on the other side?"

McQuint nodded. "The forest path is the only way."

James shook his head. "This is goddamn stupid. Ed, you guys can't be serious." He tried to contain his emotion, but the last words began to climb in pitch as his throat tightened, his lips wanting to quiver, his eyes became misty.

Ed put a hand on James' shoulder. "Remember what was said. These horses have a special bond with us. They'll find a way to join us again."

While not everything was resolved, Ed turned and the next question was one that didn't need asked aloud by anyone: who would go with on the first climb? Ed followed the rope until its end, and started doing some math in his head.

"Would you say," he asked Gwendolyn, "that we could fit six or seven on the rope at a time?"

His question was met with a frustrated sigh. "If you want this to end quickly, one way or the other, seven."

Ed shook his head at this. "We can't risk it. Two groups of six will have to do it."

McQuint scratched his head. "There's only eleven of us, Ed."

Gwendolyn answered for Ed. "I'll have to come back down and lead the next group up. Unless one of you wants to do it yourself?"

This was not met by a response from anyone in the group. Gwendolyn nodded in victory.

Ed continued, "That means one more goes with Gwendolyn."

"Who?" asked Browning.

Joven piped up, "We don't have time to put it to a vote."

"Which is why I'm going," proclaimed Johnson.

"I don't think so," was the reply from McQuint.

Short of everyone taking weapons out and starting a fight, everything that could have been done to slow down the process happened. Insults were slung, threats were made. Gwendolyn, meanwhile, whispered to the others to remain silent, and she had them all take hold of the rope.

As Ed argued with the others, Gwendolyn began to ascend the mountain. The hooked end of the rope was a good twenty-five feet up, so anyone who lost their grip would feel the pain when they landed.

James was right behind her, followed by Amanda, Laura, then Jaenen. They all were a tad nervous about the climb, but the playful nature from Gwendolyn leaving the others behind calmed their nerves a bit.

They scaled up to the spot where the rope was hooked relatively easy. No one lost their footing, and no loose rubble or rock fell beneath them.

It was Joven who first discovered what had happened and pointed up to the spot where Gwendolyn and the others had stopped.

She did, indeed, know her way around the mountain. There was a flatter spot where the five could rest for a moment. Gwendolyn took one look down at the six men left behind and smirked.

This was met by a laugh from Ed, while everyone else couldn't muster a word. Rather all that could come from it was incredulousness.

Fortunately, the six made the climb as well, Gwendolyn asking that the group of six split in half so that they did not put too much pressure on the rope. Talen, Browning, and Johnson went first, with Ed, Joven and McQuint being the last ones to reach the first landing.

Gwendolyn had them repeat the process twice more, different folks going up the rope in different groupings, save Gwendolyn, who always led. The second climb was less steep, maybe ten feet off the flat landing.

By the end of the third climb, the eleven were now a good sixty feet off the ground. Luckily no one had acrophobia. The arrival to this point was a small victory for the Mainmen, but their climb had only begun.

"Where do we go from here?" asked Laura.

Gwendolyn had already begun leading the group along a manmade trail that ascended on the mountain for a good fifteen feet. Then there was a hole that led inside the mountain. Gwendolyn entered, and everyone else followed.

9. The Caves

For nearly two days, it had been nothing but searching. Page after page was turned, but nothing was found that would be of any help to Aunten.

With the exception of the fight between Nerenger and Jenik, Aunten was successful in his isolation. He had ordered no distractions while he was going through the library. Jenik's overambition did worry Aunten, but knowing that even for people who had both lived and died once already, fear was a powerful force that could benefit anyone seeking a higher position.

If Jenik overstepped again, Aunten knew Jenik would flee rather than surrender and see himself thrown back into hell. Were that to occur, Aunten very much doubted that he would go to the trouble of finding him. He'd rather see Jenik live out the rest of his days knowing that he would always have to keep a head turned or an eye open. This pleasing sensation helped keep Aunten's mind at peace.

Turning his attention back to dull literature, Aunten was up to the fourteenth entry in the generic "history of Winterlon" series by unnamed scholars when he finally found what he was looking for.

It was not near as monumental a moment as Aunten had hyped it up to be. He merely ripped out the page and got up from the table he had sat at for what seemed an eternity.

As he called for someone to fetch him his horse, he read the page fully for the first time. The title was unmistakable: "The Killing of Aunten Schritz".

The scholar had made it a more or less mundane death for the Deadman who now read about his own demise. The warrior, Halun Leman, had taken Aunten's life then rounded up his followers, their deaths quickly following. Leman had the chance to remain at the capital, and one day perhaps even work his way up to being crowned as governor, but his lack of diplomatic upbringing told him not to chance it.

Instead, the same sting of destiny that had overtaken Aunten after the killing of Kildeno had overtaken Leman, though with the opposite result: instead of ever-ending villainy, Leman was given ever-ending heroics, wishing to travel to the furthest ends of Winterlon to rid it of darkness.

He read to the last three sentences of the page when he was greeted by Sienel and Fiernan. The close proximity with which Aunten was reading the torn page told Sienel everything he needed to know.

"I trust you've found what you sought," he stated.

This was greeted by a hand from Aunten on Sienel's shoulder. "I have, my friend. Have you heard anything more of the mountain men to the north?"

Sienel shook his head.

Fiernan stepped forward now, asking, "Should we investigate?"

Aunten smiled. "Do what you do best, Fiernan. If there is a problem, solve it. As violently as you see fit."

Sienel asked, before Aunten turned away and headed for the stables, "And what of Nerenger and Jenik?"

Aunten did not turn back to his comrades, but said as he walked away, "Jenik will pay the pittance through killing our foes. See that he does."

Turning his attention back to the page, Aunten learned that the last known account of Leman, deep in the Lanzman forest, near the end of the known maps of Winterlon. Leman had wanted to cross into the unknown, but sent off every follower of his so that they would not be tempted by an unknown evil.

This curiosity became all that Aunten could think about as he made his way toward the forest entrance, three days' ride away. What evil could even the great and powerful Halun Leman be wary of?

* * *

It was almost two hours of journeying into darkness when Gwendolyn, who led the group, stopped. She had a series of torches along the way, each a few minutes apart, depending on how far she had to travel into the caves before reaching her destination. The one she held now was getting low, so she traded it out for a fresher one.

"How many of those have you gone through?" asked Johnson.

Gwendolyn smiled and replied, "More than I would care to remember. I have to make them out of the hairs of Herenshi. And I've killed enough to bring them to extinction. At least extinct in this mountain."

Herenshi were moderately sized creatures with thin tusks used to penetrate their prey, and each tusk had a small hole from which venom would pour, further wounding and after a few moments killing the enemy. James, Amanda and Laura did not ask for details, but couldn't help but let their imaginations run. Their descriptions would not match that of reality, but most of them were worse.

Gwendolyn lit up a few candles that were sitting in various spots, and soon everyone could see her abode in the cave. There wasn't much, but a few spots where skins of animals hung, a fire that was nearly out in a corner, some books and papers in the opposite corner, and a small table with two small chairs around it.

"Where do you sleep?" asked James.

Gwendolyn sighed. "I just find a spot near the fire, grab a skin, and drift off."

It wasn't a very nice way to live, but for Gwendolyn, it had been her reality for several years.

McQuint asked next, "Where do we go from here?"

Ed answered, "Further into the mountain, I'm sure. We do have to gain elevation at some point, correct?"

Gwendolyn nodded. "But not immediately. It'll be another three hours before we reach the stairs. From there, it's an hour up, then back out. Hopefully the weather will cooperate, and it'll be a climbing day."

Talen was the one who had to bring the bad news. "Regardless of the day, we need to climb. Have you gone up only on climbing days, Gwendolyn?"

There was no answer immediately. She had to think before replying to Talen. "There is a reason they call them climbing days. I have not been the first to find out why. You risk my life as well as yours should you forgo the warnings."

Ed shook his head. "I recognize the danger we all face, but everyone in this company is willing to choose it, rather than face a showdown with Aunten without the Benshidi by our side."

Gwendolyn had to chuckle at this. "If you can even convince them."

It was James who answered. "We will."

"What makes you so certain?"

James swallowed before answering, going off the cuff. "Because we have to. Winterlon depends on it."

Everyone was silent for a while. Then Gwendolyn had to smile again. "For someone new to this world, you seem so sure Winterlon can be saved. You don't even know all the dangers of these mountains. How about I get as many of you out of here alive as I can before you worry about saving the world?"

Laura put a hand on James' shoulder, Amanda stepping up after a moment to do the same. James took the moment to think, then nodded to Gwendolyn in acknowledgment of her statement.

Despite the journey so far, it was not a tough task to get everyone to lay down and drift off to sleep. But before that happened, James, Amanda and Laura had a quick talk between them.

"I wonder," started Laura, "if any of her papers over there would help us."

Amanda turned toward Laura. She was in the spot closest to the entry point where the group had entered, James next to her, Laura next to him. It was a little difficult for James to keep up, having to crane his neck one way, then the other to look to each speaker. Amanda replied, "But she said earlier she didn't know anything of the Deadman, or how to stop them."

Laura replied back, "I know, but maybe she was lying."

James tried to ask something, but Amanda was ahead of him. "So suddenly you're the best judge of character when it comes to perfect strangers?"

"No, I just mean I think she wants to join us. Look at her place here, it's a mess."

"Some people live in a mess to survive."

"For a while, yeah. But after that, you get up on your feet and you make everything better."

Once again James tried to interject, but he failed. Amanda jumped in again, saying, "Okay, okay, so there's a chance she joins us, but what makes you think she has anything that will help us kill Aunten?"

Laura was still for a while. "I don't know, but I think we should check it. Before we leave, of course."

Amanda agreed. "In case she does join us and we never come back."

James' neck was hurting by this point, and he had to crack it a few times to relieve it. Laura jumped and let out a small shriek when this happened.

"Ahem. Sorry," he said.

Amanda laughed and rolled over, facing the empty cave they had entered in. This just left Laura and James awake.

James now turned to Laura, and it was for a great time he stared at her face, which he could look upon now for a while without turning away. The fire was still going, and the spot they had picked was illuminated enough for her eyes, cheekbones, and smile to be clear to James.

"Why are you looking at me like that?" she asked.

James couldn't help but smile. "I don't know, I guess I had to admire it."

"What?"

James' eyes went wide. "Uh…your brains, of course. I think you're right when you say that Gwendolyn might come with us."

Even with the low lighting, James saw her cheeks go crimson. She looked away, briefly. But then she couldn't help but put on an awkward, girlish smile, the kind of smile that a schoolgirl would have when approached by the handsome jock.

"James? Do you mind if I ask you something?"

He shook his head.

Laura continued, "You didn't have a girlfriend back in Ohio?"

"I have never had a girlfriend. Hell, I haven't even been kissed."

Maybe it was more of a daring instinct than anything else, but Laura got up from her spot for a moment, and planted one right on James' cheek. Quickly, she covered herself back up and turned her face toward the ground, perhaps in embarrassment, but more likely in a state of childhood glee.

James took what felt like a millennium trying to decipher what had just occurred. Finally, he put his hand up to his cheek, almost exactly on the spot where Laura had kissed him.

In reality, not much time had passed before Laura sprung up again, this time with a look of regret coming over her face. "I'm sorry," she apologized. "I felt like I was at a slumber party, or playing truth or dare or something. I didn't really mean it."

James shook his head. "You don't have to say sorry. I just wish I'd had a little more warning so I could enjoy it."

Laura laughed, and smiled at him. "Next time." Then she lay back down and turned away from James.

James smiled for a while, not even taking notice of Laura laying back down. "Next time," he said to himself. "Next time." Then it dawned on him. "Next time?"

But he wouldn't get a response out of Laura now. She was pretending to be asleep, and James knew better not to force the issue. Maybe he'd read too many books or seen too many movies, but it never ended well when the guy got pushy after the lady started hitting on him. Instead, he chose to lay down himself, and stare up at the cave ceiling, stalagmites only an inch or two long posing no threat to him as they stared back. Pleasant dreams would once again come to him, he was sure. For the first time in a while, he couldn't wait to get to sleep, not from pure exhaustion, but from the promise of good things to come.

* * *

There would be no pleasant awakening for the group, though. Gwendolyn sprung up from her spot, furthest from the entrance, when the first noises echoed toward the group.

The sounds were unmistakable: a group, exclusively men, most of whom sounded gruff and weary, was headed their way.

The host lit all the candles in her home, and slapped everyone awake. "When they get here, say and do nothing."

Everyone else in the group had no time to react after being woken up, some rather rudely from a deep sleep. But everyone was able to hear the noises coming toward them, and were quick to stay silent when they otherwise would have protested.

Ed shot a glance at James and whispered to him, "Keep it safe." He was referring to the Mainmen sword, which stayed in James' possession for the time being.

James nodded, and held it close to him, and prepared to move it so it would be quicker for him to access, but Gwendolyn motioned for everyone to get down. She then pulled a sword of her own, and began loudly sharpening it against a stalactite that looked like it had been worn over the years with similar moves against it.

The noises grew louder and louder, until finally a few shadows began to come up on the cave walls. Amanda and Laura moved behind James, and Browning, who was sleeping not too far from Johnson, did the same for a moment, but then moved behind McQuint.

The first one appeared finally from around a corner, his shadow decreasing in size leading up to his reveal. He kept marching his way up toward Gwendolyn's entrance, and wasn't but a few feet away from Amanda when he took notice of the company.

"Say," he said, "I didn't know you were not alone," he said in a high, squeaky voice. His was the exception to everyone else in his group, whose voices were lower, and very, very gruff, almost as if they had been battling a head cold for years.

Gwendolyn gulped a few times to herself as the rest of the mountain men came into her cave, and after a few tried to touch her guests, she stopped sharpening her sword and waved it toward the intruders. Most of them only laughed and kept their distance, but still put their filthy digits away.

James took notice that some of the men had only three or four fingers on each hand, and a clear space where one or two had been before, but were now missing.

One of the mountain men stepped forward even more so. He was dressed in a skin of a dark black animal, one that he had killed ten years prior. His name was Kloven, and he was the self-appointed leader of the mountain men in this particular interior. He had gone up against several attempts at a takeover, but won them all. He had a sizeable scar on his left cheek, and a burn mark on his forehead. His left ear lobe was missing a large chunk, but everyone could see his right lobe was meaty and intact. His eyebrows were thick, and matched a brown beard, growing everywhere around his face. The ones closest to his feet noticed his toenails were almost pitch black, and he had dirt all over his feet.

He spoke at last when he was close enough to face Gwendolyn. "What do you think you are doing?"

"Kloven, I've taken prisoners," Gwendolyn answered.

Kloven stepped forward once more, now nearly stepping on Jaenen's abdomen. "You've broken the code. You know mountain men do not take prisoners. We kill."

Gwendolyn struck back, "I am no mountain man, you know that well. And I believe they can deliver leverage."

Kloven scoffed, "Leverage."

Gwendolyn knew Kloven wouldn't leave it at that, and explained further, "They can be worth a lot of money. Look to their pocketbooks. You will find them full, I am sure."

She motioned at James, who for a moment forgot what this might mean. He looked to Ed for help, who looked down at his clothes. James then remembered that he, Laura, and Joven's clothes made them appear as if they were better off than the rest. It was a risky move, but he figured he had the drop on the mountain men.

James sprung up and patted his jacket, as if to clean it. "I say, this is a terrible condition to keep us in. Darling, stand up."

Laura, who wasn't piecing any of this together, shook her head at James.

"Sister, if you don't, father won't save you. Just me," James replied, and winked at her, facing away from Kloven and his goons.

Laura slowly got up, but didn't start acting the part yet. She couldn't act in this moment; she was frightened beyond belief.

When the mountain men got a better look at her, and her green dress, they began to voice approval, some making kissing sounds and others licking their lips.

Gwendolyn stepped forward and now stood behind James. She tapped his shoulder, James turned, and he was met with a punch above the nose. It wasn't a hard punch, but enough to get him to fall back down.

"You shut up. You're nothing but prisoners, both of you."

Out of instinct, Laura squatted down and looked at James' face, afraid she would see him bleeding. She was surprised, and the surprise showed on her face, more so than she would have liked.

Kloven was right where he should not have been if this charade was going to work. "He doesn't bleed."

Gwendolyn turned toward James, and he looked back up at her. She took her sword and cut at his arm.

James yelped in pain. It wasn't a deep pain, but enough to get him started.

Gwendolyn rose back up and faced Kloven. "Now he does. I dare not damage my prize any further."

Kloven looked into her eyes, questioning everything. "Prize or not, I have not known a day when Gwendolyn Asfair of the Mainmen was not afraid to make a man bleed from her rage."

115

Gwendolyn straightened up even more, trying to keep everything going, but she knew it would be to no avail. "Are you saying I'm going soft? Because if you are, Kloven, I'll make sure you see the error of your ways."

Two mountain men, without instruction, stepped up toward the group. They held a sickle like weapon, sharp and pointed right down. One was an inch from striking Amanda's face.

Kloven put on a small smile. "Some mountain men are missing. The lone survivor claimed they fought against eleven warriors. They wore Mainmen clothing, and had among them two women. That was the reason for my visit. Two of your guests are women, and minus one man, the warriors seem to be accounted for."

Talen, thinking back to what transpired a few days ago, was now facing Amanda and James, who were looking back at him, the act broken. His rage was also showing. Laura, in the meantime, was still fixated on James, trying to do something for the cut on his arm.

Gwendolyn shook her head. "I know nothing of this. These travelers claimed to have come from Virk. They couldn't have killed any of your men."

Kloven held up a finger and shook it at her. "The missing mountain men are *from* Virk, Gwendolyn."

Gwendolyn gulped, and her eyes went wide for a moment, but she caught herself, and tried to hide it. It was no use. So instead, she raised her sword.

"You step away from them, Kloven. You and your men. I will find no trouble in killing any who touch them."

Talen had had enough. "Let us touch them first. With our weapons." He then let out a small yell, and he, Ed, and Johnson reached for their bows and arrows and let loose on the first few men.

James was quick to act, remembering Amanda was in danger of being stuck with the mountain men's weapons. He bent down and pulled Amanda close to him just as the mountain man tried to end her life. The sickle bounced off the cave floor.

Gwendolyn, once James had ducked out of the way, raised her sword and struck at Kloven, who had already placed a hand on a sword. The two engaged in a lengthy duel while the others in the cave went for their weapons.

"Ed!" cried James. He then took out the Mainmen sword and threw it toward Ed, who caught it after replacing his bow.

Ed motioned for the three to move away from their spot while Jaenen and Talen advanced. The other mountain men began to charge forward, lining up with the sickle carrying mountain men.

James found himself engaged with the one who had tried to kill Amanda. He took out his sword, more comfortable with it than the Mainmen sword, and swung at the mountain man with all his might. He almost lost his balance, and realized his training was not being utilized. Before anyone could criticize him of that, he recovered, and went to break the sickle at the shaft. He was successful, and then put his sword into the mountain man's throat.

Amanda, not willing to just lay down, engaged with two mountain men after getting up, throwing a dagger into one's left eye, and trying to stab the other with her remaining dagger. She was unsuccessful, but pivoted away from a sword strike and moved to retrieve the embedded dagger. The enemy she struck fell to the floor, twitching, but she took no notice. Instead she had the bloodied dagger at the other's throat, and backed him against a cave wall. When he hit and reacted, she saw her chance, and stabbed him with the other dagger, right in the medial. Wanting to make sure, she removed the dagger and stabbed up and down from that spot, repeatedly, until the mountain man dropped his sword.

Talen and Jaenen fought against several mountain men, and aside from a short stab to the shoulder for Talen, neither met much challenge. It wouldn't be until minutes after the battle was over that he would take notice.

In total, about twenty mountain men had come with Kloven, and everyone except Joven managed a kill or two. For Joven, unfortunately, he had been struck with an arrow in the upper arm. The pain was excruciating, but Talen, who was nearest to him, managed to remove it with ease and stop the blood flow for the time being with a ripped piece of his cloth.

Laura was the last to start engaging, for her weapons had been stored away in a separate spot the night before, not too far from the bookcase. Taking a moment, she shoved as many loose papers as she could grab and a couple of books into her pack, hoping in vain one of them would be of some use. After this, she loosed a few arrows into the throat of an enemy who was about to take care of Browning.

For McQuint, Johnson, and Browning, they also had good fortune, killing twelve of the mountain men between them. All of them fought bravely, with McQuint and Browning both shooting one arrow per enemy, and eliminating them on two occasions each.

When Kloven began to see there was no hope in victory, he started striking harder at Gwendolyn, but her resolve held, and she matched with strikes twice as hard as the ones she received. Finally, when the two swords were locked, she pushed forward and knocked her enemy backward. Kloven nearly tripped over one of his dead men, and hissed at his enemies before fleeing.

Ed went around and made sure everyone was all right, panting a bit from the battle. He had mostly used the sword after being reunited with it. His last stop was with Joven, whom he had taken notice of during the battle. When Joven gave him a nod, saying he was all right, Ed turned to his host. "Gwendolyn, we need to leave now."

Gwendolyn smiled. "No shit, or so the Earth travelers would say. We can beat them to the stairs, Hotean, but we must leave now."

"Them?" replied Amanda, almost breathlessly.

Joven replied, "We killed them all."

Gwendolyn shook her head. "He'll get more. And quickly. Johnson, give me that torch." She pointed toward one that was nearly worn down, but it seemed the best of what was available.

Johnson did as he was told and flung it at Gwendolyn.

Using the nearest candle, she lit the torch and started running out of her cave entrance. Everyone else quickly followed.

10. Up and Out

Gwendolyn wasn't wrong. It would be a very short window for the group of eleven to get to the stairs that led to the mountain's peak. Kloven could have hundreds of mountain men ready to attack them along the way if everything went right for the adversaries.

There were not many options for the crew to avoid Kloven's men. That was the problem with running around the caves of the Wise-Mountains; it was a straight shot, and not too many winding curves or ascensions.

After ten minutes of running, the group was already nearing exhaustion. It wasn't just the distance and the length of time that wore them, but the terrain as well. The soles of their feet were not always running over a solid, flat surface, but rather bony, edged circles that would hurt if ran over too quickly. The rocks in-between were also the perfect size to trip over, and too many of those would mean Kloven catching up.

"How much further?" asked Joven, who began panting as soon as the last word was out of his mouth.

Gwendolyn sighed after catching her breath. "The stairs are not for another few hours."

Amanda, once she had the air capacity to speak, made several grunts of discouragement. "There's no way we'll make it."

Talen wiped his forehead, tried his best to then wipe as much of the sweat on his hands onto his tunic, then replied, "She has a point. We cannot be expected to keep this pace forever."

Browning said, "And neither can they. Surely they have slowed down."

Gwendolyn shook her head. "For a moment, yes, but now that we've killed so many, they won't forget."

Gauging the area, Ed didn't like the idea. "That may be suicide."

Gwendolyn slowed her pace, came to a stop, and took a moment to catch her breath. The rest of the group did the same.

"I'm sorry," Ed continued after he saw a look over Gwendolyn's face, one of incredulity.

Gwendolyn now worked up a few chuckles, which were quiet at first, but grew in volume over time. Soon she had let out a loud, quick laugh. It echoed through the mountain, and many of the party were tempted to put a finger to their lips, but the laugh continued, the echo lasting for seeming minutes before fading into nothing.

"You have the fortitude to tell me my plan for defense is suicide? Really, Hotean? It was you and your pack that was willing to commit suicide hours ago with a dangerous climb. Now something that might have a better chance of survival you consider too risky?"

Gwendolyn stepped back toward Ed, who was at the back of the group, making sure no one was left behind. Ed's face hardened as Gwendolyn approached.

"Do you wonder why I left, Edward? Do you truly? Joren and the others who led the cause had their hearts in the right place, but not always their heads. They were willing to sacrifice themselves to do even the smallest good deed. I don't survive in these mountains among the monsters because I did the right thing, or the noble thing. I did the logical thing. I survived. And if you want your cause to survive, you need to focus on the spots ahead, not behind."

With that, almost with precision timing, a new noise began to fill the halls of the mountain. Sounds that were at first low and deep, but soon grew to be monstrous, and moderately toned. It was a drone-like noise, one that rattled the loose ground and even loosened a few stalagmites. Luckily, they were not directly over anyone.

"What the hell is that?" asked Laura.

Gwendolyn smiled, then said, loud enough to be heard over the drone, "Up against the wall, flat!"

Everyone did as they were told, and soon they found out why. From out of the walls of the cave, at first microscopic, then growing in size, were Olma, a race of creature that can grow and shrink down to many sizes. At one moment, they could be big enough to make a spot on one of Winterlon's two moons, and soon they could be too large to fit on the back of a dicopomorpha echmepterygis.

By the time they came out of the walls and rejoined, they almost filled the whole passageway. Realizing the limitations, they shrunk, until they could move more easily. They began to move quickly once they were the proper size, and went right past the party, except for two who sniffed at McQuint and Jaenen.

"They just want some meat. Give them some," advised Gwendolyn.

Jaenen, who had heard of Olma, but had never seen any, was shaking so hard he could barely remove his pack and find what he was looking for. The Olma grew impatient, but soon realized what his potential friend or foe was searching for. Jaenen threw a moderate slab of cow meat away from the group, and the Olma, still droning, went for it, then followed the others.

Once the area had been Olma free for a few seconds, Gwendolyn stepped away. Everyone else did the same.

"Jesus Christ. When was someone gonna tell us about that?" asked Amanda.

Ed, now seeing what the whole explosion had been about, smiled in admiration. "That's quite clever, Asfair. You bought us plenty of time."

Talen filled in the blanks before the three youngsters could spout more questions. "They only live in caves like this. Too much sunlight at once can kill them."

James sighed. "Thank God for that."

Gwendolyn continued, "They normally are docile creatures, but they hate certain obnoxious noises, like screams and laughs. Olma are part of the reason other creatures don't live in the caves, like a Herenshi or a mountain boar. Or worse yet, a Tridevoir."

McQuint couldn't help but notice the type of meat Jaenen had thrown. "Guess we're not eating cow meat any time soon." He shot a disappointed look toward Jaenen, who matched it with a stare, as if to ask, 'what did I just do?'

She motioned for everyone to keep following her. The pace would be a moderate one, for it was best to leave the interior of the mountain as soon as possible.

* * *

Jaenen had ended up surrendering a whole meal to the Olma, and indeed it was of his favorite, the cow meat that the group had been looking forward to. He heard complaints of it loudly along the way as the group traveled, or at least as loud as the group was willing to get. They feared the Olma would return and surprise them further.

Two hours after the Olma had saved them, the group stopped and had a meal, mostly of blund, as there was no reason to risk their position by trying to get a fire started. Jaenen especially sulked in this time, even though he knew he couldn't blame himself too harshly.

Not long after the meal was over, the group started to see mountain men in the passageway as their destination neared. The Olma may have prevented other obstructions in the way before this point, but these mountain men were not in with Kloven's group, and were not aware that at any moment there was still a danger that Kloven and his followers could spring up behind them.

At first, James, Laura and Amanda were keen on keeping at least one hand on a weapon of choice in case the mountain men sprung into action, but when they saw everyone else tamely pass the strangers, they did the same, their hands at their sides.

Not all mountain men were ravenous, dangerous Neanderthals. Some were able to survive in the mountains off the food sources within and around. They were respectful of the people around them, knowing they had to live the same lives, fight for the same food. Even though these strangers wore fancier clothing that covered virtually all of their bodies, they didn't feel any pressure or aim to attack them.

And finally, after nearly three and a half hours of running and walking at quickened paces, the group now saw the stairway that led to the mountain's peak. The stairs were uneven, some very flat, others raised. Some were separated by a short distance, and others it would appear as if a jump were the only way to reach the next. As far as the group could see up, the stairs continued.

"Damn," said James. "A Stairmaster could really have helped me in situations like this."

Laura let out a chuckle at this, but Amanda and everyone else looked a little confused. James just shrugged.

"You guys don't know, no surprise. Par for the course, I guess."

Wordlessly, the group started the climb; there was no need for Ed, Talen or Gwendolyn to say that the longer they stayed at the bottom, the greater chance Kloven could catch up with them.

Throughout the stair climb, there were many unhappy moments where someone would nearly lose their balance and begin tumbling backwards. Of course, there were no railings or landings to speak of, so anyone who went backwards would keep going backwards, until they reached the bottom or died.

Browning struggled a few times, and McQuint and Johnson had to keep saving him. By the time the last step was almost within view, both of them had lost count of how many times Browning had nearly fallen.

James and Amanda both had a couple of tricky moments that nearly ended in catastrophe, but they were saved by Ed, who trailed the three, or Joven, who was in front. Joven's wounds began to get the better of him by the end of the climb as well, and at a few points he had to stop to adjust the cloth that was beginning to grow redder and redder.

Again, it felt like an eternity, but soon a light began to grow above the group as they realized the outside world was approaching. Jaenen was the first to clear the last step, and it was only a few paces before he was on the mountain's peak.

The group slowly massed together and looked at their next target: getting over the tall, jagged mountain that sloped into the next country of Winterlon, Dulon. Dulon was where the group would find the Benshidi.

Browning looked to the top of the mountain. He had never seen anything like it, being from the capital and never leaving. "How do we get up there?" he asked.

Gwendolyn sighed. "You leave that to me."

She started to step forward, but to her shock, and everyone else's, an arrow suddenly whisked into Browning's neck, going in one side and the head poking out the other. He slowly grasped upward to where the arrow was, then felt to his knees, and consciousness left him soon after.

The arrow had been fired by a mountain man, and right beside him was Kloven. A total of fifty-seven men were by his side, and many of them were armed with sickles and swords.

Amanda and Johnson were quick to go to Browning, hoping they could do something. Johnson took a couple of looks at it, then shook his head. He picked up Browning by the shoulders and started to drag him out of the way.

Kloven, meanwhile, stepped forward, and faced his enemies. "Olma. Not bad, Gwendolyn. But I knew you couldn't go the quickest route. I did."

Laura looked to Gwendolyn in question. "The quickest route? What's he talking about?"

Gwendolyn would have answered, but Kloven beat her to it. "I'm talking, girl, about the path that leads to the top. It's a steep climb, but it is quicker."

Ed closed his eyes, fearing the finality of defeat. Gwendolyn had chosen the safer path, but it might have led to their destruction.

The mountain men were growing anxious. Two of them stepped forward and prematurely fired arrows at the group. Everyone managed to find a safe spot, though.

Kloven turned around, unsheathed his sword, and stuck it in the first man. "You don't start until I tell you!" He turned to the other and stared in astonishment, then motioned for the man to come up to him. His demise was the same as the first man's, the sword running through his gut.

"Kloven, you might as well do it now. No use in upsetting your men," taunted Talen.

The leader turned and faced his enemy again, and let out a small laugh. "You're a bold one, to say that to me. I fear you never will be allowed to barb me again."

With that, he raised his sword, and swung it forward to signal his men to attack. All of them started to charge the small group, who were quick to get their weapons ready.

Luck was still on their side, as it had been with the previous encounters with the mountain men. James and Laura fought side by side, and fended off thirteen foes. Both suffered a small cut from a sickle or blade here or there, but managed to fight off the rest.

Ed, Amanda, and Gwendolyn were a few feet apart, but all armed with swords, hacked away at all who came near. None of them had any wounds by the end of the fight.

Talen ran down all the mountain men in his path and began a fight with Kloven. Both men were well skilled with a sword, but it would be a long duel before it was decided.

The other four who could fight stuck with bows and arrows and picked off the rest of their enemies. A large arrow hit the mountainside near Jaenen, and the explosion put a few painful slivers into his leg. He excluded himself from the rest of the battle as he sought a solution to his pain.

Joven, despite the wound from his last battle, fought bravely, and ended up with the highest body-count of the bunch, fifteen dead mountain men.

After almost fifty of the men were gone, the rest backed away from the fight. Two were hit by arrows in the back, and were added to the growing mound of bodies. The rest had no choice but to flee the way they came, down the steep mountain. No one from the group knew if the mountain men would survive the fall.

Kloven and Talen continued their duel, one striking, the other blocking, for several moments after the other mountain men fled. At one point, Kloven saw victory after nicking Talen in the shoulder. Kloven let out a yell, and ran forward to try and land the killing blow. All that happened was Talen dodged it, and punched Kloven right in the face, making Kloven spit out a worn, yellowed tooth.

While trying to catch his breath, Talen struck him across the chest, then lopped off Kloven's left arm, above the posterior cutaneous nerve. Talen then kicked Kloven backward, the latter landing on his ass.

Gwendolyn rushed up to end the fight at this point. "Spare him, Wadenston."

Talen, who was nearly out of breath by this point, slowly pivoted his eyes away from Kloven, and stared Gwendolyn down. He then saw, out of the corner of his eye, that McQuint and Laura were over by Browning, who was shuddering.

Gwendolyn turned to Kloven, disgust in her voice. "When we return, you will let us pass, lest we kill you right now."

Kloven, despite the ways of the mountain men, had to face his new reality. He nodded.

Talen turned back around and rested the tip of his sword on Kloven's Adam's apple. "We need your *word*."

Kloven choked out, "You have my word", before gasping in fear that Talen would still end his life. But Talen retracted the sword after nicking at the skin, causing more bleeding from Kloven.

James and Ed were the next ones to join their comrade, Browning, who knew the end was near. Still, James was not accepting the fate of his party member. "There has to be something we can do."

Laura shook her head, tears coming to her eyes.

Browning could not get any words out, though he tried. Before he went still, his eyes went to McQuint, who was on one knee beside him, and a small smile came upon both their faces. Only then did Browning stop shuddering, and his life was extinguished.

No one in the group wanted to move. None was ready to pass this moment and continue the journey. In this moment, the journey be damned; they were going to mourn their brother in arms.

McQuint let out a few sniffles, lowered his head, and kissed Browning on the head. His other knee fell, and he held his place for a good twenty seconds. He then lifted from Browning's side his sword, held it flat in the air above its previous owner, and bowed to Browning's body. The sword had now passed to McQuint.

The sun was warm, but the group took a long time to notice. Being inside the mountain for nearly a day, they hadn't been able to warm themselves very well.

But now it didn't matter. The sun would still be up when they finally did move again, but none of them would take much notice of how far it had moved as so much of the day was lost.

11. The Summit

It was quite a sight for the twelve Deadman. No time while being alive on Winterlon had they come anywhere close to the Wise-Mountains. All of them were thankful that Aunten wasn't here; he would make them go on about their business and pay no mind to the wonderous view.

Sienel, however, did grant them a few glimpses before announcing, "All right, that's enough. We can't keep our master waiting."

While traveling, the group would keep their hoods up to keep anyone they met in fear. Now, with no one around but the occasional mountain man trying to gather food, they were free to expose the horror underneath, the ghastly stitched-together skin tissue that all but kept their facial muscles and skulls showing.

Most of the Deadman had appearances like this. All but Latren, whose skin beneath the septeal cartilages was missing. From there up, though, his skin remained. His was a fairly light shade, not as pale as some of his fellow Deadman, but not as dark as Sienel's.

In life, Latren was the youngest of Aunten's closest followers, and had always wished to be a Mainmen. After trying again and again to be a part of the legacy, he joined Aunten after he vowed to take up the mantle left behind by Kildeno.

Now he had a chance to do in death what he could not do in life: be a man who was a part of a creed and fulfill the wishes of those above him. He took no exception here when looking deep into the eyes of the passing mountain men.

Finally, one stopped and stared back for a long while. Latren's light green eyes returned the favor, and gradually he began to move toward the man. When they were only a few paces from each other, the mountain man took a step forward, showing he wasn't afraid.

By this time, more mountain men had begun to move outside, coming down from their places as sunset began to approach. They were usually looking for their supper now, but the distraction was one they would put up with for now.

With no words between them, the mountain man and Latren continued their showdown. Finally a tilt of the head from Latren made the mountain man's brow furrow, and he planted his feet.

Now, he spoke. "I'll fight ya."

Latren smiled at the man, or at least the skin that was not uncovered gave the impression of one, then with his left hand sliced at his opponent's throat. The nails from the end of his fingers seemed sharp enough to cut through rock, to say nothing for a few centimeters of skin protecting a man's veins.

The other mountain men took this death seriously, and began to group up. Latren finally made a sound, a higher, funny sound that couldn't be made out by any, except those closest to him. He was keeping his head down, the expression continuing on his face being the only thing they could see of him. After raising his head again, they found out it was a small laugh that went on for a time, high and chilling.

"Let that be a lesson to you all", he said when he had finished laughing. "We are not to be intimidated by our hosts. Or else you will end up like your brethren."

A few mountain men stepped forward, humility on their faces, not hostility. One of them recognized Sienel, and gave a nod to him.

Sienel stepped forward. "You are the one who told of the missing men," he proclaimed, and motioned for the man to step up to him.

The mountain man was confident, for now, though after Sienel put his bony, ancient-looking hand on his shoulder and started to walk with him in a friendly manner, his outward appearance would be the equivalent of skin crawling.

This mountain man's appearance stood out slightly from the others. The skin he wore was stitched of five different animals, and done poorly. The tail of one would bleed into the back of another, then the thinner fur that would be around the animals' legs seemed to be covering his mid-section, with the thicker fur covering his upper chest. His face was also more smooth than several others, especially compared to Kloven. His mustache and beard were trimmed, where most others ran wild. His eyes and mouth were softer, not as ready or willing to scare visitors.

Sienel turned to him after a moment, his face haunting from crow's feet that seemed to dip so far down his face they were almost opposite the bottom of his nose. "Give me your name."

The demand did not help the mountain man's outward appearance, though his face remained content. "I am Sanuel."

Sienel nodded. "Sanuel, tell me where Kloven is. He is still your leader, is he not?"

Sanuel replied, "He was chasing after the woman. And her company."

This made Sienel freeze. This news gave his countenance several expressions, first one of confusion, then one of anger, but then he calmed himself and asked, "Would we know this woman?"

"Gwendolyn Asfair," replied Sanuel. "She used to ride with the Main—"

"The Mainmen", Sienel finished. "I might have known."

Sanuel's coolness now began to fade from his face and match the rest of his exterior. "May I ask, Sienel, what my reward is for this news?"

Sienel shook his head and put a finger up to his lips. "Those who ask for rewards too frequently never get them. Have patience, my friend, and Aunten himself will absolve you of all your troubles."

The eyebrows of Sanuel went up, the only hair on his face that was not as cleanly barbered. "Perhaps, without being too presumptuous, you may clue me as to the details. Let my dreams be filled with them, friend."

The word 'friend' coming out of Sanuel's mouth was higher pitched than the rest of his dialogue. Everyone, especially the other Deadman, could see that he thought he was on thin ice. Sienel acknowledged this with a friendly-looking smile.

"A place in the capital, and maybe even a rank. Food to stuff your belly to bursting, a woman to bear your seeds, and a long retirement after all of Winterlon has been purged."

Sienel's promise gave the most confidence to Sanuel yet. He bowed and walked away now, hope filling him as it had not in years.

Kinven, another Deadman, stepped up to Sienel. "Why does he speak so well? The other ones barely manage a grunt."

"Kloven and Sanuel are not true mountain men," replied Sienel. "They started with happier lives, but came here. Why? We'd need to ask them."

Kinven asked next, "Where to from here?"

Sienel turned to the other Deadman, who gathered around them. "We find Kloven. And hope he has the head of Gwendolyn Asfair in his fist."

* * *

A slap in the face from Talen started a conversation between him and Gwendolyn. She took it like a champ, knowing it was coming following Kloven's murder of Browning. She was on her knees while Talen and Ed stood above her.

"Are you this morally adrift, Asfair? To lose us so much time and a man? You really must be unwilling to support the cause in any way."

Gwendolyn remained silent while Talen spoke, and Ed soon felt the need to hold him back from any further violence.

"My friend," he started, "if we don't take her at her word, we are betraying our oath."

"Shit on the oath!" bellowed Talen, loud enough to echo through the surrounding mountaintops. "The people of Winterlon who act like this are not worth saving."

Amanda saw that the slap from Talen had broken the skin, and now a small streak of blood was coagulating under her right eye. From the battles, she already had a gash of dried blood above one of her shoulders, apparently from a wound she had not counted earlier. Amanda tore off a small part of her kirtle and walked over to help Gwendolyn. Ed and Talen watched as it happened, but said and did nothing.

After cleaning the wound and wrapping the newly made rag around Gwendolyn's shoulder, Amanda cleared her throat. "I'm not sticking up for her, but there had to be a reason for taking the way we did."

Gwendolyn gave Amanda a curt smile, then motioned with her head to look over toward the spot Kloven and his followers had appeared not too long before.

James and Laura also saw what was happening and followed Amanda. McQuint, Jaenen and Joven stood behind them and did the same. Amanda reached the spot first, and nearly lost her footing. She suddenly started breathing rapidly, and held her hands over her heart, which as the group got closer, they could seemingly hear beating faster and faster.

Then they realized what the cause of it was. The spot was an extremely steep cliff, and from it nothing short of a one-hundred-thirty-five-foot drop that was littered with the remains of those who fell. The six of them could see now that some of the corpses looked fresh, meaning that Kloven had more men with him to start, but the ones they fought braved the climb and lived to tell the tale. There was also a chance, though none of them could say for sure, that the last surviving men who abandoned Kloven could also have been at the bottom.

Amanda reached out her arms to those around her, and they helped her back away from the spot. "I was just surprised," she kept repeating, trying to explain herself. "I was just surprised. Just surprised."

Ed didn't even bother looking where they had been. "I see no reason to bicker and badger each other over Browning. We will miss him dearly, but he wouldn't want us to wallow in his death."

He then bent down to one knee to be at eye-level with Gwendolyn, and she returned his gaze. "As long as you won't kill me now, I'll take you the rest of the way."

Ed nodded, but Talen shook his head. "She owes us more than that. For the loss of a man, she will take his place."

Gwendolyn raised her eyebrows and chuckled. "You really want me to stick around after we reach the next summit? I'd just as soon throw myself from the top."

Johnson, who had been keeping his ears open, decided to step up now and join his other Mainmen. "After what just happened between you and Kloven, I'd imagine life for you here being difficult. The mountain men will take every opportunity to avenge their leader's humiliation. You'd never be able to sleep, or go where you wanted, less you desire a fight to the death with his devoted."

This point was accompanied by a sigh of relief from Talen, who now saw that shy of Gwendolyn killing herself, would probably be best off with the company.

Johnson ended his point by adding, "Joining us may extend your life the longest."

Gwendolyn shook her head. "I make no promises, but lets us revisit this when we reach the bottom of the mountain, in Dulon."

Everyone nodded, except Talen, whose face became more and more smug with every passing moment.

James and the others stayed where they were while the conversation went on, but suddenly James heard something behind him. It seemed a whisper, and he couldn't figure out what it was. Then, the Wiseman materialized before him, beaming at him as always. He appeared to levitate off the ground, above the drop-off of the cliff.

"I see you have made it to the first summit. I'm proud of you, my boy," the Wiseman started.

James smiled back at him, but only for a moment as he reminded himself of the loss of their party member. "After we lost Browning. After what you said about him, I thought he would be safe."

The Wiseman shook his head. "I may know all, but some of it comes to me later than expected."

James couldn't help but chuckle. "In other words, you were wrong."

The Wiseman had a quick response. "There is no way to count the infinitely small ways in which the future changes. It could easily have been you who took that arrow, or Amanda or Laura. Or he could have gotten a luckier shot and taken two members of your party."

"Well, the next thing we're going to do is go down to the bottom of the mountain. Do you know how many of us make it?" asked James.

The Wiseman nodded, but wouldn't say. "I cannot tell you the future, James, lest you wish it to change."

A contradictory look came over James' face. "You told me about the battle at the Canyon."

"So I did," was the reply. "But I never told you who would win. The future can change rapidly based off of what is done now and what is not done. You saw what could have happened at the Canyon. I wouldn't dare show you what would have happened had you come up to this spot from the climb."

James shook his head. "I honestly don't wanna know."

The Wiseman laughed now. "You are still as wise as ever, James. Now, as to our visit here today, I wanted to reassure you."

"Of what?"

"Of Edward's decision to grant you his sword."

This took James off balance. He hadn't even thought of that. "I don't get it."

The Wiseman beamed at him once more. "You realize that when Ed ordered the clothes you now wear, he knew what sizes to get and what materials would make them up. He wanted *you*, in your size, to be the one who looked highborn. He has trust in you enough to do that. Just as easily, he could have had his son's clothes be yours, but he didn't."

James thought otherwise. "He could just be protecting him."

"True, and that was part of his decision. But he sees what I saw in you, James, why it is you I visit and not anyone else. You still have a ways to go to becoming a great warrior, my boy. Between now and then, dozens of your allies could perish or be at your side in the darkest hours. But the point is, you have nothing to fear of your party members. They respect you, and see you as a bright spot of hope in the fights to come."

Laura had been consoling Amanda in this time, but now saw that James was off by himself, near the edge of the cliff, seemingly looking off into the distance. She started walking toward him.

The Wiseman appeared to look behind James, his eyes drifting over James' shoulder. "Do not turn back yet, but she is coming to you. We will speak soon, James."

As the Wiseman disintegrated, James turned around and saw Laura. He was surprised to see the worry in her face, and gave an awkward chuckle.

"I didn't know what you were doing," she said.

"Oh, just, you know, talking to my friendly, neighborhood apparitions. Same shit, different day."

Laura's expression didn't change. "Did he say anything important?"

James didn't change his expression either. "Nothing different than what he always says. The optimist, like last time."

"Oh," was all Laura could reply with.

"But he did say," James added, "that it would have been more of a disaster if we'd taken this climb. He wouldn't say, but I'll bet that a lot more of us didn't make it."

Laura nodded. "Well, Ed says we're ready to start a climb to the next summit. Then it's down the mountainside and into Dulon. And we're leaving in a few minutes, so get your things and get ready."

James started to do as he was told. He then saw that as Laura was walking, her posture was a little different than before. "What's wrong?"

"I think it's the books. They're heavier than they looked," she said. "They weren't so bad at first, but now they're weighing me down."

James took a while to piece this all together. He'd forgotten Laura's interest in the books and papers Gwendolyn kept. "Maybe we should take some out and look through them, see if they help or not."

Laura blew a raspberry. "Yeah, now's a good time. Ed and the others would leave us, and we'd have to try and climb ourselves."

The point was made, but James added, "Then I can take a few books myself, you know, lighten the load."

Laura didn't even think twice about it. She opened her pack and took out the three heaviest books, and plopped them on the ground in front of James. Then she sighed in relief. "Much better."

James, meanwhile, struggled in fun to get the books off the ground. He grunted and put on the appearance of a bodybuilder trying to lift thousands of pounds. Laura laughed at this. Amanda and the others around them did the same.

* * *

It had been decided that Browning's body would be left behind at this part of the summit. There was no desire to carry it with them since he would have preferred to be buried at the capital, which would not happen anytime soon.

Before the climb began, everyone paid their last respects to their fallen comrade. Each lingered for a moment or so longer than the one before, and Ed was the last to pass him by.

James and the others from Earth would normally worry about the body freezing at the summit of a mountain, but given Winterlon's inversion, they realized the sun beat down harder on the mountaintop, and absorbing all the heat at the top made the bottom feel cooler.

Gwendolyn would lead the way. She sized up the climb, knowing it would be difficult. At least the weather was on their side. "I've only made this climb on three occasions before today."

Jaenen stepped up alongside her and also took a look up. Straight up. "How tall do you figure it is?"

Gwendolyn shrugged her shoulders. "Tall enough to take an hour. If we are not too hasty."

While the first trip up the mountain had been relatively easy, this one would not be so. The only way to throw a loop of a rope upward and have it latched on to ease the climb would be if balance was set. There was no place except the ground the group stood on now to do so. Rather than do that for the first part of the climb and abandon the rope, which might be needed later, the decision had been made to free climb the mountain. As dangerous as the decision was, there was no other way.

"Maybe we can wait and see how the conditions look in a few minutes. I'd rather not start a climb if the atmosphere turns sour," warned Gwendolyn, whose words made virtually everyone in the group turn their heads to the skies.

Sure enough, a few clouds were moving from east to west, but far south. While no one from Earth was a meteorologist, they'd done enough cloud watching in their time to guess that these would not be a problem.

Talen visually protested to this. "We've already lost time with these mountains."

Ed countered, "The Benshidi aren't going anywhere."

This silenced Talen for now. James noticed how his mood had been very, very sore for the last couple of days. There had been several moments during their training that Talen had been outright hostile to the youngsters, and especially to James, but he had apologized for it later on. Looking at him now, James saw no sign of apology with him. Perhaps moving on to their next goal would help with that.

"How best do we start the climb?" asked Joven.

Gwendolyn finally took her eyes from what was above her and looked to Joven. "You put everything else aside and you start. Just as you do with any challenge in life."

She then turned back to the mountain wall and put one foot up, reached her arm, and balanced herself to the point where she could reach and hang.

Laura pulled Ed aside and asked, "Why can't we all be connected by rope, like last time?"

Ed responded, "The distance between us will be larger. We have no rope long enough to do so. And if someone in the middle should lose their footing, they'd take everyone behind them for the fall."

Laura gulped at this. "Uh, you guys go ahead. I think I'd feel a little better about this after I empty my bladder."

McQuint grumbled. "I'd feel better after I empty my stomach." He headed off as well, out of sight of the rest of the company.

Gwendolyn was now about fifteen feet off the ground, and James could see the consternation in her face as she tried to remember the different places she could safely get a hand or foothold.

Jaenen generally asked, "Did anyone ask the last time she did this?"

No one answered, worsening everyone's expectations. They all knew something was going to go wrong.

Gwendolyn took another couple of minutes before stopping, now about forty feet away from the rest of the group. Everyone was back now to see where she went. "You start where I was, go up three spots, over two, up one, and back over two. The spacing should work. One at a time!"

"Wait!" cried James. "Shouldn't we have someone behind us if we've never climbed before? So they can, you know, save us?"

Gwendolyn had to think about this idea for some time. "Perhaps. Just don't crowd each other. It'll be a recipe for death."

Talen decided he would go first, followed by Jaenen, Ed, and Amanda. James would follow, but the rest of the order was left to question. McQuint and Laura were the most squeamish about the climb, but

143

both remained at the bottom for a while, along with Johnson and Joven.

"I think I should bring up the rear," said Joven. "My dominant arm is the injured one, so if anything happens and I had to let go..."

Laura shook her head. "Don't think like that. We're all gonna make it."

While this conversation was going on, Amanda got ready to start the climb. Everyone before her was going fine, and once Talen was on the spot closest to Gwendolyn, she started moving up again, straight and not deviating for several minutes.

Amanda turned back to her friends, and a shudder came over her. "I don't think I can do it."

James came up to her, offered his arm in a hug motion, and Amanda came in close. "We're right behind you," he said in comfort before letting go.

Amanda had a tear coming down her face now, which she instinctively wiped away. She then took three deep breaths, and shakily put her leg into position so she could grab the rung above her and start.

James had decided to be the brave one and not have someone behind him who could likely save him if he fell. The confidence that the Wiseman had given him before seeped in, and before he knew it, he was on the third step, Amanda slowly going for the fourth, where she had to go over to the left.

McQuint was the loser in the deciding match of who would go first between him and Laura. Part of it may have been intentional to have Laura be in a better position, but he also had a small fear that if James or Amanda fell, Laura would not be able to hoist them up and support her own weight.

He spit out some leftover vomit from his mouth before finally getting into the first spot. Johnson shook his head and started after him.

"How are you so experienced in climbing?" Laura asked.

Johnson turned back to her and replied, "I've had to climb away from some sticky situations." He laughed heartily and continued upward.

Joven scoffed. "I think he means jealous husbands."

This humor did not sit with Laura, not because she didn't find it funny, normally she would have, but the daunting task of the climb blocked out anything else. "You'll catch me if I miss?"

She turned to Joven, fear in her eyes. Joven nodded.

Laura stepped forward, looked up, and once again had to ask a question. "And you'll be ready if I do?"

She didn't turn back to him, not at first. After she heard no sound, she did turn, and saw that he was looking up, fear in his eyes. Laura's eyes shot up to see what was happening.

As soon as she did, Joven grabbed Laura's shoulders and pulled her back. Laura ended up on the ground from the force of the pull, but had she remained where she was, she would have been crushed by fallen rock.

Up above, Gwendolyn had forgotten to go up instead of right. "Shit!" she swore to herself.

Talen was two moves behind her, and took quick notice of the false move. "Out of practice, are you?"

Gwendolyn shook her head violently, as if to tell herself to wake up. "One little mistake. Don't do what I did."

Talen scoffed. "It's a wonder we do anything you do."

The falling rocks did not boost Laura's confidence. "How the hell am I supposed to climb after that?"

Joven sighed. "Just do what she said. Don't think about anything else. Don't think about falling. Don't think about missing a step. Just climb. Pretty soon, we'll all be at the summit and headed back down."

Laura shook her head. "There's gotta be another way."

Joven put his head down. "If there is, I don't know it. Neither does Ed or anybody else up there."

Johnson was on the fourth step, and looked back down at the two last members. "Are you coming or not?" he cried down.

Joven put his hands in Laura's. "Trust me, when we head down the mountainside, there will be something waiting for us that will make the whole thing worth it."

Laura's eyebrows went up at this. "What do you mean?"

Joven turned his head in a humorous way. "You'll have to find out for yourself."

Finally, all the tension broke, and Laura put on a smile. She turned back toward the mountain, and didn't look up. She closed her eyes and walked forward a couple of steps, thinking it was the only way to keep from looking toward everyone else. She minded her steps so she didn't run into the fallen rocks, and reached her hand out so she could tell when she was at the base. When she hit it, she opened her eyes, tilted her head up slowly, and stopped when she saw where her hand was supposed to go. She hesitated at first, but finally picked her leg up and got a hold of the gash and started.

Joven breathed a huge sigh of relief after she got to the first spot, just a couple of feet off the ground. Then he waited until she was at the second spot before starting. He wanted to keep her confidence up to a point where he wasn't going to hound after her every step of the way.

Up above, aside from the occasional odd timings from some when moving to different spots, the climb went surprisingly smooth. And so it went for the first half hour.

Aside from Gwendolyn's wrong choice that caused some rocks to fall away, Jaenen and Amanda did have a couple of close calls. Jaenen's foot slipped as he was going from a spot on the left to a spot on the right and slightly above. He ended up hanging for a moment, but he soon got his foot back into place, and managed to move on.

Amanda's worry was when she turned her back to the mountain for a moment to check on James behind her. She had been doing this routinely, and James had always been a spot behind. This time he was again, but Amanda's pack, which kept being brushed upon the mountainside, finally started to loosen from its position. When she turned around to move to the next spot, it almost fell off her back. Losing it would mean losing all the food, armor, and weapons she couldn't have on her person. She reached out and grabbed it as it fell, but in doing so she had to put the rest of her weight on holding on, and she bumped against the mountainside hard as she did.

James glimpsed this and shouted at her, fearing the worst. Luckily, she was able to put one loop of her pack into her mouth, move on to the next spot once she had recovered, and had enough balance to put the pack back in its place. She took her time doing so, and had to stop for a couple of minutes before she could gather the courage to continue.

This stop was fine with James, Laura, and McQuint, who deep down were still terrified at the feat they were attempting. Joven and Johnson, however, feared that if Amanda couldn't start again, she would strand everyone else. Ed feared he would have to backtrack down and get Amanda to the next spot, which would have been extremely dangerous. Soon enough, she did start up and Ed took a deep breath.

Around that half hour mark, the sun was starting to fade. Everyone looked and saw why this was happening: some clouds were starting to come from the north and block it out.

Then the wind picked up. Gwendolyn shivered at this, sensing it first. "Everyone," she shouted down, "the weather is about to become much worse. Don't kill yourselves, but if we don't move faster, we might not make it."

The echo from her yelling took a while to reach down to the last of the crew, and Laura couldn't help but respond back, "She's joking, isn't she?"

So the crew moved a little faster, copying Gwendolyn's moves; left and right, up and over one direction, then the other. Again no major accidents occurred, save a rare misstep that would be easily corrected.

After another ten minutes, the terrain on the mountainside became less smooth, and more jagged. There were certain spots where it would appear a big rock formation or two had been separated from the rest of the mountain. Gwendolyn knew that if the rain and wind were enough of a factor, more could fall away, and risk the lives of everyone. But with these holes came more support for making it to the top, more space to go to with the next moves upward, left to right, or right to left.

McQuint was afraid after he felt a few drops that he would throw up again, but he held it together. Laura's fear also got to her again and again until she could see the next moves had more room for error. It did help her get confidence up.

Then it happened. Gwendolyn put her arm against the mountainside to make her next move, and she felt the rock begin to crumble beneath her. She looked down below and saw that most everyone was on the left side, clear of any debris. All except for Jaenen. "Jaenen!" she yelled down.

He looked up in surprise, but that was all the warning she could give. She leaped to her next spot, nearly missing. Luckily, she twisted her legs into a fashion where she could keep from dangling. From there she was able to get back to a position where she was comfortable.

As she leapt, the rock gave way and fell. Jaenen let go, fearing he would be crushed, and screamed. He fell for a few feet before an outstretched arm grabbed the back of his hand, right above the wrist.

It was James Realms who saved him. He had seen it coming, and been able to extend himself out enough to grab Jaenen without losing his own balance. James was able to pull them both over toward the left and evade the rocks.

To get out of this predicament, Jaenen saw that if he went back over to the right under his own power, he could barely grasp a spot, and move from there upward back toward the rest of the group.

He succeeded, and there was no time for thanks or welcomes. On top of the risk of falling rock, the rain also made everything more slick, furthering the risk that someone's foothold would loosen and they would go down. But it never happened, somehow.

The rain continued, but no further rockslides or loose rock fell on the group. After another twenty minutes of near-perfect climbing, though at a slower pace, Gwendolyn reached over the top of jagged rock and felt the smooth landing. She pulled herself up, and lay on her back for a few minutes, breathing heavily, utterly exhausted.

Talen was only a few seconds behind her, and remained on his feet after reaching the top. Next came Ed, Amanda, and James, all getting there one after the other. Amanda and James embraced, no words able to be spoken.

Jaenen came next, beaten and bruised from his trickier path. He slumped himself against a rock formation that sat on the top of the summit but only reached up a few feet. He motioned for James to come over to him.

When James was within a couple of feet, Jaenen reached out and pulled James in, embracing him. "You saved my life. I can't repay you."

James, out of breath, finally managed, "You'd do it for me."

Jaenen put a smile on his face. "Would I?"

This caused everyone up on the summit to laugh. The extraordinary effort taken to reach this point was enough to cause Amanda to go for her pack and pull out some mobwin meat.

"Wait a minute," she said after taking a couple of bites. By the time she finished chewing, McQuint had slowly, humorously inched his body up to the summit. He lay on his back for a long while, like Gwendolyn, catching his breath over and over.

"What is it?" asked Talen.

"Did anyone take the stuff off of Browning? Like his food?"

Everyone shook their heads. Ed replied, speaking for the first time since the climb, "It is customary for a Mainmen to not be robbed after death, save a weapon that they would have wished to be passed along. McQuint taking his sword is acceptable."

Amanda nodded, but added, "We could have taken the food at least. That would save us a little bit."

It was meant to be a little humorous, but no one except James took it as such.

Johnson came next, and was the only one who was seemingly not out of breath or acknowledging the feat he had just accomplished. He just stood by while everyone else recovered.

Laura came next, but had some difficulty with the jagged rock, ending up cutting her left arm on it and bleeding. The gash went a little deep, and that worried her. Ed and Talen saw to her wound, and helped clean it and bandage it with a rip from Ed's clothes.

Joven was the last to reach the peak, and when he did, he had to do so slowly, because his left arm had gone numb. His right, non-dominant limb took a pounding during the last part of the climb, and he was very winded, like much of the group.

Ed finally gathered everyone up and said, "I fear having to say this, but we should not rest here. It'll be much cooler down at the opposite base, and we have to leave now, or else we'll lose the light we have."

Everyone looked up and saw how the rain was continuing to fall, and the sky darkening more so than it was during the climb.

Gwendolyn concurred. "Yes. Trying to go down the steep side in the dark is risky. You might take a tumble and kill yourself so close to the end."

James shook his head. "I don't wanna do that."

12. Dulon

The end of the climb did leave everyone exhausted, but knowing that the steep descent on the other side was safer, it was a surprisingly quick result. Despite the close calls and the situation, everyone was joyously celebrating at the bottom of the mountain. And now the group had entered the country of Dulon.

The three from Earth embraced, Amanda almost collapsing onto her two friends, from a mix of exertion and hungover fear.

"I can't believe we free-solo'd that bitch," said Laura, who let out an uncontrollable, high-pitched laughter after catching her breath. Everyone else couldn't help but laugh along with her.

In a moment of relaxation, James closed his eyes as the group hug continued. His back was to the distant horizon, with the other two facing it. After a few more seconds, he opened his eyes. He realized that everyone else was quiet. Now he saw why.

For a few seconds, James couldn't believe the sight before him, and he awkwardly tried to turn Laura and Amanda's heads to face the mountains they had just conquered.

At first, they both had an expression of complaint, not understanding why James was doing this. When they finally turned their heads, they saw an awesome sight.

The steeper, back sides of the Wise-Mountains were bare stone, but had been painted over with depictions of the Wiseman, and different tales through the history of Winterlon. Some mountains were covered only with a partial drawing, carrying over to the neighboring giant. Others had two or three smaller paintings covering the side, all of which told their own story.

The mountain range went for several miles, and the depictions were big enough to be seen from a great distance. The one they had climbed down was bare, or so they had thought. It turned out the black stone was painted over, part of a black portal in the painting.

James immediately saw that the Wiseman's face and body matched what he had seen in real life, or what he had been convinced was real life. And the portal was an exact match as well.

Gwendolyn was the only one of the company who had seen the sight before. She was complimentary of their time and awe, though, and let them take their time to see everything.

"Another reason why the mountains have their name," said Joven, who had a wide smile on his face from the first sight, and would have one for a long time after. The legends had always said that the Wiseman had created these mountains after trying to rule over Winterlon, as a final act of creation before leaving the men and women to do as they pleased.

Though one detail that James did notice that differed from his interactions with the Wiseman was the facial expressions in the paintings. Almost all of them were of a stern older man, not a beaming, happy one. Instead, it was almost as if the Wiseman used to be a crueler man, and had softened in extended old age.

The tales these paintings told were not just of the Wiseman's deeds, one of which looked like the creation of Winterlon itself, but some were of great battles between warring factions. Sword was clashing with sword, spears thrown into enemies and pools of blood spilt upon the ground. To the left of the group was a representation of several men and women, dressed in smart, wealthier clothing, bowing before a man, though his back was turned from them.

"I wonder about that one," said Jaenen. "Who is the man who would turn his back on his followers?"

Talen stepped up to him and put a hand on his shoulder. "That was supposedly the time when the Wiseman had forgotten the people of Winterlon. After the end of the Deadman's reign."

The three youngsters turned to Talen. "How do you know that?" asked Amanda.

"Well," Talen started, "the Benshidi are Wiseman-fearing people. They take the practice of worshiping him very seriously. I wouldn't take his name in a negative way around them if I were you."

The idea wasn't lost on anyone, but it would be good information. There would be more to know about the people they were about to call upon, though, that was more useful.

* * *

It had taken him several days, but he had arrived at his destination: the end of the Lanzman forest. Given the information he desired, Aunten Schritz now was trying to find the last traces of his sworn enemy: Halun Leman.

The maps of Winterlon only went as far as the forest to the east. What lied beyond it, however, was a mystery to most. The word around the capital, and throughout most of Winterlon, was that it was a swampland, occupied by few and taken as a complete waste. No one in their right mind would go beyond the end of the 2,000-mile forest, unless they desired madness.

Supposedly that is what had happened to Halun. The page Aunten had ripped out and read through multiple times only stated that Halun went as far as he could by going around the forest, then ended up stranded in the swamplands. Nothing had been heard since. Perhaps he still resided there, the end of his days on Winterlon slowly creeping up on him. On the other hand, his skeleton might be happened upon, laid to rest sometime in the last two years.

Now with no further to go, there was a real chance that this would all come to nothing, but only time would tell. So far, the observations were true of the landscape. There were a few trees, and the soil soon turned soupy, with water sitting on top, gradually turning from a dark shade of blue to an even darker shade of green, moss filling the top of the water, few disturbances on the flat surface.

Aunten's bare feet squished against the soft soil with each slow step. He was sure not to find many living creatures who could speak to him, and each step further east lessened the chances of meeting an intelligent soul.

After a couple of hours wading further and further into the swamp, he soon began to find more and more life among the pools of water. Every ten seconds or so there would be a fish that would splash out of one small pool and into another, sometimes leaping across fifteen feet or more to find the next pool. And these were no tiny bluegill or perch.

These fish were approximately fifteen pounds, about one and a half foot long, grey in color, and with sharp, inch-long scales that protruded from their bodies. Anyone trying to catch one with their bare hand would be in for a painful experience.

One of the fish happened to cross Aunten's path, and hit him in the shoulder. Rather than just bounce off the taller, meaner creature, the fish's scale hooked onto Aunten, embedding into his skin and tried to reach around and bite with even sharper teeth, sixteen on top and sixteen on the bottom.

Aunten was only slightly annoyed by the fish, took a moment to admire its tenacity, then removed it from his shoulder and grasped it around the top and bottom with all his might. The fish was known as Tailas, one of the deadlier and unnatural fish in Winterlon. The Tailas fell limp, it's mouth hanging open, all thirty-two teeth on display. Aunten then threw the fish back into one of the little pools, then reached his pale hand into the pool and with force pushed down until his hand fell flat against the bottom.

Quick as a flash of lightning, all the pools around him began bubbling, and dead Tailas floated to the surface. This brought a smile to Aunten's face, and he continued his journey into the swamp.

Nearly three hours into his wade, Aunten finally did come across someone who was alive, and on two legs. The woman was dressed head to toe in cloth, even covering her entire face. The cloth was thin enough that she could see him coming, and was quick to back up, turning away.

"Wait,", he yelled, loud enough for anyone miles away to hear. She could hear him, though cloth also covered her ears.

The woman stopped, turned back toward the awful creature, and remained silent.

"You must help me. I seek out the great warrior, Halun Leman. Do you know of him?"

The woman remained silent. She did not remove any of her cloth, but instead turned her face toward the ground.

Aunten normally would have killed her for noncompliance, but with no one else in sight, he could not risk walking many more hours before finding someone else who could help him. "I promise no harm would come to you. All you need is to give me his whereabouts. Or final resting place, whichever be true of him."

Still the woman was not responding at all. For a moment, Aunten was worried she was an apparition, something that truly was not before him. He took a few steps toward her, and she stayed her ground.

It was still a few more moments before the woman, who had with her only a burlap sack that looked half full of whatever she was gathering, reached into the sack and pulled out some food. She dropped it at her feet and backed away, as if to offer it to the Deadman.

"No, I cannot take any gifts. I can only visit him. Or where he remains."

The woman began to shake her head, the cloth covering her head shaking with her, and gradually dropping away. Finally her eyes were exposed, green eyes. Aunten could guess from her moderate height, slightly hunched posture, and apparent flabby skin that she was aged about fifty, maybe a little older. But her eyes were younger looking, and the skin on her face was fresher than what could be guessed elsewhere.

After she saw that Aunten would not take the food, whatever it was, Aunten was not familiar with it, she snatched it back off the ground and put it back into her sack. Next she took out a stick and began writing symbols on the ground.

Aunten took another step toward her, and the woman did not move. The symbols she was drawing out began to make themselves clear. The first one was a side-view of a face, with the person's lips opened. The image next to it appeared to be an "x" shape. Aunten began to put it together.

"You're mum." 'Mum' being the Winterlon word for mute. "If the devil has graced with me a gift, it is hidden still. Can you understand my words?"

The woman began to draw another symbol on the ground. This one was of a closer view of an ear. She began to write lines going into the ear, as if to represent sound. Aunten still was unclear, so he spoke clearly and articulated even more than normal.

"Can…you….understand?"

The woman's eyes only caught the last word as she finished drawing the symbol. She turned her head to the side to indicate she didn't understand.

Aunten repeated it twice more before the woman was able to read the lips enough to catch what he meant. She nodded.

Aunten gave a slight sigh. "You understand some, then. You are of help. If you had parchment, I could write the name down."

But the woman shook her head. Aunten could not know from the woman, but she had been mute from birth, and her hearing largely impaired due to two close thunderclaps near her as a child. She could hear the mysterious, ugly man, but only somewhat. And it would be difficult to make everything known.

"Can you take me to someone else? Someone who can help me?"

Aunten's question was responded by the woman shaking her head. Instead, she began to walk the other way, and Aunten began to follow her, not too closely and not too far away. It would be after a meal and several minutes afterwards that the two would be able to understand each other. She would indeed lead him directly to Halun Leman.

* * *

Ed had convinced everyone to travel another couple of miles north after reaching the bottom of the Wise-Mountains. The Benshidi keep was only a few more miles away, or so they were to be believed.

Before the journey started, however, one matter had to be settled: Gwendolyn's place in the company. While she was confident she would not be a permanent member in their quest to end the Deadman's new rule, she had agreed to continue with them to the Benshidi keep at least, and stay there a few days until the wrath of the mountain men could be contained. She agreed that the rest of her life the followers of Kloven would try to kill her, but her thinking was that she would be able to take them.

As for Kloven himself, his word would only be kept as far as when the Mainmen would return. In retrospect, Gwendolyn told Ed she'd wished that one of his men had been around to hear him give his word, because the chances, she said, of surviving a wound like the one he took were fifty-fifty. If he died, his followers would show no mercy when they returned. Time would tell what would happen when they did get back.

Gwendolyn also advised that going back down the mountain would be easier, since they couldn't go down the way they came. One of the mountains further to the west could be scaled up from the bottom, and they could slide down back to the first peak, where Browning died and the second fight with Kloven happened.

And so the number in the company remained at ten. Her clothing was not in the same scheme as the others, but the light blue cloak could pass as that of a servant.

James' quick thinking in the caves of the mountains had impressed Ed, and he had gathered in

Laura, James, Amanda, and Joven as they sat by the fire that night, eating the last of the mobwin meat they had.

"First, we must prepare for anyone who comes upon us, as I'm sure will happen. The Benshidi scouts will be numerous, always looking for outsiders. When they see your clothing, they will recognize they cannot kill us all immediately."

He handed James back the Mainmen sword, and continued. "You and Laura being siblings, I think that is a good excuse. Joven, you may perhaps be a distant relative."

"An uncle," Laura suggested. "I never had one on Earth. I can say I have one now."

Joven chuckled, "I agree, niece. If it was your parents who were taking you, it would be more apt to have a wagon of some kind. Though horses would be apt for a situation like this."

James began to worry about this as well. "I wish they were here, too."

Ed shook his head. "You worry too much. To travel through the Lanzman forest and come out on the other side of the Wise-Mountains is several days journey for the horses. They would have to come to the keep to be reunited with us."

This still was a worry to James, who felt like he and maybe the two girls were the only ones with connections to their horses, at least connections like pets.

Ed continued, "As for what to say when something comes up, I think the worse attitude you two have towards us, the more distain you show, the better. Make us feel like we'd like to retaliate."

James smiled. "I know I can do that."

This brought laughter from everybody. Then Amanda asked, "Ed, do you really think these Benshidi people will help us?"

"I am hopeful," he replied. "Legend tells us that the Benshidi were once very strong warriors. Once that is in the bloodline, it is hard to get it out. Even generations of peace cannot contain it."

Joven agreed, adding, "I would not be surprised to learn if there was in-fighting amongst the people as far as violence goes."

At this point, Ed started to say something, but struggled. Laura caught this. "What?"

Ed sighed. "There is something you three need to know about the Benshidi. The outcome of our whole journey may depend on it."

The mood turned more serious now. Everyone's attention was laser-focused on their leader.

"The Benshidi are a proud race of Winterlon. They look down on people from Earth, so it is very, very important that you three not tell them this."

This revelation was a bit of a shock for the group. "Why?" asked James.

"That I do not know. Being one of the oldest living peoples in Winterlon may have something to do with it. Through the years, the Benshidi have gone through several stages of isolation. They will be neighborly allies one day, then sworn enemies the next should your paths cross. Their pureness as Winterlonians may be what makes them strong, or so they would believe. So again, I must stress, do not allude in any way that you are not originally from here."

"Then why bring us here?" asked Laura. "Why not go somewhere else?"

She would have asked why Ed couldn't have left the three in Longell and came back for them after getting the Benshidi on their side, but then there would have been no way to let them know if the Mainmen group had failed, or been killed. And from there, James, Amanda and Laura would be stranded in Winterlon with no way of going home, no other warriors to help them in case Longell was attacked, and no one to lead them to another cause if they wanted to keep fighting.

Ed nodded in acknowledgement. "It was a risk, but one I was willing to take. And one that I knew you would be willing. The Benshidi at our back would be the first sign that the countries of Winterlon can ban together. Aunten and his Deadman may seem insurmountable at the moment, but they can be killed, don't forget. All of us together stopping them brings greater odds of success."

Joven chimed in again, "And our course leading us north was a natural way to start. The journey south to Geinishaw would have been treacherous considering Aunten's assumption of the capital. His forces may have caught and killed us easily then."

All of this was something the three from Earth would think about over and over. It was true that all the forces of Winterlon together stood a better chance of killing the Deadman than just a few, but the personal attitudes would be hard to put aside at first glance.

13. The Keep

The next morning the group was off to a slow start. They all had some of the wheat blund that Maryann had prepared before they left Longell. James thought it tasted good, but could have used some butter.

Not more than a mile down the way there was a small cloud from the north that appeared. The cloud was traveling south, and soon Johnson, who was in the lead, determined what it was.

"Horses," he cried out to everyone, hoping the advancing group wasn't close enough to him to hear. Luckily the group had been traveling in the order they planned, with James and Laura next to each other, and Ed and Jaenen carrying their packs. James kept the Mainmen sword, but that was all he would carry.

Joven also was empty-handed, Gwendolyn carrying his pack on her back. He would be the one to address the riders, but Laura and James would drop in complaints every so often to keep up appearances.

This was a big gamble, for Ed and Talen knew that if the charade worked, they would have to drop it once they were before someone like King Linus. Ed would then take the lead and address whoever would see them. They were hoping that whoever that was would be appreciative of their small deception, and appreciate how difficult it was for them to cross the Wise-Mountains.

After a minute, the horses arrived, three of them, each with a rider armed with swords and bows and arrows. The first rider dismounted, and the other two remained. Each rider took a portion of the group, one at the back, one at the middle.

All three of the riders were dressed in white, except for the insignia of a red fist, or what appeared to be a fist, on their chests. Out of the knuckles came swords and spears, though they were faintly drawn in, not extremely clear, especially from a distance. An odd symbol for a peaceful people who wished to be left alone.

The dismounted rider approached Joven on foot, Joven remaining silent until the rider asked a question: "Who do I have the privilege of meeting this morning?"

Joven nodded at him and extended an arm, which was not taken. "My name is Kahlen Virdon. I travel with my niece and nephew, Clarice and Ronald. Twins born twenty and one years ago."

The rider examined that, the two youngsters playing their roles well, looking annoyed. "And what is your destination?"

Joven cleared his throat before answering. "We seek an audience with the Benshidi. Their father, Lord Yale Virdon, has a message for the king."

All this while, the rider had been harmless enough, his arms by his side, nowhere near his weapons. At the word 'king', though, he went for the handle of his sword. "I fear at this time that may be impossible to grant."

"May I have your name, sir?" asked Joven.

The rider did not comply right away, instead turning his attention to the other two riders and to the rest of the company. "A lot of bodies to be traveling with, and all armed quite heavily, from the looks of it."

"Well," Joven started, "you never know when we might run into the Click. Our Lord use to hunt them for sport, until last year, when one returned an arrow into my shoulder, and his."

The three from Earth were familiar with the Click, a group that were the Winterlon equivalent of Native Americans. They lived in simple terms, and hated all who were advanced to them. The Mainmen army had decimated a bunch of them one night while the group was staying at the Mainmen camp.

The rider now examined Joven's hurt shoulder. "It seems a recent wound."

Joven sighed. "It has bled on and off since. It happened to start just as our journey began. Damned thing."

Now it seemed that the façade was beginning to crumble. The other two riders now had a hand on their weapon of choice.

"Will you let us pass?" asked Laura, trying to hide some of the panic in her voice.

"Boy!" cried James. He was asking Jaenen generally, but Jaenen was being stared at by one of the riders. James saw a small dirt clod on the ground, picked it up, and threw it at Jaenen, hitting him in the forearm. "Boy!" he shouted again.

"Bring me some water." James' tone was very snotty, and he paid no attention to the riders.

Joven started laughing at the situation. "The spoiled little shits. You know the kind, sir."

The rider questioned him further, "May I ask where Lord Verdon is headquartered at the moment?"

"The northernmost point of Virk. No easy task passing through the Wise-Mountains. We need not see only the king, anyone with stature willing to see us would acknowledge that."

This gave the rider some pause. "And why bring the children along?"

This brought a chuckle from Joven, who motioned for the rider to come in close so he could speak a little softer. "These two are infamous in Virk. Anyone who would see them knows that our Lord only sends them when he cannot come himself. It's a way for everyone to know that what he says is to be taken seriously, for if the children's journeys are not happy ones, he hears of it."

Laura sighed. "Come, let us be on our way. We aren't supposed to break for another hour. We are losing precious time."

The rider motioned to one of his comrades by hitting his chest twice with a tightened fist. The rider closest to Laura suddenly took out his bow and armed it, aiming it at her.

"Whoa, whoa," cried Joven. "You have no idea the gravity of the situation you are about to create."

Ed and Talen, not too far from each other, were preparing for action. If the game was up, they would make sure it would end with the riders' deaths, not theirs, no matter what it would bring at Benshidi.

James then took out the Mainmen sword and brandished it before the rider who had an arrow pointed at Laura. "My father didn't teach me to fight for nothing."

The threatening rider was taken aback, not by the action, but after looking closer at the sword. "Al", he cried.

The one who had been speaking to Joven came back to his ally, and saw the sword as well. "We'd know that sword anywhere."

Ed had tried to get James' attention after the sword was out, but it was too late. Now he had to consider whether or not to stay silent or try and intervene.

"The Mainmen sword going to a lord's son? Quite unusual. Did you win that off of someone?"

James saw now that these riders were probably not going to buy anything he said, but he thought up, "Twas a gift from my father on my birthday, my, my twentieth birthday."

The leader, Al, wasn't convinced. "Let me see your hand, boy."

James showed Al the hand that was not scarred.

"Both of them," Al protested.

James looked to Ed, turned his attention back to Al, and shook his head.

Ed stepped up to Al and showed him his dominant hand, the right one, and the scar.

"Then my suspicion is now proved correct. You *are* Mainmen."

"And we would very much appreciate an audience in the keep," Ed said.

The riders chuckled to each other. Al thought about it a moment. "We're not due back to the keep for another few days, but we'll take you there. When the king hears that the Mainmen were brave enough to cross the Wise-Mountains, it will excuse our return."

The rider, Al, then got back on his horse and motioned for the others to follow him.

"How far is it to the keep?" Amanda asked to Ed.

"I'm not entirely sure. It's only supposed to be a days' journey after the mountains."

It was about nine in the morning when this all happened. It would be closer to four in the afternoon before they would arrive at the keep.

* * *

For Kloven, the aftermath of his fight with Gwednolyn was nothing but a painful memory, one that he would not forget. A couple of his men were hiding on the cliff when he and Talen were dueling, and went back up after they realized the fight was over. Incidentally, none of them heard Kloven give his word that the Mainmen could safely pass the mountains on their way back.

They had gotten him down off the top of the mountain and had to cauterize the wound quickly. The missing limb's nerves were still getting used to the change, but perhaps that was just in Kloven's mind.

Not more than an hour after the cauterization, he was told by one of his followers that he had visitors. They were twelve Deadman, whose appearance frightened him at first, but only at first. He had seen many ghastly sights in the past, some of his own people were nightmares when he was younger, though there was a large difference between someone living off the mountain and a resurrected being whose body looked and felt like it did not belong among the living.

"I have had many troubles today, being visited by the Deadman I hoped would not be among them," Kloven started.

This brought nothing but cackles from the Deadman, whose sadistic laughter only managed anger from the weakened Kloven. He tried to reach for his sword with his missing limb, but that only brought more laughter from the Deadman who caught this image.

"Ask your questions and be on your way," he warned sternly.

Sienel stepped forward. "One would have thought the great leader of the mountain men would have been able to handle a few Mainmen. Too bad they are still a threat."

Kloven huffed at the notion. "If they hadn't have gotten the drop on me, I would have been able to wipe out the remainder."

Sienel suddenly grew impatient. "It's all fun and games for someone like you, knowing that we cannot humiliate you any further, but I promise, should you decide not to disclose the truth to me, Aunten will find a way to embarrass you further."

Kloven's face fell, and he turned toward his associates, who looked away from him as he continued. "They had help. That bitch Gwendolyn Asfair."

Sienel said, "So we've heard."

"She was once a proud Mainmen, but has for several years been leaching off of our stock, killing any who get in her way. It was she who was responsible for my…loss."

Now the Deadman began to be pleased. Korah stepped forward. "Just the woman?"

Kloven thought back. "The company is larger. I believe among them are Talen Wadenston and Ed Hotean. It would fall under assumption that one of them now leads the cause."

This was good enough for the Deadman. "What of the others?" asked Jenik.

Kloven shook his head. "Unknown. All but one of them escaped us, and given our honor and code, we must grant them safe passage back when they return."

Unfamiliar with the ways of the mountain men, Latren stepped forward to assert dominance. Kloven stayed put while his followers backed away. "What code?" he asked.

"Well," Kloven started, "when one faction defeats another, if the loser is left alive, they must show their thankfulness in being spared. In this case, safe passage was their goal. I cannot kill them when they return."

Sienel nodded. He had not been the wisest of men while he was breathing naturally, but he had heard something along the lines of the honor codes kept among the mountain men. "Where were they headed?"

Kloven thought a moment, then shook his head. "I would say over the mountain. She did not risk a climb up to the first summit, so she must have been saving her strength for the peak."

Fiernan chuckled. "When they reach the peak…"

"Nowhere to go but down," finished Nalop, the Deadman who, save Sienel, held the longest life of any of Aunten's servants.

"They make for the Benshidi," Sienel added, and a large, ghastly smiled filled his face. "I pity all the lives who they will betray to us."

Nothing more needed to be said. Sienel and his company of ghouls knew where they were headed, and what they would do when they arrived.

* * *

While the Benshidi were indeed pacifists, their isolationism took priority, and eliminating any threats to the kingdom was to be done without any prejudice. The three riders who were now escorting the Mainmen to the keep knew there was a small risk of punishment from their superiors, but such a rare sight as Mainmen in Dulon would make them forget about the broken rules.

The company had learned that Al, the head of the scouts, was short for Aljen, who had held his position for thirteen years. The other two scouts were Melbun and Rickard. Both of them had been appointed in the last three years, after the two other scouts had been devoured by beasts from the Wise-Mountains.

Aljen had a white beard that fell to the top of his stomach, unkempt, as if he had started growing it in his youth and never trimmed it. The apparent origin of his character would be Asian, though in Winterlon everyone of all races were mixed together without true rhyme or reason. His face was beginning to show wrinkles, not just on his forehead, but also on his cheeks. Despite showing his age, he still rode well on his chestnut horse, and walked with a full stride, not showing any signs of slowing down.

On the flipped side of the age coin, Melbun was seemingly younger than James. He had been the one who James had targeted, and called for help. His voice was higher, suggesting his age to only be about fourteen or fifteen, perhaps even younger since his voice hadn't dropped yet. He had no muscle, but his black hair was long enough to curl. His eyes were green and his nose was pointed, sticking out from the rest of him.

The third scout, Rickard, was somewhere in the middle, in his late thirties or so the group guessed. He had a full beard that almost matched his blonde hair, the facial hair being a shade or two darker. He was the most intimidating of the three, with a frame and height to challenge Talen. In fact, Talen's dishwater blonde hair and age might have suggested that somewhere down the line of history, these two might have shared a common ancestor. Their looks were that close.

Early on their way, though, the group had discovered that Rickard was common to griping. He repeatedly asked Al why they had to take the Mainmen and slow down their pace, as normally riding back to the keep would have taken half the time or less. Al had told him just to be quiet several times. The back-and-forth nature suggested that Al was used to Rickard's whining, and had to live with it.

Laura managed to remain close to James all the while, and they occasionally shot worried looks to one another when the scouts began to stare at them, not breaking eye-contact for a good time.

Along the way, Al had been curious and asked them for their real names, which they disclosed.

The group came to a hill, and once at the top they could see for the first time the keep of the Benshidi. The building was close in shape and size to a fourteenth-century castle out of Europe, and the group could see a drawbridge that would lead inside. The stone was old, starting to wear down. Some green moss covered some of the top stones, showing age.

"Well," Al started, "the man you will see is Hunter Poldon. He is second in command of the Benshidi, and you'll have to convince him if you want to seek an audience with the king."

Ed approached, now with the Mainmen sword back on his person. "If he does not wish to see us?"

Aljen tilted his head in anticipation of what came next. "Then you will have made this for nothing. And if Hunter is in a sour mood, your party may not even go back complete."

Amanda was not happy with this. "So much for pacifists."

The group took the path down the hill and not more than twenty feet from the drawbridge, which was upright and locked, did Aljen signal for the group to stop. He whistled, and someone from above began to lower the bridge. Once it was down, just a foot or two in front of them, the scouts went first, everyone on foot following next.

A few men and women dressed in the same garb to the scouts went to see them, some of them shocked to see that they were not alone. One of the women stepped forward.

"Where did you find them?" she asked.

Rickard answered, "Just a few miles into the border. They crossed the Wise-Mountains."

This brought some laughter from the group, but Talen stepped forward and showed his hands. Once everyone saw the insignia of the Mainmen, though, they quieted down.

"Damn my eyes! We haven't seen a Mainmen in..." the woman trailed off, her eyes not leaving Talen's hand.

"True enough," said Al. "When I was a young child the Mainmen tried to form an allegiance with us. Since then I believe our lands have been emptied of them."

Rickard got down to business. "Is Hunter free? They'd very much like to talk with him."

The woman nodded. "I'll show them the way."

She was black-skinned, like Amanda, and tall, easily clearing six feet. Her clothes were free of any war damage, and appeared to only be worn down by time. Her hair was black, but with blonde highlights, something that fascinated the three from Earth.

Once all the Mainmen and the scouts were inside the keep, the drawbridge was raised again back into locked position.

Talen soon found himself in conversation with the woman. "We have traveled a great distance," he started, "to seek help in the coming conflict."

The woman chuckled to herself. "The Benshidi were brave warriors in the last generations. Now we grow weaker and weaker by the day, our strength committed more to staying alive than to bloodshed."

"May we know your name?" asked Johnson.

The woman replied. "Ramona. My name is Ramona Klein."

During the walk, everyone peeked around the inside of the keep, which looked in better shape, as if the people had taken more time and energy to preserving and keeping up the interior than the exterior. The stone was newer, no mossy spots showing. It was lit by torchlight, even during the day since the drawbridge blocked out a lot of natural sunlight. The civilians who were dressed in white as well, though they lacked the insignia, looked peaceful enough, most of them moving food or supplies around from place to place.

Without too much trouble, everyone could make out a marketplace by the shouts and shoving around of people wishing to buy and sell food and other items, mostly animals. Another place was a steel mill, where weapons could be ordered. Currency was exchanged, James could see, and the customer walked away with weapons, not of war, but of cultivating the soil. There were weapons in the shop, but mostly hung up and not of interest to the people standing in line.

Otherwise, there was a stable where horses stood, looking on to the groups passing by. A young girl was feeding them one by one, the horse next to her impatiently waiting for their meal. Soiled straw was being replaced by fresh straw from another youngster, though the face and features were a little obscured, so they couldn't tell the gender.

The group also saw some small restaurants and taverns, their design not too far off from the one they had visited earlier, Moser's. Not everything that was served looked all that appetizing, almost every dish seen was vegetable. Once in a while they would see meat, but seemingly it was bought by those whose clothes were less stained.

Soon enough the group was stopped in front of two big doors, made of oak. The doors were guarded by two armed men. They saw Ramona coming and prepared to open them. Once open, which took a good deal of strength, she led them down a darker hallway, lit by fewer torches and blocked from sunlight.

Each side had about seven or eight doors, each guarded by one Benshidi soldier. The mood of the place was much more foreboding than the open area they had started in. Now there was a sense of being shown a mysterious, almost forbidden zone where few could pass.

"May we ask who presides here?" asked McQuint.

Ramona nodded. "These men and women guard our hierarchy. The leaders who oversee our currency, our policies, laws, travel, agriculture, war. Each one appointed by King Linus and meeting with him once a week."

The end of the hallway came to a stone wall, with a separate hallway on each side, each curving around to a new hallway on either side, each leading straight on. Ramona took the one on the right, and passed by three sets of doors on both sides. The way was lit, but it was darker than the previous hallway.

"And who presides here?" asked Joven.

Ramona shook her head. "That is for us to know and you to learn, if you need to."

Gwendolyn cleared her throat. "I take it we cannot pass those big doors unless accompanied by you."

"Or someone else with permission" added Ramona. "Yes. Count yourselves in great fortune. Very few of our people ever pass through them. Let alone strangers."

After the end of this hallway, another path led them to the right. Once around the corner, the torches were fewer in number still. One lone soldier stood by a door on the far-left side. Five on either side in this hallway, all made of a stronger material than the doors past.

Ramona signaled for everyone to stop. "Stay," she warned, then went up to the guard. They exchanged some words, then she came back for them.

The end of this hallway was met by a large flag, spread out on the stone. It was the same as the insignia on the soldiers, the red fist with weapons on the knuckles. Though the design was a bit different than the ones seen earlier. James figured it to be the original flag, perhaps renovated sometime recently.

Ramona now stood before them again. "Follow."

She led them to the third door on the right, and knocked four times, all in rhythm. Then it was silent for about twenty seconds or so, before the door opened, seemingly on its own; no one was there to greet them on the other side.

Ramona waited for the door to be completely open before stepping inside. She motioned for the others to follow her, but made sure they stopped at a certain point.

The interior of the room was a little different than the others. Tapestries covered nearly every inch of the walls, which went about twenty or twenty-five feet high. Looking up the ceiling was also covered in tapestries. All of them were of different colors and shades, none of them repeating. The floor, made of wood, was the only surface not covered.

Inside on each of the four walls was a guard, looking on in a constant state of attention. They had one hand on a sheathed sword, the other at their chest, held on the same spot.

As for the second-in-command himself, Hunter Poldon was seated in a comfortable chair, similar to a throne, but when he stood to greet his guests, everyone could see a red cushion for him to be seated on. He wore white as well, but his chest, where the insignia was borne on the others, was bare. Only on the bottom of his long sleeves, down by his wrists, were two small insignia of the red fist.

For his appearance, Hunter was a man beginning to show age. He couldn't have been more than sixty-five, though he was clean-shaven, and his salt-and-pepper hair left to age gracefully, or at least as gracefully as possible. His face was one of moderate welcome, but he did not smile before the group. His height was only about five feet ten inches or so, maybe an inch or two one way or the other. His eyes were brown, his teeth straight, and pretty clean. Most everyone in Winterlon had the teeth of a person who did not always have access to toothpaste.

"The hour grows late this day, and now I see we have guests. Ramona, please remain."

She stepped forward and sat opposite Hunter. The group saw a large bed where he would sleep, Ramona now seated on the end of it.

"The leader of the group may step forward," Hunter said now, seated back on his chair, but only after Ramona was seated.

At first Joven and James both looked to Ed, afraid of whether or not to tell the truth to this man.

Before anything could be decided, Hunter saw through the charade. "You both look to him, let him speak."

Ed took a breath, stepped forward, and took a bow to the second-in-command. "I am Edward Hotean, leader of the Mainmen. We are pleased to be seen by you, sir."

This brought a smile from Poldon. "In all my years, I never thought I would have the Wiseman-given grace to see a Mainmen, let alone ten. No wonder you brought them to me, Ramona. Thank you.

"You may call me Hunter if you wish, Edward. While I may be the second most powerful man in the keep, only His Grace keeps the formalities."

Ed was now standing. "A pleasure, Hunter. You may call me Ed. I bring with me what remains of the Mainmen. We are here to warn His Majesty of the Deadman, who have risen and taken the capital."

Hunter nodded. "Word spreads through Winterlon of the return of Aunten Schritz, and his ascension. I am a man of history, Ed, so I know that the Mainmen and Governor Slank never saw eye-to-eye."

Ed turned around to see the others. "If it pleases you, Hunter, perhaps you would like to hear from my compatriots. Nearly all of us have the same story to tell."

Hunter was pleased by this. "Every man and woman has only the one experience. They cannot tell what others have seen or gone through. Let them speak."

Gwendolyn decided to step up first. "I am Gwendolyn Asfair, former Mainmen. The people of Winterlon, even beyond the capital, are beginning to act in accordance. They all have at least a moderate fear of what is to come with a Deadman rule."

Talen introduced himself, then added, "In our best hopes, the Benshidi may join us in this war, as allies, of course."

Hunter leaned back in his chair now. "I speak freely, and in honest, when I say that it is long overdue for a time to come when the Benshidi are back on the battlefield. And never a better time than the present."

This brought a look from Ramona, who stood and took a couple of steps toward Hunter. This caught the attention of the guards, all of whom simultaneously grasped their swords tighter.

"Hunter," she began, "you know of His Grace's view on this matter. We remain a people of peace."

"And we need not do so in times of war," said Hunter. "The pendulum swings ever back and forth. Our people have profited from peace, but soon that time will end. They will be just as ready as I am to defend ourselves."

"But He will not see it that way. His Grace will only banish you, or worse, for warmongering."

Hunter laughed. "The greatest crime in the eyes of King Linus. But I am not alone. When we have spoken, Ramona, you have also told of your fears. As well as I, you are aware of how diminished our force is."

Knowing that there was a chance the King could hear of this conversation, Ramona's appearance eased, her countenance now more open and telling. "True enough, Hunter. I fear that if you tell His Majesty of their coming and he agrees to see them, they will tell of our views."

Amanda shook her head. "We won't tattle on you."

This brought a curiosity to Hunter and Ramona's faces. Ed's face tightened for a moment, but only when he was sure that neither of them were looking at him.

"Tattle. A strange word to use, Earth based. Where did you learn that?" Hunter asked.

Amanda, looking around for help, tried to hide her mistake. She had momentarily forgotten the words spoken to her, and James and Laura, about how the Benshidi felt about them. "I, um, I'm not sure. It was somewhere, but I'm not sure where. Back over the mountains anyone from Earth is mixed among the people. Words get thrown around quite liberally. Some of them, like tattle, just stick."

Ramona looked on with a bit of a question in her gaze, but Hunter was satisfied. "Earth brings only creatures that we cannot say are equals. Their civilization, so we are told, crumbles with every so called advancement, and strengthens only in number, not in deed. The Wiseman graced them with advanced technology, but kept their minds archaic. With us, he has graced us with better minds, and perhaps it is for the better we lack their tools."

"Do you know of how to kill a Deadman?" James asked.

This was met by a curious look from Hunter. "A strange question, as if we hold the answer."

"It's the only sure way to win the war," James added. "Maybe you have knowledge that we couldn't find."

Hunter wasn't sure. "Perhaps. In our library. There are more books than I care to count there. Several of them are old enough to have been written five hundred years ago, when the Deadman ruled the world."

Laura got excited with this news. "May we see it?"

Ramona replied, "All in good time. The library is not restricted, but guests have been known to try and steal our history books and try to learn our fighting techniques. The guards there will not be very receptive to you having free roam."

Joven decided to speak next. "Regardless of finding that, we fear that the whole of Winterlon may depend on gaining allies in the war. With the Benshidi at our side, Aunten will see that his enemies grow in number."

Talen agreed. "Each day Aunten will grow stronger, and the people he rules will become more obedient. Time is a luxury we will not have in this war."

Ramona stepped closer to Hunter, the guards now relaxing their pose, knowing that there was less conflict in this meeting than there was moments ago. "Perhaps they have a point," she said to Hunter. "The stories must have fallen on His ear by now. He must acknowledge this, and with your word, He may indeed heed the warning."

Hunter was less hopeful. "Ending peace is a difficult notion. One that does not happen in an instant. His Grace will likely not hear what we are saying, instead He will hear what we are not saying."

This brought confusion to the group. "What do you mean?" Laura asked.

Hunter added, "His Grace may be becoming a bit more paranoid in his age. He has been on the throne for thirty years. Each day on it brings the image of someone usurping him. After so long a time, He may imagine me or someone else as trying to take it with a simple suggestion such as this."

Jaenen asked, "What will you do?"

"I will speak to him on your arrival here. He will know that you come not demanding anything, merely asking for our services. I must warn you, He will not be receptive to it. Not without a lot of convincing. But if the Wiseman be graceful, he will ask for a public appearance."

Ramona saw the confusion in their guests' faces. "Meaning He will not only see you but us as well, and perhaps other members of his callen."

'Callen', Ed would tell the others later, meaning "cabinet", another word from Earth that was transcribed to something similar in Winterlon.

"And the public," added Hunter. "A good king gives at least some credence to his people, but will stop them at their wrongheadedness."

Jaenen ventured, "And, if Wiseman be good, the people may convince Him if he may be…misguided?" He chose his words carefully, not wanting to give an impression to their hopeful eventual host that was anything less than respectable.

Hunter, though, was all smiles, seeing that these travelers were well-meaning. "In open conversation, I can say He has been wrongheaded in many circumstances. None of them have been disastrous mistakes, but this could end up being one."

Ramona then asked, "What shall we do with our guests in the meantime?"

Hunter got up from his chair and clasped his hands together. "Set them up with fine rooms. Let us not be unkindly hosts to them. Order any meal you would like, sleep how you would like, use our privies at your disposal, whatever will make you comfortable."

The guests all said their thanks and began to exit, Ramona leading them back the way they came.

Privately, Hunter Poldon was not so optimistic to the idea of King Linus being receptive. His selection of peace over everything else had not been unwelcomed in his rule, and there had been few conflicts in that time that had opened the opportunity for the Benshidi to once again become warriors.

Indeed, about the only time that King Linus' peacekeeping was in question was three years ago, at the rise of Kildeno. Even then, Linus' prediction that Winterlon would not fall was true, though many lives could have been spared if the Benshidi had intervened. Now the world was faced with the challenge of the devil himself, and his spawn. A truly greater enemy than Kildeno, whose infamy was not unknown to the Benshidi. It would take a great, great deal of words to convince their ruler that the time of peace may be at an end.

14. The Audience

James let the other guys clean up before him. Wordlessly they had decided that it didn't matter anymore if they wore their new clothes since the cat was out of the bag, so going back to the traditional brown Mainmen robes was fine with everyone. They also asked a couple of Benshidi delegates if it was all right to be armed, which they were told was fine, except in the presence of Hunter Poldon or King Linus.

Next, James was fascinated to learn that the Benshidi had the equivalent tools for shaving hair, and James decided that it was time for his excuse of a beard, which had grown in patchy and uneven, to go. He had help from a couple of Benshidi men who used the tools every other day or so, and with that there were no nicks or blood marks.

He took some time to reflect alone in the quarters, which were fairly large. They were complete with about twenty beds that appeared as bunk beds, one up top and one on the bottom, though the shapes of the frames they sat upon were circular and made of wood, the mattresses sitting on top, but if not squared away would slide off the frame.

James Realms thought about everything that had happened in the past few days. Getting through the Wise-Mountains, completing the climb, the death of Browning, and now meeting the Benshidi. It was a lot to comprehend, and so much more than he was used to, especially compared to his mundane days back on Earth where all he had to worry about was Graney's department store.

He heard the door to the quarters squeak. It brought him back to the present.

"I would have knocked but the door was already open."

Laura's voice sounded more soothing than normal to James. Even the ordeal of being taken by the Benshidi guards had had a toll on them. They felt closer afterwards, separately both James and Laura thought about the "more than friends" line, but now they had to actually hash it out.

"That's okay," James responded after a few seconds. He stood up and welcomed her with a hug.

"We're here," she said. "Finally. And now we need to wait even longer before we find out what we're doing next."

"Yeah," James replied, but only with that. He wasn't sure what else to say. Luckily, Laura was in a more conversational mood.

"Have you checked out this place? The taverns and the marketplace? It's kinda neat. They have their own coins and barter trading system. It's like the ones that we learned about a little bit, but they have different names, and sometimes the biggest things sell for the smallest amounts. I couldn't figure it all out, but it was kind of strange."

James again didn't know what to say. So Laura continued.

"Have you tried their toilets? It's like an actual toilet, not porcelain or whatever but it's the same idea. They have water run through the bottom and it's like an actual sewer system. I won't give the gory details, but it was a lot nicer than what we've been through."

This brought a smile to James' face. All that had happened, and rather than near-death experience after near-death experience, and the actual death of a company member being at the top of Laura's mind, instead it was money and toilets.

James motioned for Laura to join him on one of the top bunks. Before turning to do so, he finally asked, "What about Browning?"

Laura's face changed as quickly as her mind did to the more serious topic, though James' back was turned. "I think he would have loved it here. He really was a strong man. We'll miss him."

James was now on top, finishing the short climb up the ladder to the top bunk. "But it was actually seeing a man we'd spent time with dying. I know we all lost people in the Canyon, but this was different. This was someone who slept by our sides, laughed at our jokes, ate food with us. Other than my parents, I can't think of losing someone like that."

Laura had finished the climb and was now next to him, both their feet dangling off the side of the bed as James was partway into his last sentences. Laura continued, "It's kinda funny, losing dad was like that. I didn't really put it together until now, but yeah. It's almost like a brother or sister moving away, getting married and out of the house."

James had to ask, "You didn't have any siblings, did you?"

Laura shook her head.

"Me neither," James replied. "Ever since the end of the battle, I've kind of felt like all of us were a big family, in some ways."

"What do you mean by that?"

"Well, I just mean that you and Amanda, well, I— I don't know, I shouldn't say anything."

"James," Laura said with approach, "if you want to stay true to your word, no secrets between us, you can open up."

James sighed, a big sigh. His mind began to race in many different directions, because he was afraid what he was about to say would be the end of everything. The end of all the goodwill he had bought up to this point with the girls, especially with Laura. Her kiss the other night had not been nothing, no matter how much she had pretended that it was. Maybe she would be very receptive to what he was about to say. He'd have to find out.

"God, I don't know." That was all he could manage.

Laura, her eyes reading him like a book, had clearly been here before. "You do know. What do you want to say?"

At this point, she made a move that James had not expected. Without realizing it, her hand had moved to his back, and she began to stroke back and forth in comfort. It made James hold his breath for a minute, not sure what to do. It was an intimate moment for him, not experiencing anything like it before.

Her eyes became so inviting, full and deep. Anything he needed to say at this point, through the near-hypnotic effect, he could make pour out of his mouth. He looked away for a moment, but only briefly. Then he locked eyes with her again.

"I—I just wanted to say that you two…you mean a lot to me now."

Laura's eyes seemed to shift back to where they had been before, she seemed a little taken aback by what he had said.

"Oh." After saying this, she put on a warm, welcoming smile. The friendzone smile, or at least that's what James would have called it.

Knowing that if she felt anything more than he did, this might be the end, and knowing that he may have missed his chance entirely, he doubled back. "And, and…um. God, I just gotta say it. The way you do what you do, when you say anything to me, my heart lights up." His speech began to pick up more rapidly, the timbre of his voice growing higher with seemingly every word as he became a little more nervous.

The smile that now came across Laura's face was more flattering. Again, as if a couple of boys had said this to her earlier in life. "Your heart lights up, huh?"

James now had a big smile of acknowledgement in his face. Maybe she *did* have at least an inkling of feeling for him. "Yeah! I mean, right, but…maybe over time, when things go on, and we make it out of this war, we'll be together."

It was now Laura's turn to be a little nervous. "I can't say I haven't thought about it." Her voice became a bit huskier and whispered with each word, and James might have, if his mind were not preoccupied, noticed that this was her way of showing how nervous she was.

"And what did you see?"

Laura shook her head. "I see different things all the time. Sometimes we're together, and sometimes we go our separate ways."

"Am I ever with Amanda?"

Laura nodded. "Yeah. I've seen that a couple of times."

Now was the key moment. "And how did you feel? When you saw that?"

"A little cold. I love her, she's smart, brave, confident. She has things I wished I had."

"And…am I one of those things?"

Laura didn't say another word. She just nodded, looking forward, and James could see a slight wetness start around both her eyes. Before anything else could happen, James made his move. He delicately put his hand on her left cheek to get her to turn and face him, then moved that hand down to the front of her neck, then moving further back until it landed on the back of her neck. Then he brought her head in toward him, closing his eyes. She did the same.

The kiss seemed to last a lifetime. Both of them were, after a little bit of an awkward start, beginning to enjoy it, and making it last. When at last James came up for air, a sign that Laura may have wanted the kiss after all, he put his hands back by his side. Laura took a moment to recover, then put her hands on James' shoulders, caressing back and forth for a few moments, then she went back for more lip action.

This kiss, though, would not quite go on for as long. Sure enough, there was a knock on the door. And it was the last person they both wanted to see.

"That King Linus guy will see us."

Amanda choked out the sentence in awkward phrasing, not really sure how to proceed. She stared at the two of them for a few seconds, then turned around and went back the way she came. James thought he caught a glimpse of her shaking her head, as if to try and clear the images she had just seen from her mind.

Despite the wondrous feelings that James had had in the last minute, now his heart sank, sinking so low it seemed to touch the pit of his stomach. He had not forgotten the tender moment he and Amanda had shared one night by the fire on the way to the Mainmen camp a couple of weeks ago. That night she had shared with him the details of her brother's suicide, and James felt like she had treated him in the moment as more than a companion.

Now that he and Laura may end up having feelings for each other, that may very much indeed end up ruining his and Amanda's relationship. Part of him felt the rush to jump out of his spot and try and track her down, come up with some explanation, as if his hand had been caught in the cookie jar. But the rest of him, a weird feeling of adrenaline, kicked in instead, letting him stay where he was, letting Laura make the first move toward the ladder that would bring them down to ground level.

She did indeed go first, wordlessly. She felt just as awkward as James did, and like him was not sure what could be said to make things better, if it was needed.

* * *

Before James could have a chance to speak with Amanda, Ed had called them over. They were to meet up in front of the big oak doors, then someone would take them inside and escort them to King Linus. What they did not know is how chaotic the scene would be. For indeed King Linus would see the Mainmen, but he also invited fifty public guests, whom would be selected by the guards and staff. It was a large crowd, even for a late evening hour. There was no ceiling in the keep, not in the center at least, so the stars could be seen above, and torches were lighted so everyone could see.

"Now," Ed started, "I want you to leave all the talking to me and Talen. Maybe one of the others not from Earth. After what happened earlier today, I think we are safe for the time being, but remember what I said. Speak like we do. We have no reason to make them think twice about helping us."

After Ed had broken off to try and find some others, Amanda had turned and was now waiting by Gwendolyn and McQuint by the door. The roar of people asking patiently at first, then later yelling at the guards to let them be one of the lucky ones to see the king became deafening. James only managed a few words, even though Amanda was not looking at him.

"Look, I don't know what you're thinking, but, well, ahem—" James couldn't help but smile at himself. He was about to tell her he had actually kissed a girl, the rush of the experience overpowering him. But he cut it off abruptly and tried his best to carry on. "What I mean is, we can all still be friends."

Amanda paid him no mind. James thought for a while, but was distracted by the endless noise around him. He tried again.

"It's got nothing to do with you."

This caught her attention. Amanda's eyes went wide, and James knew he had said the wrong thing. "We're gonna talk about this later."

That was all she would say. After that, she wouldn't face him again, instead trying to engage in a conversation with McQuint.

Laura was now beside James, trying to piece together what had happened, despite being out of earshot. She wouldn't have heard anything because of the noise, though.

At that moment, the guards called for the crowd to move aside. James and Laura did as asked, she joining him on the left side. From the parted walkway, two men marched up to the door. Both of them were wearing the white cloaks with the red fist on their chests, indicating their placement as higher than civilian.

They reached the doors and spoke quickly with the guards, who stepped away from the door. They then went around and hand-picked the fifty guests from the population who would be blessed to be a part of the king's audience. They jumped for joy, jubilant in manner, while the others who were not selected turned away in disgust, some even trying to beat on the people who were selected. A few times the guards had to intervene and shove away the violent offenders.

After a couple of minutes, the guards signaled to the two new cloaked men that they were ready, and the big oak doors were opened again. The ten who represented the Mainmen were permitted to enter first, followed by the fifty lucky souls. Again the guards had to shove away those who tried to sneak in. After a while, the guards had to threaten them with a violation of peace, which made everyone stand aside.

In this time of peace among the Benshidi, a violation of peace could be written up by anybody with authority, be it a guard, a nobleman, member of the callen, or the king himself. To be charged with it was about as severe a punishment as could be handed out. It meant that the person in question was disturbing the peace to a point of violence, or deemed violence, that could threaten the pacifistic ways. The ultimate punishment, those who were found guilty of being in violation of peace were sentenced to death, in whatever manner suited the man or woman who handed out the sentence.

Back in the darker hallway, the big group was once again led past the first set of doors. Now they took a left instead of a right. Down this side, though, there were no more doors. Seemingly just a dead end. One torch lit the way.

The first man, whose appearance could barely be made out by the low light, took a step toward the torch and once in his hand, held it up close to his face. At that time he held it there for a few more seconds, then violently blew the torch out.

In a panic, the whole way went dark. The ten strangers to the keep drew their weapons and tried their best, in the dark, to circle up and fend off anyone who tried to get them.

"Traitors!" cried Jaenen.

"They're gonna kill us," Laura half-whispered, half-yelled. She caught her mistake after the word 'gonna', in the moment forgetting how she was to speak.

But soon a small light began to appear from the dead end. It grew with every second, until everyone saw that the source of the light was another chamber. The dead end was a fake, the whole stone wall able to turn and reveal the chamber. The envoy who had blown out the torch now stopped turning the wall when it hit ninety degrees, opening the way fully for everyone to enter from either the left or right side.

"Hear me, citizens and guests", cried out the other envoy. His voice was higher pitched, though still a man's. His appearance still not totally clear from the light source, but he may have cleared six feet tall, barely, and the features of his face suggested some age, as did his voice, now that it was ringing in everyone's ears due to some echo in the hallway.

The envoy would not have addressed the crowd were it not for the fact that he could see by the light source that the Mainmen were preparing for battle. "His Majesty King Linus I would not be disturbed except by those who know the way. You may try and fail as many times as necessary to get to this chamber, for only one stone out of several hundred will grant you access. The others may drop you to your death, or merely chill you at the touch. Whichever it may be, that I cannot know. I have not tried, and none that live now have, either."

His warning, with the echo and voice, was chilling to all. The citizens, who had remained relatively still and quiet during the blackout, were familiar with this ritual. Now the Mainmen knew of it. Not even Ed had been forewarned of this.

Now the other envoy, whose appearance was a little clearer than the others', looked more noticeable. He had a black beard, and tanned skin. His eyebrows were as thick as his beard, at least at a distance. His body was built massive, his muscles seemingly big enough to lift a horse over his head. His teeth were shinier, whiter than almost anyone else's they had seen, except maybe Hunter.

After some trepidation, the group began to move into the next chamber. When they did, they saw it as an awesome sight. The whole place went back two or three hundred yards, and was about fifty feet across. Giant pillars and statues graced the way, mostly made of stone or marble. Similar to the capital, which had chiseled works of previous governors, these were life size or bigger interpretations of past kings and queens. Queen Quartha's likeness was one of the last ones they saw on the right-hand side. Beneath them a blue carpet was laid, dark blue, almost going into a purple hue.

On the far end, on the left-hand side, was the likeness of a man of middle-age. He was clean shaven, and had an angular, almost European look to him. His nose was prominent, though not enough that it made the whole face look awkward. His hair parted down the middle, looking moderate in size and shape, no sign of thinning quite yet. They guessed this to be the appearance of King Linus.

All along the way on both sides plenty of torches were lit, illuminating the whole place. Before them at the end of the carpet was about ten or fifteen feet of stone floor, and then a massive throne, the cushion on it matching the color of the carpet. It sat empty now, and once at the end of the carpet, the two envoys turned and motioned for the group behind to stop. They did without question.

The older envoy's appearance now was before them. His hairline was very far back, but it still grew long in the back. The rest of his dome was bald. His height may have once been as tall as five-nine, but now he only stood at five-six or five-seven.

The group sat in silence for about a minute while the envoys took position, one on either side of a great stone door that would have to be winched open by a lever. These people had the technology of a pulley, at least, James thought after seeing this.

After they were set, the taller and younger of the two on the side with the winch, they motioned for everyone to file in on the stone floor. Everyone fit, though some of the population that were guests pushed and shoved to get toward the front, James and Amanda being a couple that were unaware that being at the front was where they wanted to be.

Everyone had filed in, and now the winch began to be turned, and the stone door, perhaps ten feet across and twenty-five or thirty feet tall, began to lift. Out of it came a young woman, perhaps the same age as Laura, James and Amanda, but more likely a year or two younger.

She had blonde hair, which grew freely and went straight down, long enough to touch her bum. Her face was delicate, her features amusingly pleasant, at least from what could be seen. Her eyes and face were looking down at the floor as she walked. Her clothes were minimal, basically scantily clad. Even by today's two-piece bathing suit fashion, this may have been unacceptable. Her breasts and pubic regions were barely covered, and despite her perhaps younger age she showed ample cleavage.

In another manner, another life, this may have been a turn-on for the men, especially Johnson, but this presentation was sad. Clearly this girl did not want to be wearing what she had on, did not want to be made up the way she was, and did not want to be before the group she had been asked to stand in front of.

The rest of the crowd's reaction, though, was another matter. All of them, even the women, cheered, whistled and clapped. All at once, the picture was beginning to form. Before the king would make an appearance, this was the warm-up act.

Once the girl was only a couple of feet away from the group, more bodies began to appear from the stone door, which remained open. Among them stepped out about twelve men and six women. Hunter Poldon could be made out, as could Ramona. The rest were King Linus' callen, representing the various duties held to a cabinet.

The eighteen higher members filled in and stood around the entertainer, nine on each side, bowing outward in a half circle. Each stood in a position where they could see the girl. Now she began to lift her head up, slowly, and her eyes began to meet that of the crowd.

Her face was delicate, very fresh. She wore perhaps a version of blush, though it was coarser and patchier, almost as if it were in chunks across her cheeks with another on her chin. Her eyes were a dark green, though from a distance that could have been confused for a shade closer to a brown color. Her mouth was average sized, maybe a bit wider than normal, but otherwise caked in lipstick. Too much lipstick.

She turned and faced each of the semi-circle of superiors around her, bowed, then turned around and did the same to the empty throne. Seeing her near-naked backside thrilled the crowd as well.

Few knew that behind the throne was a wall equipped with small peepholes between two stones, perfect for the top of the hierarchy to use to spy on the royal chamber before making an entrance. In this case, it was a perfect opportunity to watch as the girl performed for her crowd.

The man was indeed in his late fifties, nearing sixty, his face in the likeness of his life size sculpture outside. His height cleared six-three, not quite six-four. His body was in fair shape, not quite as hefty as some kings grew during their rule. He kept in fair health, taking long walks when necessary, and runs outside the keep when advised.

For clothing, King Linus I wore a black cloak with a red cape, the Benshidi insignia on the back and fur on the trim, which was draped over the shoulders. The fur was made from brentin, creatures that were more commonly found on the Wise-Mountains, but would occasionally journey into the land of Dulon. His boots were white, though, as if to say symbolically that his guards, the callen and his second-in-command were only as worthy of their king as licking his boots.

This girl had been performing for guests since she was six years old, and in the twelve years since, Linus had not grown unfond of watching her. He did not do it for sexual pleasure, as could easily have been imagined. No, the true reason he revealed to each of his audiences.

In the meantime, the act was beginning, and the girl began to perform a ritualized dance, one without music to guide her or keep time with her movements.

She had had to practice over and over until she had it right, less she be whipped and scratched for her constant mistakes. In the twelve years she had been before audiences, though, her mistakes were usually helped with a little makeup that matched her white tone, spread across her back. That was where most of the damage had been done. A few times it had been done on her abdomen as well, and once in her youth on her upper chest.

That time was truly traumatic, for the glass tips had sliced open her chest, and left several scars on her upper chest, one of which could now be seen up close on her left breast. She had been blamed for it, because the woman with the whip meant to go for her shoulder, but because the girl moved, it hit her lower. She had been told at that time by the whip woman that if her breasts were damaged too severely when she grew up, she would lose all her value, and be tossed from the top of the Wise-Mountains.

The Wiseman, though, in his grace, did not ruin her figure, though, save some tissue that bared the scars. Remembering when the day had come that she had been deemed 'big enough' to be a woman in that regard, her chest had been thoroughly examined by the king, by the then second-in-command, by half the callen, and a guest audience of one hundred citizens (just to add further humiliation), and it was decided that the damage was not too severe, and she could live to an older age, as long as she could still perform.

All of this the girl kept in the front of her mind as she moved from side to side, her head moving first left, then right, her body following as if interpretively. She would jiggle many body parts, exciting the crowd even further, and at times have to leap to the floor and crawl in slow motion, giving the audience plenty of time to gaze down upon her.

This went on for about three minutes in total, though the Mainmen group could only tolerate one. Never had James had any special interest in the idea of women parading around in near-nude clothing, had no large interest in going to strip clubs, or any desire to live in a world where women were forced to do so. He ended up looking away for some of it, though against his will Ed, Joven, and Johnson made him turn back to look at her.

Three times her eyes locked onto James', and it was no surprise that the look she gave him was one of sadness, a desire for him to help her in any way he could, to free her of this hell. And she could see by his face and expression that he was not enjoying this performance.

For Laura and Amanda, the experience was even more humiliating. Here was a girl around their age, and had gone through perhaps the worst life imaginable, to be an entertainment slave to the masses. They just hoped against hope that her exploits did not also include sex with the higher-ups.

The others watched without breaking much eye contact out of respect. The Benshidi were peaceful people, yes, but the rumor was they could be easily insulted, if they were in the wrong mood. Not wanting this to be the case, Ed set the example, and everyone followed.

After the dance ended, bursts of applause and cheers came from the audience. The performing girl was quick with her bows then ran off toward the stone door, which remained open. She disappeared into the darkness beyond it, not looking back as the cheers continued.

Now that that was over, the Mainmen could breathe easily again. A few of the decorated

Benshidi took notice of this, but did not show it in their expression.

After the applause wound down, Hunter stepped forward, and announced, loudly and clearly, "It is my pleasure to introduce His Majesty King Linus I."

Everyone went down on one knee as soon as the introduction was over. And sure enough, here came King Linus from the doorway, entering slowly, seemingly making the entrance as slow and dragged out as possible. When at last he reached the throne and turned, he spoke. "Rise."

Everyone did so as he sat. His voice was soft and gentle, but carried in the chamber. It wasn't extremely high pitched, not quite as high pitched as the elder envoy, but it was distinctive, nonetheless.

Linus had a smile cover his face. "I always take pleasure in giving credit to our opening entertainment. I hoped you enjoyed Montana."

This brought some quieter clapping from the citizens, and further amusement from the king.

"Yes, yes. Earth girls always do it the best."

The news was dizzying for the trio. Now all the clues were forming together to finish the puzzle in their minds. Ed had warned them to not say they were from Earth, Hunter had spoken of Earth citizens as if they were second class, and now this display showed them how people from Earth were treated by the Benshidi: as slaves.

All this was spinning in their heads, but the silence between Linus' revealing of this information and his continued speech only lasted about five seconds. To stay in character, all but the three from Earth chuckled along to the crowd, who were more open with their comedic displays. Even the higher-ups were laughing at this in full honesty. In retrospect, the Mainmen just hoped that no one saw the three youngsters refusing to laugh at this joke. If they did notice, it could have been the end of the line, and the three would likely have been prime targets to be taken from the group and asked to remain and become slaves themselves.

"Now, to the business at hand. I have agreed to hear the case of Edward Hotean and the Mainmen cause. May you please step forward, Edward?"

Ed did as he was asked, and went back down on one knee. James started to do so as well, out of respect, but Talen, who shifted and now was beside him, made him stop.

"If it pleases Your Grace, you may call me Ed. My friends address me as such, and I would call it the highest honor of my life if you were to address me in tandem."

Linus was pleased by this. "Yes, Ed. Now please, bring forth your case."

Settling in, Linus prepared to hear everything that Ed would say, expecting for this to be a lengthy address, but Ed left it fairly short, hitting the main points.

"Winterlon," he began, "may be in shambles. The capital has fallen, Governor Slank is dead, and Aunten Schritz has taken over. He is now a Deadman, and he has brought back twelve of his followers. We ten represent the last of the Mainmen, and we wish to continue the fight against him. The rest of our followers were killed in combat in the Arnic Canyon. We ask, nay, we plead that the Benshidi force be reassembled, your bravest and most honorable warriors brought to the fore and join us as we bring together the great forces of the world."

Linus leaned forward afterwards, in surprise. "What you ask, Ed, is something that may trouble our people."

At this, the citizens were given room to speak amongst themselves. The squabble was too random to be made out, but certain words like "Deadman" or "Schritz" or "capital" were about all that were made clear.

"No doubt even though we branch ourselves off from the rest of the world, the Benshidi are informed enough to know of Aunten's ascension and Slank's demise. I do allow a few of our scouts to be in contact with mountain men, there is a mutual agreement they may hunt our lands when food is scarce," Linus added.

"It is good you are aware, Your Highness," Ed said.

Linus' attention now turned to his decorated comrades. "I ask that Yellen Kargor and Blaine Vivsky speak on this manner."

Yellen Kargor was Secretary of War for the Benshidi, a modest, often boring position since Linus was crowned. Still, the services of a war secretary were necessary in case anyone should call forth on the Benshidi a conflict.

Kargor was a replacement for the former secretary, Niles Qan, who met his demise after falling from a tower. The old man truly was not murdered, having reached the age of one hundred and eight. Only he could be blamed for not being able to keep his footing.

Yellen Kargor stood at six feet even, and like the other men in the callen was clean shaven. His age was forty-five, and his hair remained black, no gray yet. His face was a stern one, his features seemed to be closer together than normal, making him look meaner than the average man. He spoke first.

"My Lord, I say this without prejudice, but the people we have welcomed here today are of little concern to us. They have called upon themselves to be of aid to Winterlon, and must take responsibility for their failure. Aunten will have no interest in us, knowing we mean him no harm. I advise His Grace to dismiss his guests and go about his duties."

The words of Kargor echoed in the chamber for a time, his voice being huskier, deeper. The people were not very quiet afterwards, some of them openly protesting the short speech.

Next came Blaine Vivsky, the Secretary of State. It was he who was partially responsible for the low amount of communication for this shut-off people. He had spoken with his predecessor about the mountain men, who he used to have to deal with when they entered Dulon, and suggested that they be given some leeway in their territory.

He had only been appointed in the last few months, not long before reports of Aunten's rising from the dead, again after his predecessor had died.

This predecessor, Kate Tarto, had been relieved of her duties, though. She had suggested in the years prior, not constantly, but with enough regularity that it annoyed King Linus, that the people of Benshidi open the borders of Dulon and become part of Winterlon again. This had not been done in the last one hundred and forty years, and she had argued it was well past time.

The king's reaction had been flat rejection at first, but after Kate tried to seduce him into a yes, and he saw through her disgraceful rouse, he had her head taken from her body and the rest fed to the pigs. Vivsky had been much more receptive to Linus' intentions to keep the Benshidi, and Dulon as a whole, isolated.

"I must agree with Mr. Kargor. Our people have no direct affiliation with the Mainmen, or the capital, or anyone else in Winterlon, for that matter. I say that lest the problem come to us, we keep our lines cut. Only then can we pursue a course of action that would lead to bloodshed."

Blaine was one of the younger members of the callen, only thirty-one, and had brown hair. Clean-shaven, and keeping a youthful appearance in his face, he could have passed off for twenty-two years old, or around that age. He stood at five-five, also helping his age seem younger. His voice was of a moderate timbre, not too high, not very low.

The planning was beginning to become obvious to Ed and the others. These two would be the biggest opponents in the notion of helping out the Mainmen. Linus was about to speak again, but Hunter beat him to it.

"A point of order, Your Highness. I wish to speak next."

King Linus' face sank a bit. Almost in that moment everyone knew that his plans had been ruined. "I was going to ask for public opinion next, but since you are so eager, Mr. Poldon, I will allow it."

James saw right through the facial expressions of King Linus, and knew why he was selecting the order in this way. He had already made up his mind about helping the Mainmen, and the answer was going to be 'no'. The public was likely already aiming for a no answer, but now with Hunter and possibly one other speaking before them, their response might waiver.

"Thank you, Your Grace. I speak plainly when I say that the greatest threat before us is not our enemy, but ourselves. I do not suggest anything treasonous in manner, but perhaps if we cannot get past our own insccurities we will cease to exist.

"The Mainmen are, in fact, not hyperbolically, finished. Ten remain, and they are before Your Grace. I agree with the sentiment that our Benshidi warriors were once superior to those of the Mainmen and the others causes of the world, but that was in bygone eras. Now our guards only fight for you, Your Grace, and not the rest of the world. There is, of course, no problem with that, so long as you do not take the rest of the world in account.

"For everyone else, though, I give pity. Our walls can be breached just as easily as the capital's, if not more so. Should Aunten turn his attention north, I'm afraid Your Grace may only be a slight detour in his overall goal of domination. He may, pardon me, sir, seek to have you dead. Though the Deadman being killed is something we would, of course, be all too happy to aid in, if it meant prolonging your life, as well as ours, Your Grace."

It wasn't a bad counterpoint, and even Linus' expression changed from time to time as he began to weigh this option more.

"Was anyone else up here in this capacity?" He called.

The Mainmen put their attention on Ramona, who they knew from earlier in the day felt nearly the same, but she remained silent. For a flash of a second, her eyes changed from forward glancing to looking to Hunter, who almost made the motion for her to step forward.

Instead, Secretary of War Kargor stepped forward. "May I rebut, Your Grace?"

Linus nodded. Kargor cleared his throat.

"Mr. Poldon, I say to you what many others in this callen would: if Aunten does decide to wipe out all possible opponents, what use is it to fight now and be killed sooner? If the day should come when he does decide to turn north and cross the Wise-Mountains, perhaps he would face a more stiff opposition if we took our time to set up our defenses, rather than rush out our offense into a bloodbath."

This brought nods of approval from the others in the callen and a few higher guards. Even Hunter had to turn the other way and be quick on his feet. James and a few others could hear murmurs of agreement behind them from the citizens.

Hunter finally did respond. "How do we know he is not already on his way? Since we have cut off almost all contact with the rest of the world, he and his Deadman, let alone an army, could be coming down the slopes of the Wise-Mountains as we speak. Perhaps if we were to join this conflict, Your Grace, we might split the difference: train some of our citizens in self-defense and have them man the towers, and our hardened warriors awaken from their slumber and prepare for war."

The idea brought protests from the citizens, mostly. A few tried to sound out agreement with Hunter, but it was too much of a cacophony to make anything out.

"Silence!" bellowed Linus. For the first time since his entrance, the entire room fell dead quiet. "May we please have a pair of our lucky citizens step forward? I'd like to hear their ideas."

A woman nearly tackled James and Laura out of the way to get to the front. She bowed to her king, then said, very quickly, "Your Grace, my name is Natalie Baw. I have been lucky enough to speak to Your Grace on multiple occasions, may you remember me?"

King Linus smiled, a loser smile, one that was full of shit. He wouldn't have remembered this woman if he had seen her every day. "Of course, Nathalie. What a pleasure to see you again."

Natalie's face went red and she turned in embarrassment for a moment. "As a part owner in the marketplace, I must protest to the idea of war. War is bad for business. Trading goes higher, and the people stay in bed. Our profits take the dive, and the rest of our economy suffers. I promise you, Your Grace, that the rest of our market owners will protest this war, should it be started, from the first day to the last."

The audience clapped at this, some agreeing more forcefully than others. Linus was satisfied with the answer. "Any others?"

An elder man stepped up now, more respectfully than Natalie did. "Your Grace, I'm of the eldest in the keep, I grew up on stories of the Deadman. I must say that they present a foreboding challenge to our peace. But consider, younger sir, that to gain war we must lose peace. And losing peace will mean losing more than just soldiers. The keep would be a constant target, and the innocent fall so easily."

Linus even stood up and applauded this man's answer, the rest of the citizens doing the same. "May I know your name, good sir?"

The man bowed, saying, "Evan Jennings, Your Grace." He tried to stand back up gracefully, but he struggled, nearly losing his balance. Out of instinct, McQuint and Gwendolyn, who were nearest to him, helped him up. He wordlessly thanked them for their quickness.

"I think," King Linus began, "that your word is final for this conference. I have heard all of the points and counterpoints and everything in between. For you kind people of the Mainmen, you have my respect. Crossing the Wise-Mountains is no easy task, and trespassing on our land was a bold move, but one that may be necessary given your condition. I fault you none, and grant you continued access to our best living conditions for as long as you desire. While I am in thought as to our beneficiary, or lack thereof, I will ask if there is anything further I can do for you."

Before he could stand from his throne to start to leave, Amanda stepped forward. "Your Grace?"

Ed's heart began rapidly beating when he recognized her voice. Everyone else who knew her had a similar reaction.

Linus stopped in his tracks. "May I know your name, ma'am?"

Amanda, being a lady, bowed before him, smart, knowing a curtsey had not been done yet, and to be sure, she did not do one in case that gave her away. "I may ask, Your Grace, that we be able to see your entertainer. You called her Montana?"

Linus chuckled. "That is an odd request. We call her Montana, before us she would not speak another word when she was young. Now she does not speak at all. I'm not sure what company she will keep."

James, thinking on his feet, tried to help. "Your Grace, I may now say aloud what I was afraid to say earlier. I cannot say, Highness, that during that gorgeous display she did not enter my interest. Perhaps she and I can be left alone for the evening."

This brought laughter from the audience, who knew what he meant by this. All of the callen and guards couldn't help but childishly giggle at the idea. Linus himself was all smiles in the affair.

"I guarantee you, young sir, she has not been spoiled up to this moment. For a traveler from so far away, who has come from so far a distance, I would say whatever your heart desires will be the limit for your interaction tonight."

This brought more laughter from the crowd. Deep down the way everyone was going along with this was sickening to James and Amanda especially, but they had to laugh along with them.

Ed walked over to James and shook his hand, as if to congratulate him on his bravery. He leaned in close, and whispered in his ear, "What the hell are you thinking?"

James just winked at him, as if Ed had given him a suggestion for what to do with Montana. He turned back to face Linus, who asked one more question.

"You two, may I know your names?"

Amanda and James both bowed. He spoke first. "James Cameron." The director reference almost made Laura giggle, but she stopped herself.

Amanda's reply was, perhaps following suit with James, "Amanda Snipes."

Linus signaled for them both to stand up. "James, Amanda, welcome to the keep. I will have Montana escorted to your chamber, James, in the next hour. I'll give you that long to prepare."

With a hearty laugh and a continued smile, Linus stood and began to head for the opened stone door. Once he was out and the stone door brought back down to a close, the envoys prepared to lead everyone away.

Once they were out of earshot, Amanda called the other two in and whispered, "I'm gonna get that girl out of here, whether you two help me or not."

15. The King's Decision

Silence was maintained all the way back to the resting chambers for the Mainmen. Obviously, Ed and the others wanted to confer with Amanda and James after their request. Making sure no one was watching, Ed shut the door behind him and sighed before turning to face his comrades.

"This has seriously jeopardized everything we are working toward. What can you get out of a meeting with a dancing girl, for Wiseman's sake?"

Amanda felt like she wanted to slap her superior. "I don't expect you to understand. You never went through slavery. My ancestors did. No one should go through it."

This brought a few seconds of silence from the group. Ed and a few others were ready to come back with a response, but they couldn't think of one right away. All except Talen.

"Your heart is in the right place, but your head is up your ass. These people, regardless of their positions, are the first step in our plans to rid the world of Aunten Schritz. Nothing can stand in the way of that."

Gwendolyn sighed loudly to get everyone's attention. "You saw what everyone else saw, Wadenston. King Linus will not consider our position at all. In all likelihood, he made up his mind before his ass hit the chair. The Benshidi will not come out of isolation for us, not until Aunten strikes the first blow."

McQuint agreed. "In the meantime, I commend your courage, Amanda. But I wish I knew how you plan to help her."

Amanda turned to James, who had the walk from the royal chambers to here to think it over. "I think if we can convince her to tell us where they keep her, we can get her out. Besides, did you see the way he looked at her? The lust?"

Everyone was silent. James continued.

"They look down on us, but he would be sad to lose her. Maybe we can try and get them to come out of retirement by showing we mean business."

Amanda shook her head. "We'd be using her as much as they are. James, she goes free, and that's all. We don't use her as leverage, we don't use her, period."

Talen had walked over to a table while James was speaking, and after Amanda was finished, he slammed his fist down hard enough to crack the wood and the table to split. "Then the result will be us stealing one of their possessions, a prized one. We'll be worse off than we were before we came here."

Amanda disagreed. "You said coming up here and having them join us was the goal, that it helps unite Winterlon. I don't know about the rest of the people on this planet, but I'm gonna guess not all of them are for slavery. Having numbers on our side helps, of course, but if we all have different ideas, hold different beliefs that slow us down, numbers won't get us as far as unity."

He walked up to Amanda, calming down more and more with each step, then put a hand on her shoulder. "You need to hear me. This is how adults work, girl. Sometimes you have to do something that you don't like. We have to overlook a wrong to make things right. Aunten killing more innocents than we can fathom would be wrong. One slave girl saved couldn't possibly equal that."

Amanda, in frustration more than anger, shoved Talen's hand from her shoulder, and walked over to one of the bunk beds, sat down, and didn't say a word.

"Regardless", Jaenen added, "they're bringing her here soon. We have to do something about it."

Ed shook his head. "James," he started, "you can do as you like, just please consider the consequences of stealing her away from here."

"What would you do?" he asked.

Ed's reply was a bit of a shock, but he said his words regretfully. "Do with her…what you told the king you would do. I don't mean you have to lay with her, but keep her company. If there's anything she does know that could help us, keep it in mind."

With this, Laura and James went over to Amanda, who was trying her best to not cry over the whole ordeal. Everyone except Jaenen left them to talk things over, knowing that shielding them from this information before arriving in the keep had been a mistake, and one they may have to pay for dearly. Jaenen felt he had to speak to them.

"I can say something my father can't, I'm sorry. We should have told you how they felt, what kind of people these are."

Laura, turning to a version of reason, responded, "If you had told us, we might not have come at all. In some twisted way, what you guys hid from us probably was for the best."

Amanda nodded. "It was. But now we know, and we can't un-know it. James, Laura, please. We have to do this. If we don't…if we don't teach these guys a lesson, we're dooming anyone else from Earth that they meet. We have to take a stand, even if it hurts."

Jaenen sat down on the floor while the other three took up the bed. "Let me know if you need help. But whatever you do, do it carefully. I agree, King Linus will not openly help us, but I think even if my father and Talen and the others knew that before we came here, there's still something we can gain. Maybe a few of them will join us."

With that, he left the other three to themselves. Amanda turned her attention to her friends.

"We don't have to talk about what I saw earlier, either. That's way less important than helping Montana. Jaenen's right, we have to do this slowly and methodically. James, I have an idea."

* * *

It wasn't more than fifty minutes later that there was a knock at the door of the guest chambers, and James took a big breath before walking up to it. Opening the door, it was what he had expected, one of the envoys from before, the big one with the beard, and Montana, though she was better dressed, or rather dressed period. She now just had on a brown cloak, which in the Benshidi culture was one of the lowest levels. James and the others had seen perhaps one or two other plain brown cloaks.

The man chuckled. "I hope you enjoy your evening. Feel free to share the details." An evil laughed filled the room as he closed the door after shoving the girl inside. From the closed wooden door, the laughter pervaded still, souring the feeling in James' gut.

Not looking at him, Montana sighed softly, waiting for the moment to come where James would take advantage of her. But the moment would not come. Not tonight, and God willing not ever.

"I can't believe this place," James started. "Feel free to keep the cloak on, because I'm not gonna do a damn thing to you."

For the first time, Montana's eye contact was not with the wooden panels of the floor, but with James. At that moment, from the far corners of the room, Amanda and Laura appeared. Amanda rushed in, and hugged the poor girl, and the action was reciprocated. Laura gave an encouraging half-hug from behind, her hands over her shoulders in comfort.

Amanda spoke next. "We're from Earth, too. And we're gonna make sure you get out of this place. You can come with us if you want, or go your own way, whatever you want to do."

This was met by silence from Montana, but they could all see small tears of joy start in her eyes. She obediently wiped them away and sniffled.

"Can you talk?" Laura asked, and made a face afterward like she was asking a rude question.

"Not to them," Montana said slowly, her voice and tone low. The three could tell she tried not to talk to the others she saw all too often, and was uncomfortable with this.

James asked, "So, what's your name and where do you come from?"

Montana shook her head. Still not totally comfortable, her pattern was broken slightly and her voice barely above a whisper. "I don't remember. My dad just told me that was the only word to tell them."

Laura turned to James, saying, "That must be where she's from." Then turning back to the girl, she continued, "Well, Montana's about the loveliest name for a girl I've ever heard." She tried not to be too on the nose, but it was too far.

"Don't talk like that. I'm not a child. They've told me that many times."

Amanda swooped in to save the day. "Pretty soon you won't have to worry about those guys. I'm making a promise, we're not going to leave you behind."

Montana nodded. "Thank you."

James sighed. "So, this is going to be a little tricky. We need you to tell us where you stay, so we can come and get you. It'll have to wait until tomorrow, but we will be there."

Laura then brought in some parchment and a quill that they had found when they were first shown the chamber. "If you want to draw, if that was easier, feel free."

Montana focused on this, and agreed it was best this way. "All right, so if we're here," and she drew on the paper, starting at a point on the far left of the page, and drew several lines jotting first up, then down, down then to the right, then just straight down. Finally, she marked another spot. "This is my cell."

After the confusing directions were read over again by everyone, Laura couldn't help herself. "Shit," she said simply. "They could've made it a lot easier than this."

James studied the lines a few times over. "Do you have to pass through the big oak doors to get there?"

Montana thought for a minute. "There is a way through the back of the market." She turned the parchment over and started again, marking the starting point the same way as before, then drawing a line to the market, then a straight line to the right, one line down, another line to the left, another one up, and one last one to the right, marking her cell one last time.

"This may be easier," Amanda started, "but we have to know something, Montana. We don't mean to say this in a bad way, but we have to ask. Did anyone tell you to talk to them after tonight and tell them what happened?"

Montana stood back for a moment, but her face was not one of betrayal. "You guys are smart. I'm supposed to say what happened to two people."

This thought had come into Amanda's mind early in their conversation. She added, "I had to ask. I just don't wanna chance it that you would turn us over. We don't want to end up next to you tomorrow."

Now the whole thing was becoming more real for her, and the tears of joy began to come back forcefully. "I've been here for twelve years. My dad died trying to protect me. If only he could be here."

The three were quick to embrace their newest friend. Together they sat and talked for the next few hours. Luckily the envoy who had brought Montana to them had other duties tonight, and was not to disturb the couple unless ordered by the king. At this point, the only way this could go wrong was if the trio were caught the next day when attempting the rescue.

* * *

That next morning began, though, in the armory, which was a closed off room. Every one of the Mainmen went to sharpen their blades, or repair their bows if needed. Gwendolyn had only still been armed with the sword, and while she knew at this point she may have been along for the ride, at least for the moment, she forbade Ed or Talen from adding the other weapons to her side.

While looking over the blade he had used all his time in Winterlon, the practice blade that Ed and the others had given him to begin with, he saw that blade truly was an older one, perhaps worn down and remade twice over, lasting a total of twenty years or more. It was down to the end of its line, or so James thought. In the room also were Joven, Amanda, and Gwendolyn.

Soon enough, here came Hunter Poldon to the room. The four of them tried to bow before him, but Hunter stopped them. "Bow to the king, not to me. I'll likely be at my end."

Amanda stared questioningly at him. "For disagreeing with the others last night?"

Hunter turned his attention on her. "That is part of it. I haven't held this post near as long as previous men and women, but I know that the second-in-command is the one who enforces, not disagrees with, the leader."

He reached toward his beltline, and drew out two large swords. Hunter had carried them so well that no one could have guessed he was this armed. He continued.

"I come to this room every day for practice. I know what His Grace does not, that war is coming, whether we are ready or not. I'd like my wits to be as sharp as my blades."

After a few practice slices, James went back to looking at his sword. This caught Hunter's attention.

He walked over to James, saying, "You don't seem too pleased with your weapon there, young sir."

James shook his head. "I'd rather trade it for a new one."

Hunter laughed in good spirits at this. "You may find out how quickly you will disagree with that sentiment. In my experience, using a new weapon means to learn everything all over again. Well, unless you're using a copy of what you had before. See, each blade carries a different handle that you need to grip, a new balance to get adjusted to, a level of sharpness or dullness to prepare your enemies for. It's not unlike riding a new foal for the first time."

James saw Hunter's points. "I still think I'd be a better fighter if I had a better sword."

Hunter shook his head fiercely at this. "Now we fully disagree. To think each warrior is judged by the freshness of his sword is folly. The best warriors don't carry the sharpest blades. They carry the blades that best suit them, no matter what shape they're in. They can take the weakest, oldest weapons in the world and be more lethal with them than anyone else with a fresh blade. Remember, it's not the weapon that makes the man the warrior, it's the man himself."

Amanda cleared her throat, and raised her eyebrows waiting for Hunter to finish his sentence.

"Where are my manners?" he continued. "Or woman…herself."

This brought a smile to Amanda's face.

"May the Wiseman forgive me," Hunter finished, ending his little encouraging words in a humorous way that made everyone easy again.

Joven sighed. "I've always wondered if it's true or not, but the drawings on your side of the Wise-Mountains, they were done by Benshidi?"

Hunter nodded in triumph. "Done thousands of years ago. Every fifty years or so we are charged with freshening them up, or going over the ones too far gone and telling new tales."

Amanda and James were not aware of how religious these people were, but they masked their surprise knowing that especially today they could not lead on at all that they were from Earth.

Hunter smiled. "I'll leave you to it, but James", he said, remembering his name from last night, "if I were you, I'd use my weapon until I couldn't any longer. Forget the upgrades, they'll only slow you down. And if you fall in battle, the bad guys won't take the time you did to notice how nice your weapon looks."

Leaving the room, everyone was surprised at how much of a sense of leadership was dripping off of Hunter Poldon. In another life, or perhaps later on in this one, he would make a fine king for the Benshidi people. He was, in addition, more logical in regard to their foes, and would make a fine ally in battle.

Gwendolyn sighed after he left. "You will hold onto your blade, won't you, James?"

He nodded. "I'll let the people who know what the hell they're doing guide me."

The four went into on-and-off practice for the next hour, getting used to the new sharpness of their blades, or better balance of repaired bows. They just hoped that it would be a long while before they would have to use these weapons in true combat.

* * *

Hundreds of miles away, Aunten Schritz' patience was coming to an end. The mum woman he had come across in the swamps had led him to her abode, and what he thought would be a complimentary meal from a stranger became two days of hell on Winterlon.

He had explained to the woman, as best he could, what he was after: either the resting place or the living body of Halun Leman before heading to her hovel, but she would not communicate with him further until they arrived.

By then it was nightfall, and the woman went to bed. Before doing so, she removed all the cloth from her face, so now her skin was exposed there. From the clues he had seen from their previous contact, Aunten was correct in that she was no spring chicken, perhaps nearing sixty years of age.

Not knowing where to go from there, Aunten found a place to rest as well. Deadman, however, as he learned, do not sleep. They may tire and run out of breath, but they could not fall asleep.

The next morning the woman had made food enough for both of them, barely, with what she had. In the swamps meat was scarce, so Aunten had to settle for dalween weeds. They were fairly succulent for plant-based food, and to Aunten's filed teeth anything tasted good at that point.

The hovel only measured about six feet high, room enough for the woman, so Aunten had to crouch everywhere he went. Across, it only went about thirty feet in total, with a small kitchenette next to her bed, which was separated by a poor excuse for a living room by a curtain made from torn up tall grass.

The clothes the woman wore each day were the same, Aunten could only guess that she bathed them only when necessary. In the living room there were only spots where the woman had dug in, perhaps with a small spade, and filled in the space with straw and flower pedals, anything to make the dirt below stick to your clothes less and be slightly more comfortable.

After breakfast, Aunten had again tried to communicate with the woman that he was not here for a visit, but that she was to lead him where he desired. He dare not threaten too severely or kill her, but his worn patience was beginning to show. The woman just went about her day as if he was no longer there.

He finally scoured the hovel for something to write on and something else to write with. He was able to find very old, worn-down pieces of parchment that had spaces on the back. Looking over the front, he figured that these were documents that showed someone owned the land or the hovel, though this would have been ages ago when the eastern parts of Winterlon were not endless swamps.

The legend went that when creating Winterlon, the Wiseman had started with civilization in the east, but they grew fond of living on their own, not wanting anything to do with their creator. When the rest of Winterlon was established, the Wise-Mountains came into place, cutting off the rest of the world from the eastern parts, save access through the Lanzman forest, which was about to be forbidden by the Wiseman. The effect of the mountains also was to change the climate in the east, which used to be fertile farm ground, but now were virtually laid waste to the swamp terrain and all the terrible new creatures found within, like the Tailas Aunten had encountered the day before.

He also looked around for something to write with, but found no luck. So he had no choice but to use his green, puss-like blood. Deadman, he also discovered, can bleed endlessly, their veins and arteries able to fill themselves back up on their own. So he cut his hand and used it to write the message.

The woman was alarmed by seeing him cut his own hand to communicate with her, and ran from the hovel, staying outside until he found her again. "Take me to Halun Leman" it had said. She had read it over once more, then shook her head. Aunten's fury was just short of killing her, but he stopped himself from doing so.

With all that power, he had made the few green grasses around him erupt into fire, with the woman being protected on the ground she stood on. The sight of Aunten caught in the flames and his flesh and black cloak burning also frightened her, and after he extinguished the flames with a swipe of his hand, and she saw he was the same as he was before, she went back into the hovel and barred the door with everything she could find, including a few wooden boxes and a chest that may have been a dresser at one point, but now stood empty.

Rather than blow the door down and further show off his vain abilities, Aunten patiently stood outside a window and stared at her. Afraid to move, she made no eye contact with her guest, and was petrified with fear the rest of the morning.

Aunten began to wonder if this was some sort of a trick the devil was pulling on him. He wondered out loud, "I curse you, master, to have the only living creation that can lead me be unable to speak."

In this, he found that perhaps that was the point. Anywhere else, with anyone else, he would have gotten what he wanted immediately, with few displays of power and little effort. This woman, however, would require effort and persuasion to be beneficial to his mission.

In that moment, he realized he would have to stoop to her level of communication to gain his next victory. He tapped on the glass panes of her window and waved in a friendly manner, doing his best to smile happily. The woman still did not move. By this point the sun was well past the midpoint of its arc, and in a few hours, twilight would be upon them.

Using a small display, he moved everything away from behind the door, walked up and knocked. Still frightened by everything, the woman refused to move from her spot. Aunten took a shaky breath and opened the door.

He then moved over by the woman and sat down across from her, being as friendly as he could for a tall, dark, ugly creature from the dead. "Ma'am," he started, "I will rid you of my presence once I have gotten what I came for. I only seek the spot, the current location, of Halun Leman. Once I have that, you will never see me again."

The woman finally did make eye contact with him now, though she did not catch what he said due to her hearing impairment. She could read lips, though, so Aunten started again, repeating virtually the same message now that she was paying attention, and speaking a little more slowly so she could catch everything.

After he had done so, she looked around, contemplating what to do. Aunten continued, "I see that your living conditions are less than desirable. If you would care to follow me back to the capital when it is all over, I will see that you live like royalty compared to this depressing existence."

The woman seemingly had no interest in gaining a new life in this manner. So Aunten tried a different tactic.

"Very well, how about money? The capital's bank can supply you with an endowment big enough to start a new life, wherever you desire to go."

This definitely did not interest the woman. She backed away from him, afraid that the next thing, for some reason, would be another burst of furious anger.

"How about you tell me, however you can, what you would like. I will see you get it."

Aunten repeated this again, and the woman's eyes began to light up. A small smile came across her face now, and she got up and went over to the dresser. The opened the top drawer, which was empty, and on the side unattached a small wooden piece. Inside she pulled out a drawing, and then went and sat back down across from Aunten, putting it down on the ground so they both could see it.

Studying the picture for a few moments, Aunten put it all together. The woman, some unknown time before, was not living by herself. In the drawing she had a sister, or wife, or other relative or friend, who was no longer here. The drawing was basic, but Aunten could see the woman was not too much younger than the one that he had met, and he was able to identify her on the picture as well, the woman on the right. Her eyes were easy, young-looking, and matched the woman who was sitting across from him.

"She is dead?" Aunten asked plainly, which was confirmed with a nod from the woman. "And you want me to bring her back?"

This brought a tear to the woman's eye. Yes.

To add insult to injury, one breakthrough in communication had led to another brick wall. The Deadman could do many things, and the list of what they could not do was shorter, but on that list, in addition to not being able to bleed to death or sleep was the ability to raise the dead. He explained it to the woman, whose tears multiplied. She then got up, walked back over to the dresser, replaced the drawing where she had found it, and walked outside, closing the door behind her.

Aunten wanted to tear the place apart. He was not totally uncapable of feeling. He and the other Deadman no longer had tear ducts, so he could not weep with the woman. The devil had once again trapped him in a scenario where he would need to outsmart the prince of darkness, beat him at his own game.

He let the woman be to herself for a few hours, and then she came inside and prepared supper for the both of them. It was the same as before, the dalween weeds still filling up both of them. The woman went to bed, but beforehand Aunten had tried speaking with her again after supper was concluded.

"You must understand how important it is that I find him, or where he rests. If I do not, my master will bring nothing but sorrow upon me. I fear what he will do to you may be even worse."

This tactic was absolutely ineffective. The woman's eyes became large, and she refused to look at him the rest of the evening. Aunten had to re-think his next move. Force had not worked. Threats had not worked. Asking the woman for anything else would not work. She knew her price, and would not exchange it for anything else.

Overnight, Aunten began to play out different scenarios in his head. The one he spent the most time considering was to empty the house of food, starve the woman until she agreed to help him. But he knew this would only satisfy her. Then the next breakthrough came. He knew an exchange that she might agree to.

When she awoke the next morning, Aunten had already prepared the morning meal for both of them. Then he went in for the kill. "I apologize that I cannot provide you with what you wanted. But maybe I can give you the next best thing."

Then he did something that may have made all the difference in the world. He held the information she desired, just as she had held his. After a few minutes of silence and no eye contact from Aunten, she knocked on the table, knowing he would hear her. He held out a little while longer. She grew impatient, and walked outside, shutting the door harshly behind her.

Aunten's wicked smile showed he was successful in his path. He crept over to the door and opened it, the woman facing away from him. His bony finger, figuratively the finger of death, tapped her shoulder until she turned to face him.

"Take me where I need to be, and I will reunite you with your beloved. In death."

* * *

James finally had a chance to walk the keep with Laura by his side. They had both noticed certain stops when they first arrived, but now they had a little more free rein to explore where they wanted. One of those was a bakery, where they both tried different pastries. James went with one that appeared to be baked dough covered in chocolate, though they said it was lema, and it tasted very similar to chocolate, though a little richer in taste. Laura had sliced blund with cinnamon sprinkled in. It was topped with whipped cream.

Along the way they had small talk about the journey and what was going to happen next. The time was just after noon, and they had just under eight hours to go before the rescue of Montana, or Tana, as the group came to call her.

Her story was a very sad one. She had been brought to Winterlon when she was five by her father, who wound up lost in the far north, where few civilizations can spring. He journeyed south, hoping he could find something hopeful and dream worthy, but instead he had been found by some Benshidi scouts.

The father had been suspected of being a spy, and was killed. Before his death, though, his little blonde daughter, who had turned six just a couple of days before they were captured, had been told not to utter her name, but instead just to say where she was from. Only that.

And that was how she had the name. She and her father had come from Montana. She, nor any of her new friends, could guess why her father didn't wish for them to use her name. James figured that somehow her father knew what would be in store for her, and that if she was to be addressed by her name, she would despair.

She had also told them she had not spoken a word for three years after being captured, except the word Montana. It was only after more girls from Earth were found by the Benshidi that she spoke again. Often it was them who acted as a buffer between her and whoever she would need to speak to.

In any case, as long as they could get her out, there was no doubt her best days would be ahead of her, and her past could be forgotten. Well, not completely forgotten, but James wrestled with whether or not he was glad he personally had not experienced anything like it.

After lunch, Laura found a table and had James sit down. It had taken a while, but she had news about the books that she had taken from Gwendolyn.

James was excited to hear. "Did you learn anything?"

Laura shook her head. "She was telling the truth; the books had nothing in them. Just maps and stories."

"What stories?"

"Ones from after the end of the Deadman rule. Stories about Mainmen coming around to different countries and trying to kill bad guys. None of them were that special."

James sighed. "If only we could go to their library. Do you know where it is?

Laura shook her head. "No. But James, after tonight, we're not going to have another chance."

"Then we can't waste another minute. Let's go find it."

Laura's eyebrows went up as she thought of something. "What about Montana?"

James didn't get it. "What about her?"

"Well, if we go around wandering now, and they don't let us into the library, they're gonna remember. If they see us tonight, they'll be suspicious."

"But we might never get to come back here again."

"She's not going to have another opportunity to get out, maybe ever. And if we have to make a choice, and Amanda hears about it, she's gonna flip if we decide without her. And you know what she would choose."

"Laura, it might be up to us to save this world. The other guys haven't been very helpful about asking for information. They'll fight for it, they'll break bread, or blund, whatever, with these people, but they

228

won't do anything to help figure out how to kill a Deadman. Between the world surviving and one slave girl…"

For half a moment, Laura's eyes were furious, and it prevented James from finishing his thought. But her eyes relaxed after a few seconds of looking into James'.

James leaned in, reached for Laura's hands, which were on the table, and he began to stroke them in comfort, thinking this over. "What if we can do both? Let's talk to Amanda. I've got an idea."

Before they could get very far, Gwendolyn stumbled upon them. There was some bustle around the keep. "The king's made a decision."

Joining her, they fought their way through the crowd until they found Talen, who stood tallest amongst everyone in the keep. Sure enough, the older envoy, breathless, got to the head of the pack and waited until all the ten of them were there. The rest of the callen and trusted guard would be ready for them when they got back to the royal chambers.

Repeating the same song and dance, though this time without being shocked by the blackout, they soon were before the empty throne again. Since there was no audience otherwise, Montana was not dragged out for entertainment. Instead, once everyone was in, the stone door was opened again, and the callen and guards arrived.

Hunter again called for everyone to bow as the king arrived, and his entrance was quicker and less official than normal.

"Rise," the king said once ready to sit, as before. He sighed then leaned in close to speak to his guests. "After careful consideration, I have decided that for the good of the Benshidi, isolation and peace will continue to be our path. I am truly sorry for your journey to have been spent with this result, but I will grant you three days more of relaxation and comfort. Unfortunately, outsiders such as yourselves, as pleasant and accepting of our culture as you are, cannot be permitted to stay forever.

"Once again, I thank you for your time and wish you nothing but pleasant trails. Should Aunten find our peaceful keep and bring hell and fire down upon it, and word reaches you that we survive, we will of course revisit your offer and consider further at such time."

These last words were more formalities than anything else, but something about the way Linus spoke rubbed everyone the wrong way. He was much more deliberate in his speech, quick to dismiss them. He had untrusting eyes now resting in his skull, and when they found James, they were quick to move away.

Sometime before this second audience, Ed had been informed that if the king had accepted their offer and the Benshidi had joined them, they would have had to kiss the king's hand. Since there was no agreement, the envoys just had to escort the group out.

"Excuse me", King Linus said just before the envoys began motioning for them to start in the other direction. "One last word with you, Mr. Cameron. I had heard word last night that you had had some trouble. I ask, what happened?"

James and the others had anticipated this might be a problem. They figured that such a peculiar interest had been taken in Montana that there was a chance someone would check her to see if she still remained a virgin. Sure enough, they had. This had been more anticipated after she had informed them that she had been spoken to by two parties who wanted her to spy on them. Luckily, they would all have the same story, or at least they had hoped Montana would be true to her word.

James, chuckling to himself, replied, "Not my best hour, I'm afraid, Your Highness. Even though the trail was long and the road weary, I was unable to perform. I blame myself more than anyone, though. I usually set myself up for failure when I make my sex life public."

On that note, the final exchange had been a funny one between the two companies, confirmed by a roar of laughter from the king. This brought a sigh of relief to the trio. This was the story that Tana was to tell if anyone asked. She had to tell this story thirteen times during the morning and early afternoon hours.

Once the ten guests were out of earshot, Linus called in Ramona. She bowed before him, then he said, "Have her cell guarded tonight. In case that bumbling fool comes back and wants to try again."

Ramona nodded and left without a word. King Linus, being a man of peace, did not, however, hold peace in a universal trait. He did not trust very many people, and he had been known to execute or dismiss members of his callen, sometimes without much provocation or warning. While he was not aware of the plan that had formed between the four young adults, he had a proclivity for sensing when danger was coming. He did have that sense now, but it was not necessarily around his slave girl.

16. The Rescue

Despite the momentum that was growing to save Montana, James couldn't help but feel he was fighting against a tide that would drown him. The Benshidi were some of the strongest warriors on record, and even if all three of them were to rescue Montana together, all of them could fall to their enemies' blades.

On top of that, there was public opinion that also fueled their rescue, but could also be an even more painful punishment. If the guards kept them alive, the merciless nature of the Benshidi and how they felt about people from Earth would guarantee their freedom being lost. Ed and the others would have no choice but to abandon them, lest the whole Mainmen cause be extinguished.

James felt it best in this moment to be alone. He told Amanda and Laura that he needed a few minutes to himself, and that he would come back and find them later. He walked through the keep to the drawbridge, and asked for it to be lowered so he could go outside. They had discovered earlier that this was the only way in or out of the keep, at least around the main hall.

James took about a half an hour to walk around the outside of the keep. While he knew what had to happen that night, there were so many things that could go wrong. While doing a second lap around the keep, James turned a corner and found himself back in the company of the Wiseman. As had happened before, James was furious at first.

"You could have told me that we were walking into a trap, Wise Guy," which had become his insult name of the Wiseman. "You didn't think we needed to know before coming here that the three of us would be in more danger?"

The Wiseman smiled, as always, at James. "My dear boy, you cannot say that the knowledge of how the Benshidi feel about you wouldn't have helped more than it hurt. If I had told you, you would have tried to convince the others to turn away, break off from your allies. You could easily have been left to the elements of the north, and death would have taken you.

"Remember, James, even in the darkest regimes in history, there are always those who have their senses. Not every last Benshidi civilian hates you, or Amanda, or Laura. Or even Montana. You'd be surprised how many times peer pressure has built empires."

James thought about this for a while before responding. "Good Germans." He thought for a minute, hoping the Wiseman knew what he meant, but felt the need to ask, "You were around for World War II, weren't you?"

The Wiseman nodded. "Yes. Seeing what they did also helped me in the idea of creating a new world. It's what many thought about doing so soon after V-E Day."

James asked next, "Can you tell me more about how you were able to create Winterlon? I mean, everybody always likes to imagine things. Seeing people, loved ones who have died, new and weird creatures. But you actually, like, created it. You made it real. How did you do it?"

The Wiseman beamed at him as his memory began to fill. "I cannot explain everything, James. We all have our hidden talents. Those things that we don't acknowledge but know are there. You have some talents that you kept hidden away for so long, like having the talents of a leader. Showing your skills and having others begin to trust you. I say again, James, Ed wouldn't have entrusted the Mainmen sword to you if he didn't see it himself. And you rescued his son. What more could you display to him to show your talents?"

James smiled at the compliments, but kept on it. "Did you know anyone else who could create whole worlds?"

The Wiseman shook his head. "I might tell you in time, James, but for now I must leave you with this: in times of crisis, when everything could fall apart, that is when people show you who they really are. Any hatred they harbor is unleashed, and all kindness kept inside overflows. Do not underestimate that. Farewell, James."

And as he had done before, the Wiseman faded away, leaving James alone. Maybe he was right, and it would all work out. He had no way of knowing who among the Benshidi might be open to their plan, or able to help them. He hated to leave that to chance, but it might be the only option left to them.

* * *

The next move was to be a meeting between the three youngsters. James went back into the keep after his meeting with the Wiseman, and he tracked down the two girls. Once back outside and out of earshot of anyone with prying ears, James made it clear: two things had to happen that night. The library of the Benshidi had to be located and searched for historical help, and Montana had to be freed. The questions would come down to who would do what and how.

"Okay," Amanda started, "what do you do about the library?"

James shook his head. "Gotta find out where it is. The only way to do that may be to get it out of a Benshidi."

Amanda agreed. "I guess you're gonna ask me the big question next, right?"

Laura's eyebrows furrowed at the ask. "Big question?"

"Can I do it alone?"

A moment of silence hit all three of them as the gravity of it hit them. If Amanda failed, she'd be accused and found guilty, rather quickly, they surmised, of being from Earth, or at least of having sympathy toward people of Earth. But which crime was worse?

Amanda sighed. "You don't have to say anything, of course I can. My ancestors, generations ago, helped free others from chains. I'm gonna do the same. You heard what that guy Hunter said, there's too many books for one person to go through quickly. Just wait for me. When this is all done, we're gonna have to take off fast."

Laura smiled, then added, "Thank God for Ed."

"No," James added, "thank the Wiseman."

Perhaps the stage of finding out who was doing what was as good a place as any to be interrupted. Luckily, the interruption came from a joyous sound. From the south came a thunder, and with it a few whinnies. The horses had come home.

Hearing this, a few Benshidi citizens gathered at the open gate, and were proud to see the guests that were outdoors greeting their steeds. Soon they

235

parted as Talen, Jaenen, and the others who had mounts came to greet their horses.

James was especially happy when Rohan's dark brown hide returned, his white socks sticking out from others in the pack. His snort at finding James and rubbing his nose against James' shoulder was a welcome sign as well. For the first time in a long time, an emotion so happy that it caused tears came over James Realms.

Amanda's tan horse had also found her, and was playfully nibbling at her tunic. James' tears surprised her, but she couldn't help but laugh over it. "Reunited," she said.

James opened his mouth, ready to sing, 'and it feels so good', but stopped himself knowing that no one of the Benshidi race would know what it was, and being different here was frowned upon. He instead whispered the rest of the chorus to her, which made her laugh.

Making sure they wouldn't be heard, Amanda asked him, "So how do you get to the library?"

James' answer, after a sniffle, was, "The most innocent way I can. I ask."

* * *

The basic plan of Montana's rescue went as such: Amanda would need to knock out any guards that stood in the way and get out with Montana before anyone noticed. With the horses back, it wasn't tough to convince Ed and the others to escape by horseback as soon as the deed was done.

For James and Laura, the trouble was getting permission to enter, then enough time to explore the library. With the king's reaction to their plea, the Benshidi were indifferent toward their guests now, which was a disadvantage.

Obviously, the bigger problem was that the Benshidi were advanced in their combat abilities, despite the pacifistic way they'd held for nearly two decades now. Being tough wasn't going to be enough for Amanda; she'd need adrenaline to carry through the deed. But with the circumstances being what they were, that wouldn't be too hard a task.

The night Montana had visited them, and the plans were laid out, they had all decided the second path would be better. From the back of the market, Amanda would take a right after getting through the doors, take another right, a left, another right, and one more right to reach Tana's cell.

To help her out, James decided that he and Laura would start with a distraction in the marketplace, where prying eyes would keep away from the back doors where Amanda would slip in. After the whole situation was cleared up, the other two would make for the library.

Getting to Montana's cell would then be the easiest part, unless Amanda was seen before reaching it. She had a few excuses in mind in case she did, but regardless it would chance the mission being compromised early.

Then there was the question of getting Montana out. Clearly the path taken originally, if reversed, risked running into guards who might not have been there before, or the guards who were in the way possibly being back on the defensive if they had to be knocked out. If the two made it back to the market, there was a good chance they could slip by unseen, though James and Laura would probably not be finished in the library.

However, the biggest risk of all would be that the civilians all knew Montana. If she were spotted at any point by a passerby, the whole operation would be blown. Even the cloak she wore when taken to James the first night would be easy to spot.

The solution was a risky one, and hopefully one that would not need to be questioned: Amanda would take her Mainmen armor and clothing with her. She still had everything in her pack, so she'd just need Montana to wear it while Amanda switched into the cloak, hiding her brown skin from everyone, which of course would be another giveaway.

Laura had timed everything to begin at 5:00 PM, which should have been when the market was in peak. It risked there being more people to spot the whole thing, but when else would a spill be less common?

From the time the final plans were laid down to 5:00, the three had only two hours to try and find the guards that kept the public from the library. They thought about trying to recruit the other Mainmen to help, but none of them were to be found.

Laura saw that above the two big oak doors and to the left was a balcony, so there was a second level to the keep. She looked all around but there were no stairs that led to the second level. She guessed they were only on the opposite side of the oak doors, and at the moment the two guards were intimidating, and didn't let her in.

They met up at 4:45 to have time to get ready for the marketplace shenanigans. All three of them had come up empty, but Laura surmised that the library had to be behind the oak doors, and very easily could have been on the second level. Maybe after Amanda went through the back door of the marketplace, James and Laura could sneak in after her and find another way, or better yet try and find Hunter, who may be sympathetic to their cause.

James and Laura kept their clothes from the journey on. Luckily they had had a chance to launder them after the first day, so they no longer stank of sweat and blood. The doors furthest back of the market were fairly sized, though not as strong and orderly as the two that led to the back chambers.

In front of the doors were two barrels of onions. Amanda went back and picked at a few of them for about thirty seconds, hoping the older man to her right would stop looking at the carrots. Unfortunately, he had been in this spot for about two minutes already, and was taking his damn time.

Laura spotted this immediately, and had to improvise. "Excuse me, sir?"

The old man, wearing grey clothes from head to foot, his bald head exposed, didn't turn very quickly, and had a questioning look on his face. He hardly heard her.

"I was hoping maybe you could help me. I'm looking for blund, not fresh blund, but ones that were made earlier in the week. I'm going to have it with my friends tonight, and we expect to eat it all, so we wanted to have everyone else get a chance at the fresher loaves."

As she was talking, she put a hand on his back and led him toward another part of the market. James was now left to his own devices for the distraction, and the window was a small one, for a middle-aged couple were headed for the back rows of the market.

The only option James had in front of him was a barrel of fruits. Glancing inside quickly he saw mostly miniature oranges sitting on top of apples that were mostly baseball size, though he saw a couple that were closer to the size of a cymbal.

Making sure Amanda's path was still clear, he reached into the barrel far enough to knock it over, his head sticking in it as fruit started to rush past him. The cymbal-sized apple hit him right in the noggin, and actually did feel heavy enough to leave a bruise.

Sure enough, about ten people started to rush over toward him, and soon he was grabbed abruptly and harshly by a big man, about six-eight, who weighed somewhere in the neighborhood of four hundred pounds. His head was bald, but he had a thick mustache, and some hair on his chin. James had recognized him the day they arrived at the keep, and he had been here in the marketplace.

"You messin' up my place, you little shit!" he yelled. "Pick everything up and get out of here, fore we have folks slippin and fallin' all over."

His British accent was unmistakable, but wasn't unique to Winterlon. As James was busy picking up the fruit and replacing it in the barrel, he heard a sigh from the owner.

"Now what?" His heavy footsteps headed the other way grabbed James' attention.

Sure enough, he had noticed the doors that led to the back chambers partially open. The man looked around, opened one of them and peeked inside.

James froze, unsure if disaster was about to strike. If Amanda was hiding near the door…

A slam got James back to his senses, and he shook his head and continued to pick up after himself. The heavy man waddled back from the door, and crossed his arms. He looked around, and spotted someone to the left of the entrance to the marketplace. After a few moments, he started waddling that way.

Laura had caught most of this, and now free of the older man who looked at carrots, saw who the owner of the marketplace was going to talk to: Ramona.

* * *

Inside, Amanda had gotten away without being seen. She breathed a sigh of relief and looked to her right, knowing this would be the path. The passageway, she could see, led to a dead end, but it was perhaps one hundred feet away. She took a few quick steps to see how the sound went. It reverberated, enough to cause an echo down the passageway; her steps would have to be a bit more nimble.

All the adrenaline rushing inside her, Amanda felt like it would be days before she reached the end of the passageway and made the only left turn. From there directorially it would be easy to reach Montana's cell, but doing so with little resistance was nearly impossible.

Time went by so slowly, and her steps seemed to make smaller and smaller progress as they went. The torches also, to her eye, seemed to dim more and more the closer she got. In reality, they burned brighter and brighter the closer she got to them, but the anxiety of the moment made it feel the opposite.

Sure enough, she made it to the end of the passageway, and stopped, peeking around the corner to see who else was there. To her astonishment, no one. She breathed another big sigh of relief after turning the corner, loud enough for it to echo around her. A torch burned bright on this side of the wall, though she didn't immediately notice. After a couple of pants, a new noise reached her ears: a door closing.

She'd been made! Amanda slunk against the wall quickly and held her breathing down to a minimum. But she soon realized the closing door was not from her left side, up the passageway, but from her right, back the way she had come.

Then the footsteps began to echo down the passageway, inching closer and closer. Their strides were bigger, the distance closing second by second. The idea hit her, and she knew she had to time it just right. She silently stepped toward the upper passageway until she had about four or five paces to take before she was at the end. She was going to head back the way she came and turn the corner at the same time as her foes.

She made sure her weapon was secured, not too open for the others to see, but within grasp in case she needed it. Then she took the necessary steps to round the corner.

However, when she did so, the footsteps were still far away. There was a good ten feet between the two guards and Amanda. She was unable to hide her surprise.

"Excuse me, maybe you can help. I'm a little lost," Amanda started.

The guards, both of whom were unfamiliar to her, looked at her with disgust. "You aren't to step foot back here alone," one said.

Amanda looked down at the ground. "I'm sorry, I got separated from my group. Ed Hotean, maybe you know him?"

The guards looked to each other, not recognizing the name. "You will leave with us at once," the other said. The one who spoke first was about three inches taller than the other. Both were male, and both had dark skin, a darker shade than Amanda's.

She decided to give the appearance of giving up, and took a couple of steps forward. The guards turned, knowing she would follow. That's when the anger boiled over.

The adrenaline having never left her body, Amanda braved enough of it to unsheathe her sword and hit the taller guard over the head with it, not penetrating into his skull, as she may have liked to have done, but instead the blunt force of it knocked him down.

The other guard, the shorter one, noticed the fall of his comrade, and unsheathed his sword. The blades clanged as they fought, briefly, but Amanda soon found herself outmatched. His movements were quicker and more dangerous than hers, and her parries couldn't counter the full impact. Soon enough his strength overpowered hers, and he was able to knock the sword out of her hands. It's clatter on the stones below reverberated louder than anything else thus far.

In a panic of fight or flight, flight won, and Amanda took off, turning the corner before the guard recognized what she was doing. Remembering the torch on the other side, using the last of her strength, she quickly grabbed toward the bottom, which was hot, and waited for her foe to turn the corner himself.

Once he had done so, the first thing he felt was a cool blaze that intensified immediately. She couldn't have planned it better; the guard had walked directly into the outstretched flame, his face caught immediately. She hadn't noticed before, but the man did have facial hair, which was now in danger of being consumed by flame.

His voice, which was deeper when he spoke before, now came out in small yelps. Afraid she would have to deal with more guards, she shushed him, and reached into her pack for a dagger.

Once the man had recovered enough, a huge burn mark on his cheek and part of his facial hair gone, he noticed the blade at his throat.

Amanda summoned the words, though deep inside she feared her life would end this night, at the hands of the man she held now, or at the hands of other men and women who would stand in her way. "Take me to her cell. Maybe I'll let you live."

No other choices before him, tears began to go down the man's cheeks, a couple of them searing into his burn mark, causing more pain. Amanda also noticed the strong scent of urine as the man voided his bladder in fear. Hours later, she still wasn't able to say where, but Amanda produced a laugh of satisfaction that sent chills down even her own spine.

The acknowledgement that this guard's life was in her hands now, and someone part of something so evil and disgusting being reduced to this was justifying. He led the way as she stayed close behind, the dagger ready to go into his spine if he dared try anything. No more words were needed to verify she would do so.

* * *

Before she could reach the doors to the back passageways, James got Ramona's attention.

"Excuse me," he started. "I was hoping I would run into you. My friend and I wanted to see your library."

Ramona gave a look of dissatisfaction to him, then she looked around the marketplace. "Which friend would that be?"

Sure enough, here came Laura, as if on cue. James grabbed her shoulder and pulled her close to him so they were now side by side.

"And may I ask," Ramona continued, "why you choose now to seek out the Benshidi knowledge?"

James cleared his throat. "I think we may be pressing off tomorrow."

"I wouldn't count on that," said a familiar voice. Sure enough, here was Al, one of the three scouts who had taken the Mainmen to the keep. "Mr. Realms, nice to see you again."

Ramona's eyes went wide for a moment, but she controlled herself. She had been present when James had named himself James Cameron. Al, Melbun and Rickard had all gone back to their duties as scouts after the Mainmen were inside the keep and in the hands of Ramona. Now they had come back, not knowing what had transpired.

In this moment, giving away this knowledge would have been a crucial error. Clearly these two were up to something, but she didn't know yet what it was. Now she had a chance to find out.

"Aljen," she greeted him, drawing attention back to herself. "I suppose you could be good enough to grant our friends a trip to the second floor. They wanted to see our library."

Not being the fool, Al knew there was a mischievous quality in Ramona's nature, and she would not be taken for a fool either. Despite not being present for the past few days, Al let on that everything was still calm.

He nodded toward her, saying afterwards, "It would be a pleasure. You two, follow me."

The whole exchange brought nothing but tension to Laura and James. The questions were many: where was Ramona having Al lead them? A trap, death, something worse? How was Amanda getting along in the back passageways? Before either Laura or James could begin to piece together dreams of fear and destruction, they had reached the big oak doors, and the two guards before them departed and Al and his two guests were through them.

* * *

As badly as things might have been going for James and Laura, the situation looked downright dire for Amanda. Not only was the plan already off on its timing, now she had a passenger with her, one she had to hold at bay with a dagger. He led the way, each small step seeming to take longer than the last to complete the motion of walking down the passageways.

After the second turn, where they would be going down a new passageway, then at the end taking a right, supposedly able to see the cell at that point, Amanda's patience began to wear even thinner. She moved the blade from the man's back up closer to his Adam's apple, and put a slight amount of pressure on it when it touched. "Any slower and I kill you where you stand," she said with menace.

The guard's reaction was to keep moving at about the same pace. Deep down, Amanda knew what had to happen. She had the jump on the guard earlier, but each step gave him more time to think, and more time for an opportunity to arise. All together they had spent about seven minutes to walk the length of three passageways, a small task that could have been accomplished in a minute or less.

Now they were up to the final turn, and more torches were lit at the end of the passageway, which truly was a dead end. Amanda's breaths began to get louder and louder as she felt more hopeful. So far, the girl had kept to her word. So far.

Amanda's trust was compromised, though, when she saw three guards standing right outside the cell, all of them now curious as to the sight of their comrade leading the way with a blade at his throat.

"Tourdain, what is going on?" one of the guards asked.

Wordless, Amanda and her guard continued to walk up the passageway. The timing would have to be perfect. The three new guards outside of Montana's cell would not hesitate to kill her if they got the chance. She needed to make sure they didn't.

She figured a distance of about ten feet was enough. The guards only had swords, and the distance would be about right for her to get ready to defend herself if need be. At this point, Amanda figured there were only about four or five more paces the guard she held could take before he would join his buddies.

Counting down, Amanda began to feel the adrenaline rush again, knowing it was the only fuel she could use to accomplish her goal. But then one of them stepped forward.

"Wait!" he yelled. "What do you want?"

Not expecting this, the guard and Amanda stopped at the same time. It took her a few seconds to process this. Eventually she responded, "I'll trade him for the girl."

The three guards looked back at the cell they were guarding, Montana standing up to the bars, her hands on the outside, gripping them tight.

The one who had yelled at Amanda turned back around to face her and the guard she held at bay. "Tourdain, everything is going to be all right."

This guard stepped forward now, the other two standing back by the cell still, not knowing what to do.

"Get rid of your weapons," Amanda commanded.

Still approaching her, the guard went at his hip and loosened his belt, his holstered sword falling to the ground.

Amanda looked to the cell and motioned for the other two guards to do the same. They did not move.

The guard who was walking up to her turned his head to the right, so the sound was more generally directed at his compatriots. "Do as she says, gentlemen."

Looking at each other first, the two other guards then did the same.

At this point, Amanda was still holding the dagger to Tourdain's throat, but it now was not nicking his skin.

"Now what?" asked the guard who had dropped his weapons first.

"Who has the keys?" Amanda asked.

The guard turned back to one of the others.

Amanda nodded, indicating to unlock the cell and release Montana.

"Mel," the guard directly in front of Amanda commanded, "do as she says. The quicker you do it, the sooner we're done here."

Not hesitating any further, Mel reached for the keys, which were on one of the belt loops on the floor, and went for the one to the cell.

"Can you release Tourdain now?"

Amanda shook her head. "I get her first, we get to the end of the passageway, then I let him go. I'm not gonna let you pull any tricks, asshole."

The vernacular of the girl now gave away what was really going on. The guard understood. "So you *are* from Earth. The boys and I will be rich, indeed."

Amanda looked puzzled. She took notice too that the cell was opened, and Montana was walking toward them. "What do you mean?" she asked the guard.

"Bets were placed on whether or not you and the boy were from Earth. And now we know."

Montana rushed up to Amanda and hugged her tightly, a couple of tears rushing down her face and falling to the ground.

Amanda, though, was still trying to hold the guard, but Montana made that difficult.

"Why don't you let him go?" the guard asked. "I won't cause any more trouble this night."

She wasn't falling for it. "He's not going anywhere until we've cleared this passageway. Otherwise Montana and I will turn around and you'll shoot us in the back."

The guard shook his head. "I'm not like them. I have no prejudice for Earth folk. The girl has suffered enough at our hands."

Amanda still shook her head. "Prove it. Prove you aren't going to kill us."

The guard thought for a moment, then centered his attention on Tourdain. "You can kill him if you want to. None of us are armed. There's nothing we can do to defend him."

A worried look came over Tourdain, uncertainty in his eyes. This guard was going to let him die, and it seemed nothing could change that.

Amanda had not expected this to be the allowance the guard would give up. She figured he was going to try and relieve his fellow guards and dismiss them, something to grab more attention. But to kill one of their comrades and still do nothing? She sensed a trap.

"You wouldn't let him die," Amanda said finally, shaking her head. "You're bluffing."

The guard stood as still as a statue for several moments. "His death would leave one less Earth-hating bastard inside this keep. One less for you to fight to get her to safety. One less arrow to dodge, one less sword to strike against. You're not going to find too many other guards who will offer that."

The adrenaline was still inside her, but with each moment it dissipated more and more. She knew now she would not be able to kill Tourdain. She even felt a lump in her throat and her eyes began to well up. And then, almost against her own will, the dagger she held in her hand quickly fell, and landed by her side.

Tourdain was free. He slumped to the floor in defeat and in exhaustion.

Amanda turned and grabbed Montana's hand, and the two began to run down the passageway they had come and headed back to the entrance of the market.

Mel and the other guard back by the cell began to make their way up to the guard who had negotiated with Amanda. "Hawkins, what the hell did you do that for?"

A smile came over Hawkins' face. "I just saved two lives tonight."

Nothing more was said in the matter. The three guards weren't sure what they would tell the king, but they knew it could not be the truth. His Highness would not forgive them for allowing so easy an escape for his favorite prize.

***

The end of the line. Laura and James had not seen anything that indicated they could reach the second level of the keep, but sure enough behind one of the doors in the long passageway was a staircase, winding up and very, very old. The stone was falling away on some of the steps, as if no one had gone up them in years.

Al led them up, then stopped as they reached the top. Two big doors, one on the left and right side, were there, each door large and oak, the boards also very, very old, beginning to rot. The one on the left you could even see a bit of light coming out from the missing board.

Letting the mood settle in, Al finally acknowledged the two, and pointed toward the door on the left. James gulped and reached for the handle, afraid that there would be an executioner or something worse behind it. Laura walked up behind and put a hand on his shoulder in comfort, but her hand was firm, as if ready to pull him back if necessary.

On the other side was just an empty room, a stone slab for a bed, a window that looked out over the keep, and a lit candle, the wick down nearly to the bottom. James was slightly dumbfounded.

"For your own safety," Al started from the top of the stair, "stay here. We'll let you know when it's safe."

Laura turned and asked, "What the hell is going on?"

Al said nothing more. Instead, he reached down at his side, pulling a key out of his pocket.

James had to ask, "They let a scout keep a key to *this* room?"

No response. Al shooed them in, shut the door, and locked them inside. Clearing his throat, he added from the other side of the door, "And don't bother screaming. You're alone up here."

They both feared the worst. Ed and the others would leave without them. If Amanda failed, she'd also be left for dead. Or maybe Al would come back and butcher them. The next fifteen minutes were about to be the longest of James and Laura's lives up to that point.

17. A Night of Death

Linus' night was next greeted by a knock at the door of his private quarters. Very few people had access to him in the room, all of them trusted enough to the point where they could treat him a little more informally, which was not a bother to Linus, who was always dressed down in the room.

Behind the door was Hunter, who would only come this early during a time of crisis. He usually would visit the king at midnight for private conferences, so Linus found it a little odd that he was here right before supper at 6 PM.

"Poldon. Do what do I owe this visit?"

Hunter let out a sigh before beginning. "We have a problem."

Linus only chuckled at this. "I count more than one."

"She's gone. Your slave girl."

Linus clapped his hands. During the whole visit, he was seated in front of a mirror, preparing himself for dinner, applying some light makeup to his face, a creamy color to match his skin. He also wanted to try on a few different tunics, each slightly different, some fitting more closely around the waist, others around the shoulders, and so on.

"I knew it," he added. "I knew we couldn't trust them. You were right in your assessment."

Hunter nodded. "I know Earth people when I see them."

Linus sighed. "So, what punishment do you see fit? Hanging? Torture chamber? Imprisonment for life? Enslavement?"

Hunter shook his head. "The people should decide that."

Linus agreed. "I hardly have the stomach for it anymore. If we punished every last Earth loving citizen we saw, I'd gather we'd have a third of our people in cells."

"But not her," Hunter continued.

Another sigh from Linus, one filled with lust. "The fact that that girl cannot be touched by mine own hand is proof that the Wiseman is laughing at me. Damn tradition."

"You'll never let her go?" Hunter asked.

"We've had this discussion before, Hunter. You know better than I the answer."

"So punishment will be instore for the culprits. Very well."

Linus finished with his makeup and changed the subject. "As for the reason for the Mainmen's visit, what do we plan to do about the Deadman?"

Hunter stepped forward for the first time since he stepped into the quarters. "You know my stance."

"Yes. And it's my stance as well."

"Then why don't you call the men to arms and get them ready?"

Linus was quick to respond. "You have never had to wear the crown, Poldon. Panic sets on the keep, and the soldiers will spend more time defending themselves than attacking the enemy."

"Tell the people your stance," Hunter pleaded. "Prepare them. We can win."

"When we tell the people we're pacifists, we need to live up to it. The people will always love a peaceful king before they love a warmonger."

Hunter took another step. "But the people will die if the Deadman come for us."

Linus had a small laugh as he switched tunics. The one that was tighter on his chest was not catching his fancy this night. "Until they face death, they know nothing of it. And I'm not prepared to be—"

Linus was also unsatisfied with the current tunic. He lifted it over his head, cutting off his vision for a moment. While his chest was exposed, suddenly he felt a chill, and looked down to see a red spot in his chest. It wasn't until after he saw it that his breath began to tremble.

Hunter took another step forward to twist the dagger further into his king's chest. "I know where you kept this," Hunter added.

For years, King Linus had forbidden anyone to be armed in his presence when a guard was not on duty. His only defense was a hidden dagger, one that Hunter had taken time to find.

After removing the dagger, Linus gasped, his eyes wide, and fell from his chair, writhing on the ground in pain. This continued for about thirty seconds before he went limp and moved no more.

"The king is dead." Hunter looked in the far corner of his quarters, and saw the spot where Linus always lay his crown when he wasn't wearing it. He repeated the phrase twice more, then stepped up to the mirror to take a good look at himself.

A handsome smile came over his face as Hunter liked his appearance more and more as he fixated on his countenance. He didn't even notice the splotch of blood from his former king that had splashed onto the mirror, or that specks of blood had splashed onto his tunic. The smile continued as he finished, "Long live the king."

* * *

As soon as James and Amanda were locked in the room, Al went back downstairs to speak with Ramona and see what was to be done with them. Whatever way this was going to end, violence would be involved.

He found her on the other side of the big doors, a guard with his hands over his head at her side. She had a sword drawn.

"Aljen," she started, "I didn't want to embarrass you in front of them, but I need to question your being here. Scouts rarely return so often."

Wordlessly, he motioned for her to come up to him. "May I ask what's wrong with your friend?"

Ramona turned, as if she had forgotten, then said, "We have a breach. One of the Mainmen, no doubt, disappointed in the king's decision. Help us catch them and it will be much easier for you."

Aljen sighed. "Then you are accusing me of treason for returning to the keep?"

"I won't bring the accusation to the king, but it brings suspicion on you. For all I know, you were wheedled by the Mainmen." She started down the passageway Al had come from, toward the stairs.

Al asked, "Where do you think the Mainmen were going back here?"

Ramona sighed. "You weren't there, but they were most curious about the king's prized possession."

No explanation needed. "They are sworn to protect the innocent."

"Yes," Ramona admitted, "but they are outsiders here. We'll bring them to trial if necessary. No doubt the king will see them imprisoned, or enslaved themselves."

At this point, Al noticed that the guard who they had gotten past, whoever 'they' were, was staying behind. "He isn't going to help us?"

Ramona whistled and the guard came over. Al stepped toward him, making Ramona raise her eyebrows. "What are you doing?"

Al went behind the guard, extending up on his tip toes to look at the wound. "Scouts need to know the basics for care. We have no infirmary out in the open country."

Ramona kept her blade out, sensing what was coming. Al put his left hand, the dominant one, on the wound, knowing it would recover just fine. The guard would not recover, however, from a snapped neck, which Al delivered.

As soon as his hands were free, he drew his blade, and Ramona was ready to receive him. The two were locked into swordplay for a good minute before Al was able to force Ramona back against a wall, restricting her arms and forcing her to be put in poses that could be blocked easily, and soon she was unarmed.

"I'm not going to kill you," Al stated, picking up her fallen blade and sheathing his own. "You know as well as I we cannot survive as pacifists."

Ramona, her back still against the wall, began to piece it together. Aljen was back for a purpose, all right. Insurrection. She looked down at the floor, unable to look the traitor in the eye.

"How many?" she asked, trying to keep her voice from breaking.

Al shook his head. "You'll see."

Ramona was trying her best to keep the tears back, but it wasn't working. Her voice did break when she asked, "And what will you do with me?"

The response was Al dropping her sword toward her feet. "When we restart the army, you'll be stripped of your rank. A common soldier, but you'll still have my respect."

Ramona eyed the sword, then looked back up at the scout.

He continued, "I trust my instincts enough to put my life in your hands. You saw the signs, heard our reports. You know as well as I the only way our people survive is to face Aunten head on."

She couldn't deny it. Deep down, the old Benshidi ways were at war with her current peaceful state. There was always conflict, just as there was in any warrior worth their salt. More out of that than fear she picked up her sword, and joined her opponent.

"When Hunter makes his speech," he added, "you go along with it. I knew you'd make the right decision."

To make sure she wouldn't stab him in the back, he made her walk in front of him as they headed for the rendezvous point. Most loyal soldiers would have had to be killed with that interaction, but Aljen had been chosen to deal with Ramona for his ability to reason and appeal. His skills would be used to great effect in the upcoming war.

* * *

It had taken a day and a half, but now Aunten and his mum companion had come to the end of the line. The swampy terrain seemed to go on forever, but now there was a great tree, seemingly as if out of a portrait, in the middle of the swamp. It grew strong and tall, no sign of decay or withering from the horrible conditions. It was the final resting place of Aunten's enemy, Halun Leman.

"So this is where you ended up," Aunten said on arrival. "All this time, and see who is still standing."

The mum woman now saw what was to happen, and feared the worse. Not for her, but for Winterlon overall. The tree represented the spiritual life of Halun, which still prospered well.

Aunten turned to the woman, and motioned for her to step up. Tears coming down her face once again, out of fear of the future, both hers and everyone else's.

"Come, child," he said, extending his arm in comfort. "It will be over soon."

The woman finally stood at the spot Aunten wanted her, right at the base of the tree. She shivered now, despite being all covered.

"I can tell you from experience," Aunten taunted, "that death is not as painful as you would imagine. Once the pain ends, the rest is just the afterlife."

He took out his famous sword, and without hesitation decapitated the only person he had been in contact with in the last several days. Her blood spilt on the ground, headed toward the tree.

That's when it happened. As if there were holes in the ground, the blood went down to the root level of the tree, and in seconds, the roots began to be infected. A line of red began to go up the bark of the tree, a rot around the line following it.

The line traveled up to the limbs, which began to sink under the pressure, and soon there was a large, loud creak as the tree began to die. The right side of the tree drooped, and the ground began to pop as large, once healthy roots began to surface.

Toppling toward the ground, the tree gave way and crashed. And with it came a boom that resounded across the swamp, across the nearby Lanzman forest, across the capital, across the Wise-Mountains, across the countries, even up to the Benshidi keep. No one but Aunten would know what had happened for many days. In this fell swoop, he had used enough of his power to extinguish the spiritual life of Halun Leman. For the man who had taken his physical life, Aunten now returned the favor.

Now Aunten sighed heavily, knowing that the enemy that had taken him to hell was gone, never to return again. The devil had tormented him with many obstacles that he had overcome. Now he was free to rule Winterlon and combat only his living foes.

***

Amanda knew it was a bad sign when the passageways back to the marketplace were empty. Even the guard she had just knocked out was gone. Once on the other side of the door, they should be fine.

They had not had a chance to change outfits until they got to the door. Even though the whole plan had gone astray, there was still the final obstacle of everyone spotting Montana once in the marketplace.

Amanda got her pack off and took out the armor she was going to give to Montana, saying, "What's the first thing you want to do when we get the chance?"

Montana had had many years to think about the opportunity of being free again. She didn't take much time to think about it. "Learn how to ride a horse, by myself at least, then take it out in the open country, camp out by myself for a few nights."

Amanda was all smiles. "I'm the perfect person for that."

By this point Amanda had her Mainmen garb off. Unlike the natives of Winterlon, she did wear clothes underneath, and Montana being from Earth originally still did so as well. While handing over her clothes to Montana, Amanda took a moment to look at her new friend. She really was a naturally beautiful girl. Her slave clothes, or near lack thereof, were not what made her the desire of many of the Benshidi.

Catching up with the necessity to get out of the back passageways, Amanda snapped out of it and got Montana's cloak on, careful to keep her skin invisible to anyone who would pass by. The hood up, her black hair would also be hidden.

Montana now had on her savior's armor, but took notice of the aroma of the interior. Despite everything they had gone through, she found humor in the situation. "You probably should have washed this first."

Amanda laughed, a tang of nervousness in her throat. "When you go into battle on a hot day, there's gonna be some sweat."

Now dressed and ready to go, Montana stepped up to Amanda and gave her a big hug. "No matter how this turns out, you've given me the best moments of my life."

Amanda patted her on the back, still embracing her. "The best is yet to come."

They patted each other on the shoulders, Amanda doing so first before Montana mimicked the action, to pump each other up and complete the riskiest part of the plan.

"Here we go," Amanda said, not wanting to overthink anything before going out to the marketplace. She opened the door enough to take a peek. The big man who had harassed James and Laura was off by the front entrance, so they would just have to go by the customers unnoticed.

She whispered at Montana to lead, and she did so, moving as naturally as she could. Had they had more time, she might have gotten a chance to get used to the weight of the armor and how it changed her posture as she moved, but the opportunity had not presented itself.

Amanda was slow behind her, a dagger hidden in an interior pocket of the cloak in case things went very bad. After the first few steps, Amanda had wished she had spoken with Montana and formed a better plan, perhaps if one of them had gone down one isle of the marketplace and the other on the opposite side so as not to attract attention.

Regardless, they both made it about halfway through when someone bumped into Montana, an older gentleman who excused himself and moved on. This would have been the end, except a middle-aged woman had glanced up to see who was speaking.

"My goodness," the woman said, a brown-haired, blue-eyed and short one at that. Her clothes were worn pretty well, and her hands, which slid out of her sleeves, were full of sores. There could have been many, many guesses as to what profession she held to make her as worn as she was. She reached up to touch the armor, asking, "Is that genuine?"

Montana froze, not knowing what to say. She had never spoken a word to any of the Benshidi, so her voice would not be recognized, yet she held her tongue in fear of saying something that would extend the conversation. Instead, she bowed before the woman, who became even more fascinated.

"We've only heard tales. Who is to know the next time the Mainmen will journey to our keep? I wish you well on your way."

Given this opportunity, Amanda had snuck around the other way, bumping into a few figures here and there accidentally, all of them hardly taking notice. By the time she had neared the entrance to the marketplace, Montana had begun to walk away from the woman, who followed her. Amanda's heart sank.

"Before you go, could you perhaps lend me a tad-hip for my troubles? I can afford almost half of what I could last month. That damned man keeps raising his prices. At least a couple of colliers? Something? Anything?"

Montana never turned back to face the woman. Amanda was tempted to turn back and tell her off, but she knew there had already been too much bloodshed. Especially with that first guard gone, perhaps ready to come and catch them at any moment, the best path forward was one without conflict.

The woman curled her fingers together and made two fists, and began to curse Montana. "Good deeds go far, you remember that. Next time carrying one out will bring you good fortune."

Her voice escalated with each word, or so it seemed, and drew the attention of the marketplace owner. The big man looked first at the woman, then followed her eyeline to see the woman in armor. He brought his fat fingers to his double chin, stroking in question.

Amanda caught his gaze, and knew what was coming next. The big man began to take strides toward Montana, ready to question her, but there came a large boom from the direction of the big doors on the other side of the keep.

The noise was the doors being flung open, and voices clattering up and down the passageways as guards began to run toward the busy part of the keep. Seeing the opportunity, Amanda stepped up to Montana, grabbed her gloved hand, and told her to run.

The two crossed back and forth from the gathering crowds and headed for the private quarters where the Mainmen guests had stayed. They dodged all others as long as they could, but did hit a few citizens as they tried to get as close as they could to the big doors.

Amanda reached out, the door to the quarters open, and flung it open even further, finally reaching the bunk beds.

"Quick!" Amanda commanded. "Take off the heavy armor and hide under. We'll come get you when it's safe."

Montana did not speak a word. Fearing she would end up right back where she started, she obeyed.

Amanda, however, realized that she might bring attention unless she changed back into her Mainmen robes. Hiding away from the open door, though everyone bustling around probably would not have taken notice, she changed quickly, and ran out to see what all the commotion was about. Deep down, she feared she may never see Montana again. In the last moments before joining the crowd in the keep, she tried her best to keep tears out of her eyes, tears of fear she would not see her friend after this.

* * *

While Montana and Amanda were making their way through the marketplace, James and Laura were stuck in the chamber on the second floor.

"We're not gonna die here," she said to James, for about the third time since Al had locked them in.

James shook his head. "If not us, they'll kill them. Simple as that. They knew. Somehow they knew."

Laura sighed in frustration, sitting on the stone slab as James stood at the door, waiting for it to open. "If you really believe that, you're delusional. They'd have to be mind readers to know what we were doing."

"Laura, what if we never get to that library? The secret to killing Aunten could be in there, and we'd never know."

"It could have been just a bunch of papers, like those books we swiped from Gwendolyn. Even as pacifists, if they knew the Deadman were back and knew how to kill them, they would have come forward."

"But look at how they treated Montana. They're a proud people. Maybe they just wanted to save all the honor and all the glory for themselves."

Laura got up from the slab and took a couple of quick steps toward her friend, but her pace slowed and her manner simmered as she put a warm hand on his shoulder and massaged him. "We're both upset. When he comes back, we need to talk it over with him."

James' breath trembled in anger, but he agreed. "We need to. Whatever happens, no matter how badly they try to punish us."

Laura motioned for James to go over to the slab. He did so, Laura joining him, and the two leaned in, both internally afraid of what came next, but hoping against hope that Al or whoever came to collect them would listen.

After a couple of minutes of silence, they both heard the key enter the slot, and the door opened. Al was back, and he had a very different manner about him. Wordlessly, he motioned for them to get up from their spot and exit the chamber.

Laura didn't hesitate, "Al, look, we need to get to that library. The whole fate of the world may depend on it."

Al had his back turned as he led them back down the stairs and down the passageways. "All in good time. When did He approach you?"

"He?" James asked.

"King Hunter."

The new title to their potential ally caught them both off guard. "You did say 'king'", Laura stated.

Al kept moving. "There are many allies here in the keep that agree with the Mainmen notion that we join the fight, and tonight we do. King Linus was a jagged block that had to be removed."

"Oh my God," Laura said, which made Al stop in his tracks. "It was a mutiny."

Al turned and faced the two. "You both come from Earth, correct?"

Laura nodded.

For a moment, Al was unsure if he could add anything, but he ended up saying, "We'll see what the new king says about people from Earth. And we'll see what he does with your other friend, the one who took the slave girl."

James worried about Amanda, but couldn't help his curiosity, asking, "So you've been planning this? You and Hunter wanted him dead?"

Laura picked up. "And we gave you the opportunity."

They couldn't see it, but Al was smiling. "You catch on quick. Linus couldn't see defeat coming, but we could. Me, Hunter, Secretary of War Kargor. You'll notice he hit Hunter pretty hard back at the meeting. The perfect cover. He's been itching to go to war since Linus appointed him."

Laura chuckled to herself. "So like Julius Caesar, the king is killed by the hand of his most trusted. But you'll join us?"

"We need to settle things here among the people first, but when you need us, we'll be there."

This development was perhaps the last thing that James had expected. Laura and he joined hands as they walked down the last passageway toward the big doors.

"What happens now?" she asked Al when they stopped.

"The new king will console the people. It's very important for you to understand, what he says was planned months ago. If it is not all truth, it is for a reason. We'll let you join with the Mainmen. You'll bear witness to a historic moment. It's not every day that a new monarch is crowned."

There was a chill that went down both James and Laura's spines at the last sentence. The outcome was one that they preferred, gaining allies in the fight against Aunten, but in doing so they had betrayed their fallen king and deceived their people.

Deep down, James was nervous about what would happen after this speech. These people looked down on him and others from Earth, yet they were firm believers in the ways of the Wiseman, who would not approve of their conduct. They were a peaceful people, and yet their leaders had murdered their own king. Who knew what they would do when joined with others in battle?

* * *

The boom that Amanda and Montana heard that saved them from the wrath of the big man was the great doors opening and Hunter and his group of mutineers arriving victorious, ready to meet their subjects.

Hunter, still dressed as he was when he killed Linus, was middle of the pack, surrounded by guards whom he trusted with his life. He had not put the crown on yet out of respect of his predecessor, and that was by design. He would have to break the news to the Benshidi citizens, and doing so in too hasty a manner would backfire.

James and Laura separated for a few moments, but were able to spot Talen out of the crowd and met up with him. He greeted them and looked around, calling out for Johnson and McQuint. The two had been having beers all afternoon, and were easy to spot.

Ed, meanwhile, was halfway across the courtyard, closer to the entrance of the keep. He had been on the watch with Gwendolyn and Joven for Amanda and Montana to return. Jaenen was off on his own, somewhere in the mix of everything. It would be several minutes before he would be found by his father as that group moved up toward Talen and his group, who were closer to the big doors.

Amanda emerged from the quarters, being hit by citizens left and right as she tried to make her way toward any familiar or friendly face. After several minutes, she realized in fear there were none to be found.

Hunter, meanwhile, in this moment of 'emergency', would be placed on the top of the spire overseeing the courtyard to address the people. The way to do so from the floor of the keep was to climb up a few jutting bricks in the wall and then use a rope to reach the top. A couple of guards were there to secure him.

Leaning against the wall, partially in defeat of not finding any other Mainmen, but also out of pure exhaustion, Amanda was not afraid to shed tears, looking away from the chaotic scene. She was afraid she had failed her new friend and might have been abandoned by her old friends. Where were James and Laura? Had they been allowed in the library? Had something gone wrong and now they were captured?

Person upon person was looked at carefully by Ed and his group, and only citizens they were unfamiliar with met them. Then there was a call.

"Dad!" Jaenen had spotted Ed, and the two rushed for each other, embracing as they caught each other's gaze.

"Do you see the others?" father asked son.

Jaenen shook his head. By this time, the others had gathered around him. They still searched, hoping the easiest person to spot, Talen, would stick out from the crowd. No luck yet.

Ed whistled, and the three others began to follow him as he moved across the courtyard toward the front.

The whistle caught the ear of Amanda, who looked up, tears still in her eyes. Sure enough, she caught the back of Gwendolyn's hair, and saw what appeared to be a small group around her that resembled the Mainmen. She took off, using all the strength she had left to catch up to them.

Talen and the others, meanwhile, were headed the wrong way. They hoped to go closer to the marketplace at the instruction of James and Laura, who were hoping against hope that Amanda and Montana may be found somewhere in that vicinity. They hoped to overturn some boxes and stand on top to get the height advantage. Sure enough, the big man saw Johnson tip over a box of a rare fruit, huila, which were pear-shaped, bigger, but purple in color. He ran up to Johnson, pushing and shoving, berating the stranger. This was met by a punch in the face by Johnson, who easily knocked out the nuisance.

Talen, not needing a box, soon saw one familiar face: Jaenen. He called over for him, but Jaenen didn't hear. Almost everyone in the keep who wasn't stationed behind the big doors at this rate were assembled, hustling and bustling at each other to get the best spot in the house.

Unfortunately, Ed had instructed the others to break up to cover more ground, saying they would meet at the sleeping quarters after everything was over. So when Jaenen finally did hear Talen calling out, he was alone.

Amanda chased after Gwendolyn, hoping everything would be all right. Gwendolyn, however, over the noise, did not hear her compatriot coming up behind her. So when Amanda's footsteps finally did reach earshot, Gwendolyn whipped around and prepared for battle. Amanda nearly ran into her, Gwendolyn's sword turned out and slightly up, and quickly she had to back up a pace to avoid impaling Amanda.

Ed and Joven stopped where they were after the noise of the crowd began to quiet down. Hunter was about to make his first address as king.

This moment was one Hunter knew was coming, but all the same, now that it was here, it was hard for Hunter's voice not to sound too excited. It ended up being an additional touch that fed into the lies he was about to tell.

"My people, heed me, please. Let silence fall as I bear sad news."

A few moments longer before the noise level in the courtyard went from sold out arena to pin-drop quietness.

When he was satisfied with this, Hunter continued. "You may see my appearance, and judge correctly that our great leader, King Linus I, is dead."

Gasps and screams of horror came out of the audience. Many men and women broke down, endless tears streaming down their face the rest of the night.

Again, ever the actor now, Hunter waited until enough of the noise had lessened again before going on. "Your king is dead. But I say now that your king does live. He lives on through me."

Hoping for applause, but getting none, Hunter let the silence sink in for a few more moments before his speech continued. "I must say to you that in his final moments, the true nature of His Majesty overcame his senses. He pleaded to me that we surrender to Aunten Schritz. That we stop our isolation from the lands over the mountains and give in to a usurper. He was ready to have all of you die in the name of the Wiseman for the good of the world.

"My people, as I swore in solemn oath when appointed as second-in-command, I would uphold our beliefs, stand ever true to that, damning all consequences. Tonight, I had to damn the greatest consequence of all and see that our beloved king's life came to an end. I will not see your lives lost this night, nor any other."

A break here, and sure enough, some folks began to applaud. James and Laura, meanwhile, knowing this was coming, looked at the group of mutineers, who were directly below Hunter. They were all smiles, knowing every word out of their new king's mouth was horseshit, and that the people would gradually begin to eat it up.

"Now, I have also been shocked to learn that there were conspirators in this madness. One of them is your Secretary of State, Blaine Vivsky. He had been trading secrets with our neighbors, breaking the silence we swore under King Linus. He was preparing to make a deal with the Deadman, figuring which of you could work as slaves and which would be useless, which of you would be killed when we arrived at the capital. Though I am sad to say that he did so under King Linus' orders, both of whom held no quarter in betraying the trust of their people.

"So his betrayal was also met with death. We may thank our guards for their service in this matter."

Applause, more general this time, broke out, and Hunter acknowledged Melbun and Rickard, the scouts who served with Aljen, who had gone to Vivsky's quarters and had him killed while Al had convinced Ramona to stay on their side.

"Our investigation will begin for the other members of the callen who betrayed the Benshidi, for I know more than two conspirators exist. Once we have found them, rest assured they will meet a demise worse than the two we have already put to rest."

Another break as the people began to shout Hunter's name, easily accepting his new rule. A small smile came over his face a moment, but just for a moment. He still needed to address the citizens from an angle of unwillingness.

"Though I have only held the post of second-in-command for a matter of eight months, I assure you I will assume the duties of king immediately. I will seek out the best path forward by looking to our past. I am a man of history, and cannot be guided without it. As the Wiseman once showed the people of Winterlon to clean water, or taught them to build fires and houses of wood and stone, I too shall look to our great maker for guidance.

"Let us not forget, my people, that once the Deadman did rule this world, but it was thanks to the Benshidi army that the lands were rid of them. Let not our great tactics and trades of war be forgotten this night, nor any other, until once again the Deadman are returned to hell!

"And, as a man of history, I must honor the tradition of past kings and queens who have fallen. It came to my attention tonight that we have other traitors in our midst, who have taken King Linus' favorite possession. The Earth slave girl, Montana, is missing."

This news, more so than the passing of Linus, was met poorly by some citizens. Amanda, still at Gwendolyn's side, nearly passed out in shock at the words spoken. James and Laura, meanwhile, were unable to keep smiles off their faces. 'Yes,' they thought, 'Amanda had done it.'

"So, as a sign of passing from one rule to the next, the sin of taking away a king's possession will be bestowed onto those who are responsible. Come forth now, and your punishment will be favorable."

Hunter had added this addition last, so the words came more slowly, bigger spaces between phrases, unlike the rest of the speech, which was more rehearsed, the phrases, words, and silences coming together as planned.

Every one of the Mainmen were ready to step forward. Truthfully, all of them were responsible in one way or another for the folly. James and Laura soon began to get down from their boxes, ready to push through the crowd.

Toward the back, Amanda was ready to do the same. Gwendolyn held her back, though, a look of sadness in her eyes.

Likewise, Johnson and McQuint soon found Laura and James, each going up to them and stopping them. "No," they said simply. The youth had to fight against their elders, but both failed. Out of the corner of his eye, James saw Talen and someone else moving people out of the way as they went forward.

Ed was also unaware of what was happening, but soon realized Talen was stepping up. "No!" he shouted. "No. Talen, no!"

Not turning back, Talen had reached the third row of spectators, who began to step aside, knowing he was coming. A noise began to come from the crowd, one of displeasure, a hiss type of noise. They were shaming their guest for what they believed were his actions.

Talen also had Jaenen at his side. Both of them held their heads high and looked Hunter directly in the eyes, never breaking contact.

In the back, Ed still tried to inch his way forward. "Talen, what are you doing?"

Hearing this now, Talen opened his mouth and took a moment before saying, "Don't listen to a word these people say. The Mainmen do not believe in enslavement. My colleague and I did the deed."

"Identify yourselves," Hunter called out.

"Talen Wadenston."

"Jaenen Hotean."

Ed was not able to see that his son was at Talen's side. In a state of shock, he stood like a fool as the next moments unfolded. Not even a tear of sadness could come from him.

"Do you know the girl's location?"

Talen shook his head. "We rescued her early this morning. She is miles from here, far from your reach."

Hunter nodded. "So be it. Since the girl will not be returned, your punishment will not be as lax. You will therefore be held in the torture chambers as prisoner until you are declared dead."

Nothing could be done to save their friends now. The Benshidi were fond of punishments when it came to Earth positive matters. The great doors opened, and two guards came forth to take Talen and Jaenen away. When they were before the doors, they turned back, trying to find any of their friends. Jaenen especially tried to find his father, but the crowd being at ground level forbid their curiosity from being satisfied. It would be a long time, if ever, before they would see their fellow Mainmen again.

"Now," Hunter continued, "I know some of you are worried about our time of peace coming to an end. Fear not. Our souls are to be met with a great test. One that—"

His speech was interrupted by a cry from outside the keep, a sound that pervaded the cool, chilling night air. It resembled an animal of moderate size being killed. After a moment, all the lights in the keep went out, and soon all the people were in total darkness. Screams and cries went out. Not knowing what it was at first, but then gaining an idea, James trembled in defeat, reaching out for Laura. Their enemy had caught up with them.

18. Extinction

The crowd was yelling and screaming in the dark, no one able to tell where everyone else was. The yelling and screaming came to a stop after a few more moments when a new sound took over, one of creaking and wood splitting. The drawbridge that everyone used to enter or exit the keep was moaning, the wood splintering, as if someone were using the force of it to open the opposite way.

Pressure from the outside forced it to go, and the wood splintered, a new source of natural light from outside now entering the keep, but only for a few moments. Then the lights from inside, torch and candle lights, suddenly were aglow again.

Silence continued. A few people looked up to where Hunter had stood a minute earlier, but he was gone. In the blackout a couple of guards had escorted him back inside the interior to keep their newly declared king safe.

Twelve figures, all in black and hooded, now entered the keep. James had figured correctly; the Deadman had found them. The sight of the creatures from hell brought up new screams and shouting from the crowd, all of whom had heard the stories, new and old, of the Deadman's terrifying feats. Now they were about to witness them firsthand.

A black, bony hand came up from the first to enter the keep, and the people who were furthest in the back grew silent, knowing he was about to say something.

"Kill them," was all the figure said. The Mainmen did not know the Deadman by name yet, but the words were spoken by Sienel.

Pandemonium broke out. The people furthest back in the crowd shoved their way towards the front.

Civilians were on the ground, being crushed by the feet of their neighbors, others were trying to defend their kin by fighting the Deadman, all of whom were among the first to die.

Up at the big doors, the two guards stood still, not allowing any to pass. Eventually the people overpowered them and pounded for more help, someone to open the doors. They would pound and pound until their knuckles broke, blood stains left on the wood.

As for the Mainmen, Amanda and Gwendolyn being furthest back set them up to fight the Deadman first. Amanda, though, feared for Montana. Gwendolyn, on the other hand, drew out her sword again and was ready to fight.

"Wait!" Amanda cried. "What about Montana?"

Gwendolyn considered the option. After seeing a few citizens fall to the jagged, ugly, sharp swords of the Deadman, she nodded and the two began to creep their way over across the courtyard to the entrance of the quarters, where hopefully Montana had stayed hidden.

They made it about halfway across when they were met by a Deadman, who removed his hood to show his hideous features beneath. Jenik was the Deadman they were to face, though again none of them knew the names quite yet.

He smiled as he prepared for battle. His sword came up and clashed against Amanda's, the clash hard enough for her to drop the weapon.

Gwendolyn came in for the rescue. "Go," she said to her friend. The next blows met Gwendolyn's sword and the two dueled for a time. Jenik could have killed her at any moment, but instead loved the fight, preferring it to easy pickings.

Amanda took off once she had recovered from the encounter, and rushed through the door to the quarters. "Montana!" she shouted.

From under one of the beds, a hand emerged, shaking from fear. Amanda ran over, reached under, and pulled her out.

"Time to go?" Montana asked.

"The Deadman are here. We have to find a way out."

Montana nodded. "Where are they?"

"Everywhere. In front of the main entrance, making their way toward the big doors to the passageways. Where else can we go?"

"The marketplace," Montana answered. "Bring your friends, hurry."

Meanwhile, James and Laura tracked down Ed, who in the chaos had managed to find Joven. Johnson and McQuint followed them, and soon the six were together again.

"My boy, we have to save my boy" was all Ed would say. He still was in shock over everything, even as innocent Benshidi blood was being spilt by the gallon at the hand of the enemy.

Being together was a bad idea, and now a Deadman, Cedrik, spotted them. He slowly made his way over to the group.

James argued, "They came for us. We need to distract them away from the Benshidi. It's the only way to save them."

McQuint came back with, "Son, they're gonna kill all of us regardless. We just need to get out of here."

Laura's eyes went wide as she remembered. "The horses, they came back for us. We can get away from them on the horses."

277

James nodded. "Okay. We just need to get to the stables."

By this point, Cedrik was about ready to take a swing at them, but McQuint engaged, ready to do battle. James took command, motioning for everyone to head over to the marketplace entrance. It was the only way he knew besides the big doors to get to the passageways, away from the Deadman.

The crowd was frantic still, but beginning to be thinned out as nine Deadman began to pick them off.

As for Al and the scouts, along with a few of the other guards, the way up to the spire was taken. Ramona led the way, followed by Al and Rickard. Melbun stayed behind, content on protecting the people. He also kept citizens from escaping the same way by knocking them away with punches or kicks.

There was a total of nine of them up on the spire by the end, running back to the doors up above, where Hunter had escaped. A couple of the guards had bows and arrows, and began firing them down on the Deadman, but they all missed. All except for one shot that hit a Deadman, Korah, in the torso. He removed the arrow and flung it back by hand at the guard, the arrow hitting its originator in the skull, making him fall onto the crowd below.

Al and Rickard noticed the door was locked, so they began kicking at it and thrusting their swords butt end against it as well, hoping it would fall apart enough for them to get inside.

Amanda and Montana exited the quarters for the last time. Luckily Amanda had taken notice that a couple of Mainmen packs had been left behind, so she took the liberty of dragging them behind her, Montana taking one as well, as they raced toward the marketplace entrance.

Along the way, they saw Gwendolyn, still at war with Jenik. She looked exhausted, barely able to hold her sword any longer. Amanda reached into her pack and removed a dagger, throwing it at Jenik to distract him. The dagger missed, and clattered on the stone floor.

Drawing his attention, Gwendolyn was able to step back and recover from the fight. Amanda let out a scream as the Deadman started toward her and Montana.

Hearing the scream, Joven saw she was in trouble. He was the last in line to head to the marketplace from their starting point, James and Laura already at the door. Ed and Johnson were only behind a few paces, but also noticed the scream.

Johnson withdrew his sword and ushered Ed to keep going. Joven, however got his attention.

"Get him inside," he said. "I'll give you a head start."

Eyes wide, knowing he was about to make the sacrifice, Johnson screamed, "No!" But there was no deterring Joven by this point.

Amanda, meanwhile, backed away, headed toward the quarters again. She and Montana felt trapped.

Gwendolyn tried to take a step toward them to join up in battle again, but noticed her leg hurt when she stepped forward. She looked down to see a wide gush above her left knee. She'd been hit during the battle. The yell from Johnson caught her attention next, and when she saw he was going for the marketplace, started to move that way, slowly.

Joven cracked his neck in preparation. "For Slank. For the capital. For all of them." He reached into his Mainmen pack and produced his bow, fitting an arrow inside. He aimed and fired at Jenik.

Amanda backed up more and more until Jenik stopped. A small ooze came out of his chest by a hole, green in color. Looking down, the Deadman noticed it and quickly turned around to find the source of the arrow.

Joven had another arrow ready, aiming again for where the heart would be on the awful creature. The shot did hit the Deadman, but was off, hitting his arm. With more speed, Jenik began to step toward him.

Seeing the opportunity, Montana and Amanda headed toward the marketplace, staying out of sight of Jenik as he headed toward Joven.

McQuint, all this time, still battled against Cedrik, and had already earned several scrapes and bruises on his knuckles, and a gash on his forehead, for his troubles. At one point his enemy took a step back, allowing McQuint to take a large swipe toward the Deadman's stomach, but this ended up being the crucial mistake.

Cedrik took the opportunity to stab his enemy square in the chest, then lifting the sword up so McQuint's feet left the ground.

As soon as the sword pierced his body, McQuint let out a groan, one more so in frustration than in pain, knowing that he should have seen it coming. He let out smaller groans as his enemy lifted him in the air. Once he was up high enough, Cedrik stopped, smiling in victory.

"Finish it," McQuint managed through the pain. Cedrik shook his head, favoring the suffering he was causing his foe. Still nothing further. McQuint gritted his teeth, and with everything he had left, screamed at his enemy once more. "Finish it!"

Cedrik now obeyed, bringing a hand up over McQuint's throat and digging his nails in, sharp enough to tear at the skin and cause more bleeding. Cedrik closed his fist on the opened skin of McQuint's neck and removed his sword from McQuint's body, allowing a larger gash on the throat and for the body to fall to the ground in a heap. It would be about eighty more seconds before McQuint bled out, but he did so alone.

On the way to the marketplace, Montana spotted Gwendolyn, and she and Amanda helped her to the door, where Johnson stood, watching as Joven prepared to fight Jenik.

Joven fired one last arrow at his foe when the two only had about four feet between them, but Jenik lowered his hand in the spot Joven had aimed, and it ricocheted off the hand and bounced harmlessly to the ground.

His other hand still held his sword, and with it he took a swipe at Joven's neck, slitting it, and allowed his enemy to drop to his knees. He then walked on top of his body as he turned and went toward the other Deadman, who were still picking off Benshidi innocents.

Johnson let out a cry as he saw Joven go down, but was then pushed inside the door by Amanda and Gwendolyn, who took the lead. Once Montana was inside as well, they closed the door, leaving the courtyard for the last time.

On the interior of the keep, Al and Ramona had indeed busted through the door, but beforehand were distracted by a scream from down below that sounded familiar.

The Deadman had taken Melbun, who now lay lifeless on the ground. Al was the last of the two to go back to pounding on the door until they could get inside.

As for the Benshidi citizens, it was a total of five minutes before the last of them were slaughtered by the Deadman. In total, 1,450 now lay dead on the cool, stone floor. Sienel was at the front of the pack, and now approached the bloodied, big doors. With a movement of his hand, the two doors creaked again then burst into thousands of small pieces. The splinters flew in every direction, some nicking Deadman on the same side. Some green puss-like blood came from small wounds, but none of them cared.

Once the Mainmen were all gathered again, Montana took the lead, followed by Ed, then James, Amanda and Laura. Johnson helped Gwendolyn, volunteering to do so. The group that had survived Arnic Canyon had numbered eleven, but now they were down to seven. They had gained Gwendolyn and Montana, but had lost Darven, Jaenen, Talen, McQuint, Browning, and Joven. The fact that more were captured, dead, or out of the fight than began two weeks before was disheartening, and not lost on the group, even as time was precious before the Deadman would try to get them again.

"The stables are on the other side of the keep," Montana advised. "Up this way as far as we can go, then to the right, then down some stairs will get us out."

No words were spoken otherwise, mostly from the grief of the losses, but Ed especially felt the lousiest. Even though it was a group decision to head north and seek out the Benshidi, he alone held responsibility for all lives lost, all blood shed. What kind of leader was he to have allowed all this to happen?

Elsewhere, the eight Benshidi guards and scouts headed for the private quarters of the king, where Hunter would be guarded. Al and Ramona still led the way, running as fast as they could, fearing the enemy would close on them any moment.

Around one corner, Al ran into Yellen Kargor, the Secretary of War who had been in on the assassination of Linus. "Al," he managed after catching his breath. "It's a disaster. A new king appointed, and within minutes, the Deadman at our doorstep. What are we to do?"

Al shook his head, breathing hard. "Seek out the counsel of the king. He'll know what to do."

Ramona made a soft moan in protest. "I say we abandon the keep. Our people will all be dead by morning, if not sooner."

One of the guards spoke up. "The king does not leave the keep, less He surrenders it."

"Then He will surrender it," Ramona said in excitement. "Less He wishes to die in it."

Kargor huffed at this. "I was hoping to find you, Aljen, and seek out His Majesty's word. We will obey it." The last sentence came out very sternly, directed at Ramona.

The group continued, and after another few moments did end up at the door to the king's private quarters. As expected, twelve guards were in place around it, guarding all corners.

"We wish an audience with the king," Kargor demanded.

"Let them pass," they could hear Hunter say on the other side.

The guard did as commanded and let Al, Ramona, and Kargor enter. Rickard and the guards remained outside.

Hunter seemed exhausted at first sight, still in the clothes he wore as he executed his former king. "Did you see the Mainmen?" he asked.

All shook their heads. This was met by laughter from Hunter, first general, then maddening.

"Don't you see? It was them who led the Deadman to us. We would have survived, but the devils trapped us here. Now like stinking bait to the hounds, we will be eaten, while they watch. Damn them!"

Al and Kargor nodded in agreement. There was a far-off noise from outside, a sound of screaming and flesh being split open.

"They're coming," Kargor said. "Quick, sire. We must run."

Hunter held up a hand. "Let them come. I realize now this whole thing was a mistake. A judgment we had to make sooner. Linus would have had us all killed eventually. Now it will come to pass."

Ramona turned away from her new king, and exited. She grabbed Rickard and motioned toward the left passage, which would lead away from the Deadman and toward the stables.

Kargor and Al remained, but only a moment longer. Neither spoke a word, afraid to say anything in acknowledgement of their comrade turning her back, or of asking what to do next.

"Go," Hunter pleaded. "Run for your lives. Let not the Benshidi go extinct tonight. Prosper, teach our ways to your sons and daughters, while you can have them. Leave me to my death."

Both men bowed before their king, tears now in their eyes. Once they had determined they'd spent enough time on their knee, they got up and exited. Noticing that Ramona and Rickard had already left, but hearing their footsteps, they followed. They were all headed for the stables.

Not more than a moment or two after the older men had followed the others, the guards at the door of the king went to battle with the Deadman. It was truly a slaughter; guards being tossed left and right in bloody heaps as the devils continued their assault.

Finally, it came down to Sienel getting past the last one. By this time, Hunter had gone back into the corner and, for the first time, laid the crown upon his own head. In history, this was heresy. It was always someone else who would place the crown on the new king, not the new king himself in a manner of gloat and pomp. But Hunter did not want to die without knowing first just how heavy the crown wore on him.

Sienel inched into the room, his sword at his side, his eyes never leaving the man in it. He stopped when he was a foot away from him. "You are King Linus?"

Hunter shook his head. "Linus is dead. I am King Hunter I."

Smiling at this, Sienel took a moment to acknowledge his foe. "My congratulations on your appointment. It is not every day the Benshidi crown a new ruler."

Sighing, Hunter shook his head. "Kill me and be done with it. You've killed everyone else."

Sienel's smile continued. "At the word of my master, yes. You, on the other hand, will only die if you do not tell us that which we need to know."

Another Deadman, Fiernan, filed into the small room. The other Deadman began to search the surrounding passageways for others to kill. They would find none.

"Are there any Mainmen here?"

"You want to kill them, too?"

"In time, yes. But first we must know where they are. And who they are."

Hunter nodded. "You can have them. The filth betrayed us by bringing you here. Mobwin to the slaughter."

"By housing them, you brought it on yourself, Your Highness. Where are they?"

Smiling now, Hunter remembered. "Two are in the dungeons. They freed King Linus' favorite slave. Their punishment was to be kept until death. Perhaps they will favor you instead."

A cruel little smile came from Sienel's mouth. "It's a start. Thank you, King Hunter I."

With that, Sienel took no malice in killing Hunter with a stab directly in the man's heart. He had fulfilled his purpose, and now would join his people in death. It was the best he could hope for. Funny enough, Hunter fell in a spot very close to the one Linus had slumped onto when he passed. Two kings killed in the same evening, dying in the same room.

The crown fell from Hunter's head once his body hit the floor, clattered once, then rolled into a corner of the room. Sienel took little notice of this, instead turning to Fiernan.

"Fetch the two Mainmen. Once they're out of the keep, burn it all down."

As Hunter was making his last conversation with Sienel, Montana and the Mainmen had arrived at the stables, each with a horse left grabbing them and getting ready to leave.

Ed noticed they had been tied up, unnecessary considering they wouldn't leave while their owners were still in the keep. He cut the ropes loose for the horses whose owners were not mounting them, letting them run free.

Montana joined Amanda, and Gwendolyn joined Johnson for mounts and away they all went. James was glad to be reunited with Rohan, who also nickered in acknowledgement.

Before they had taken more than a stride or two, Al, Ramona, Kargor and Rickard arrived, all mounting rides and taking off as well. They went to follow the Mainmen, not for certain if that would just be for tonight, or if they now would journey with them.

Looking back now, they soon saw smoke coming out of the open courtyard, flames soon visible after a few minutes.

Once Ed and James, whose horses held the lead, also smelled the smoke, they halted and watched as the place they had stayed hours earlier now began to burn. This also gave the opportunity for the four Benshidi survivors to come up alongside them.

Kargor spoke for them. "You will pay a heavy price for the loss of our people."

Shaking his head, Johnson spoke on behalf of Ed, who was still silent after losing Jaenen. "That doesn't matter now. If your people had been more tolerant, perhaps everything would have played out differently."

James, who rode back so he could hear everything better, then did something out of instinct. "Join us. The Mainmen could always use the expertise of the Benshidi warriors. And since there's now as few of you as there are of us, it'll be better if we stick together."

Ed, whose sympathies and mind still lied with his son, who at this moment he was questioning whether still breathed or was dead, simply nodded. In this moment of crisis, there was no use making an argument whether or not they could or should join up.

For four minutes the eleven people gathered watched as the stones began to crumble under the pressure of the heat, the spires in the courtyard beginning to fall away. No screams were heard since all the inhabitants were dead, but still there seemed to be a painful sound that emanated from the flames, the sound of a people who generation after generation had been born, grown and died in the keep, were helpless as it would turn to ashes.

When they had seen enough, Ed encouraged his horse to keep going. The ten others followed, fearing the Deadman may begin a chase.

Inside the private quarters where first King Linus then King Hunter had fallen, the crown which both men had killed for was the last item in the whole keep to catch aflame. Made from bronze, it had to grow very hot before it would begin to blaze. That, more than anything else, symbolized the end of the Benshidi race. None who knew soon enough the mistakes made by their leaders would survive this night, and the heaviness of the crown would take the brunt of the blame.

To be continued…

Made in the USA
Columbia, SC
07 October 2022